HOLDING
ONTO
FOREVER

THE BEAUMONT SERIES · NEXT GENERATION

HOLDING ONTO FOREVER
HEIDI MCLAUGHLIN
© 2017

COVER DESIGN: Sarah Hansen: OkayCreations.
EDITING: Ellie: Love N. Books

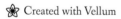 Created with Vellum

To those who have lost and loved again

PEYTON

Kyle Zimmerman, one of the top-rated quarterbacks in the league, and Chicago's most eligible bachelor is holding my hand as he guides me to his car. The schoolgirl in me is trying not to let his presence affect me, at least not on the outside. On the inside, though, I'm a ball of nerves mixed with excitement. Who would've thought a simple assignment would turn into a date? Not me. Not in a million years, but here I am, being helped into his car and anxiously waiting for him to get behind the steering wheel.

And once he does, the sweet scent of his cologne fills the small space. I find myself leaning a bit closer to him so I can inhale deeply without looking like a creeper. Kyle smiles. It's an ear-to-ear grin with a slight chuckle. I've been caught, but he doesn't seem to care. He leans forward, pulling himself away from me. It's probably best. We've just met and if he kissed me now, I don't know what I would do.

"Tell me about yourself, Peyton."

"I'm majoring in broadcast journalism. I love football. I'm a twin."

"Is your twin as pretty as you?"

"Prettier," I tell him.

"Impossible," he replies, never breaking eye contact with me. "What do you know about me?"

"Everything, yet nothing. Your rookie year, you sat on the bench but started your second year. You threw sixteen touchdowns, eleven interceptions and accumulated 3,440 yards. Your completion rate was fifty-eight percent. This year, you're pushing seventy percent and in line to win the league MVP. You've thrown for almost 4,500 yards, twenty-five touchdowns and four interceptions."

Kyle's eyes widen as his mouth drops open. "Wow, you had to go and bring up my first year, huh?"

I shrug. "You asked, but ..."

"But what?" he asks, adjusting the way he's sitting.

I run my cold hands down my pant legs to create some heat. "I don't know anything personal about you, aside from your age, where you were born, etc.... all stuff that is easily found on the internet. I'd like to get to know the real you."

"You're right, so what do you say we head to dinner and talk about who we are away from football?"

"I'd like that."

Kyle starts his car and pulls out of the parking lot. There's very minimal traffic waiting to get out the exit the players use.

"Tell me, Peyton. How do you know so much about football?"

"Well, my dad and best friend..."

"Ms. Powell-James, I'd like to see you after class," Professor Fowler says, calling me out in front of everyone. An email would've sufficed if he needed to see me after class. As is, all the males in class all make comments on how I'm in trouble, and the few other females sneer at me. Who knew

journalism is so cutthroat? I sling my backpack over my shoulder and take the steps down to where my professor is standing.

"You wanted to see me, sir?" I close my eyes at the idiocy of my statement. Of course he wanted to see me, he called me down, humiliating me in front of the entire class.

"Peyton, you're one of my best students."

"Thank you."

"Your knowledge of sports, particularly football will get you far."

"I owe it all to the men in my family." If it weren't for my father introducing me to the sport and Liam coming into my life when he did, I could've easily fallen out of love with it. Noah was there, of course, but I could've become a cheer-leader or not had anything to do with the game entirely.

"Well, make sure you tell your family that you'll be on the sidelines for this week's Bears game." The professor hands me a lanyard with the word Media written all over it. Attached to the clip is a press pass with my name on it.

"I don't understand."

"It's simple. This Sunday, you'll be representing the school and me at the game. I expect a full write-up of the game on my desk on Monday morning. Everything you need to know will be emailed to you later this evening. You've earned this, Peyton. Enjoy it."

"But why me?"

"Because you're the best." He picks up his briefcase and exits through the faculty door, leaving me in the room staring at what is surely going to be my most prized possession until I become an official member of the media. I slip it around my neck and hide it under my scarf, hiding it from anyone who may be lingering out in the hall.

As soon as I push the heavy door open, I spot a group of

my classmates. With my head down, I rush by them, praying none of them say anything.

"Hold up, Peyton." The voice belongs to Donnie Olson, the self-proclaimed God of all things sports. He thinks because he knows more about rugby and soccer, he's the king.

"Hey, Donnie."

"What did Fowler want?"

"To ask about my friend."

"Right. I forgot you're 'best friends' with Noah Westbury."

I don't stop when he mocks me. I made the mistake of telling a sorority sister about Noah. She didn't believe me, going as far as saying Noah going to prom with me was a charity fundraiser I won. And it's not like I've been able to prove her otherwise since he's been dating Dessie, which has strained our relationship by no fault of his.

"Yeah, something like that." I continue to walk across campus with him right next to me. He continues to gab about Noah and Dessie, reminding me, very painfully I might add, that he's with her and how they're all over the place, with her talking about marriage. I want to plug my ears and throw up at the same time.

"Would you look at this?" I say, pointing to my sorority house. "Gotta go!" I hurry into the house and shut the door.

"Donnie, again?" Veronica, one of my sisters, asks.

I nod and head toward the stairs. "It's relentless."

"He probably wants to ask you out."

I grimace at the thought. Something about him creeps me out. I head toward my room and strip off my winter gear. I find myself standing in my mirror with my credentials hanging down. I can't help the smile that spreads across my face. Pulling out my phone, I scroll until I find Noah's name. My thumb hovers, but I don't press. I haven't called him in *so long I honestly don't know what I'd say if he answered... or if she did.*

Instead, I scroll up to Liam's name and call him.

"Uncle Liam, I have news." I proceed to tell him, thanking him repeatedly for helping me get to this place in my life. He tells me he'll be at Noah's game, but will try to watch the Bears game as well, hoping to see me on the sidelines. My next call is to my parents. My mom's excited, and my dad is reserved. He's never really grasped my love of football but has always encouraged me to follow my passion.

The rest of the week I'm a mess, studying not only for my classes, but the stats for the upcoming game. I focus heavily on the Bears, but also their opponent, the Bengals. On paper, which means nothing on Sunday, the Bengals are favored to win. Still, I take my notes, jotting down things I need to watch for.

Sleep evades me, and by the time my alarm goes off Sunday morning, I'm a zombie. I down coffee, shower, drink more coffee, do my hair and get dressed before downing yet another cup while I'm on the phone with my mother, who is basking in the warm temperatures of the Bahamas with my aunts.

Arriving early with my press credentials hanging happily around my neck, I am downright giddy and loving every second of lifting the badge to show security that I'm allowed onto the field. Walking through the tunnel, I take it all in. While the noise level is high now, it will be thunderous when kick-off happens. People start to fill the seats, while many young kids are hanging over the railings trying to grab a player or two for an autograph. The smell of popcorn and hot dogs fill the air.

And the reason I'm here... the media outlets are setting up on every corner. Microphones are being tested, makeup done so they look perfect when they're on air. This is what I want. I turn at the sounds of applause and find the Bears coming out of the tunnel. They slap the hands of their littlest fans as they go by.

Being here early has its perks, at least it does for me since I'm the newbie. I'm the one learning. An NFL field is vastly different from high school or college and the last thing I want is to find myself tripping over some random piece of equipment or find myself standing in the wrong spot. I want to know my place on the field before someone yells at me.

As the Bears warm-up, I start taking notes, writing down everything from what stretches they're doing to how many are running full sprints. None of this is important for my article, but it keeps my mind busy and keeps me from gawking at the quarterback, Kyle Zimmerman. Each time I look at the field, his eyes are on me. The first time I noticed, I smiled and quickly went back to my notepad, but now I can feel his eyes burning into me.

"Watch out," I hear, looking up in time to sidestep an errant pass made by Kyle, who is rushing toward me. I pick the pigskin up and throw it back to him, with a perfect spiral I might add.

"Whoa, on target and everything," he says with a smile so wide that his eyes appear to be twinkling. "Sorry about that, sometimes the ball just gets away from me."

"You're the quarterback. It's your job to make sure the ball hits your mark each and every time. The ball should never get away from you. You should command it to do your work for you."

He smiles and pushes his hand through his hair. There's a bit of laughter coming from him as well, which in turn makes me smile, but I try to hide it. I know football, better than most, thanks to Noah.

"I've just been schooled by a reporter," he says, shaking his head.

"Not exactly."

"What do you mean?" he asks.

"I'm a broadcast journalism major at Northwestern, but football is my life."

His smile gets wider. "Let me get this straight, not only do you understand the game, but you can throw a wicked spiral?"

I shrug as if it's no big deal.

"I think I've died and gone to heaven." The thought that Kyle Zimmerman is impressed with me sends my heartbeat into a tailspin. He places his hand over his heart and bows. I could easily say I'm following right behind him with his dark hair and five o'clock shadow. I haven't dated much since I moved to Evanston. In fact, dating in high school rarely happened either. Most of the guys always thought that Noah and I had a thing, and while there was a time in my life that I wanted us to be, we're nothing more than best friends or at least we were.

"Have dinner with me after the game? Win or lose, you and I go out and enjoy each other's company."

"We barely know each other."

Kyle steps closer. He smells like man mixed with sweat. "I'm Kyle," he says.

"I'm Peyton." His much larger hand engulfs mine, covering it completely.

"Peyton as in Manning?"

"As in Powell-James, but if you're asking if my father was a Peyton Manning fan, the answer is yes." He wasn't exactly, but when Elle and I were born, Peyton Manning was one of the best quarterbacks in the league and his brother Eli was a rookie. I think for my father, being saddled with twin *girls, he wanted to do something to compensate for being the only man in the house. I never asked my mom why she allowed our father to name us after the Mannings... probably because I know it still hurts her sometimes to talk about him. Even though she loves my dad, Harrison, I know she misses my father, Mason.*

"I like it," he says, winking. "I gotta go to work." He motions toward the field with his head and that's when I make the mistake of looking. His teammates are standing there, gawking at us, with a few of them trying to hide their laughter behind their hands. If they had their jerseys on, I'd make a note of who they were so I could be sure to mention any screw-ups they had during the game. Luckily for them, I'm not a Bears fan and I don't have their roster memorized.

I try not to watch as Kyle runs back toward the rest of the team, and when he looks at me over his shoulder, I can feel my cheeks turning red. Of course, it could be because the wind is blowing and it's cold despite the sun being out or it's because I like that he's taken an interest in me.

And I really like that he's taken an interest in me.

While Kyle's car is small, he's leaning toward me, listening to everything I have to say. We haven't even left the parking lot yet, and his hand has moved closer and every few seconds I can feel his finger brush against my knuckles.

"I'm kicking myself for not throwing the ball at you until today."

I want to roast him for admitting that he was trying to hit me, but I let it go. "Today was your only opportunity. I was on an assignment. This was my first Bears game."

"And we lost."

I shrug and keep my eyes on him as he inches us forward.

"What are you in the mood for?" he asks as he brings his

car to a stop to let traffic go by, turning his head left, then right and when he looks at me, he winks.

"Someplace quiet, where we can talk."

Kyle smiles before pulling out onto the road. I barely recognize the sound of a truck horn blaring and tires screeching before I look out my window and see the word MACK heading straight toward me. As the grill of the truck smashes into my side of the car, I raise my hand to protect my face from the flying glass and I wonder if this was what my father did all those years ago when he met the eighteen-wheeler that took his life.

2

NOAH

*T*he crowd is deafening as I take the field. I don't need to look up at the scoreboard to know that there is under two minutes left and we're down by seven. Of course, if our last touchdown hadn't been called back for a bullshit call, we'd be tied, although, my mindset wouldn't be much different. This is our hurry-up offense that we practice the most. Some teams are better at it then we are, but we're young and still building the expansion team. Truth be told, no one expects us to win, and when we do, the sports analyst have a field day, jumping on the temporary bandwagon of the Portland Pioneers.

I'm used to the haters and have had to live with them badmouthing my dad for the past fifteen years. Being Liam Page's son hasn't been easy. Despite what critics say, everything that I have done, every achievement has been earned. My father was adamant that I make my own path, determine my own future. He didn't want me doing something I didn't want to do.

There was a time when I thought baseball was going to be my calling. My coach and somewhat step-dad, Nick, was convinced as well. After we won three consecutive state titles behind my pitching, the colleges were ready for me to commit to them and Major League teams were ready for me to sign my life away on the dotted line.

When I sat my parents down, which included Nick and Aubrey, I told them that I wanted to play football even though our high school team never made it past the first round of playoffs and the colleges weren't scouting me. I had a few small offers, but nothing that stood out. My parents supported my decision and were the ones to drive me to Notre Dame weeks before school started so I could walk on. It was the best decision I had ever made because within six games I was the starting quarterback and once the season was over I was offered a full-ride in exchange for three years of playing football with them.

After my junior year, I was encouraged by money hungry agents to enter the draft. My coach knew this was happening but never said anything. He didn't have to. I could see everything he was feeling in his expression. He was sad and worried that his star quarterback was ditching out a year early. It's not unheard of for an athlete to leave school early, but that wasn't for me. I made a commitment to the school that took a chance on me and really wanted to lead them to a bowl game. I did, but we didn't win. Still, it was one of the best decisions of my life.

And now here I am in my fourth year in the National Football League and the starting quarterback of a team that just wants to win. We have the tools in the players that we have. Our coach, Bud Walter, is one of the best but isn't here for the long haul. He's had a storied career and will be retiring soon, but until then he demands one hundred percent from us each and every time, and we do everything that we can to give it to him.

I stand behind the center Alex Moore. He's one of my best friends, not because he's meant to try and protect my ass from getting tackled or sacked each play, but because he's a stand-up guy who doesn't give a shit that my father is famous. I yell out my cadence and tap Alex on his ass in the event that he can't hear me. Once the pigskin touches my hands, I'm backpedaling with my arm cocked and ready to fire. My targets are the wide receiver, Julius Cunningham, who has been in the league for five years or Chase Montgomery the tight end. Chase is one of the best in the league and asked for a trade once the expansion team was announced. He's from Portland and wanted to be at home so his ailing mother could come to his games.

A monster of a tackle comes rushing toward me as I release the ball. I'm hit and thrown to the ground before I can see if it lands in Chase's hands. By the roar of the crowd, it does and I scramble to stand so I can get back to the line of scrimmage only to find Chase dancing in the end zone.

Coach yells that we go for two and I'm contemplating his thought process as I hurry toward my offensive line. Going for two means our opponent has to score. Tying the game means we can go a few more minutes. I have never second-guessed Bud, and I shouldn't be trying to now. I call out the play and resume my spot behind Alex. Once again my cadence is repeated and the ball is put into play.

The field before me is clear and I fire a rocket of a pass to Julius who catches it flawlessly in the end zone. My arms go up as I run toward him to celebrate, which is cut short because now we have to go back on defense.

"Westbury," Bud yells my name as I reach the sideline.

"Yeah, Coach?"

"Next time run more time off the clock."

I nod and walk toward the bench and sit down. He's right. I should've run some small routes instead of opening it up for the deep pass. Now we have to hold them on defense. I have faith in our cornerback, Cameron Simmons, but he can't cover everyone.

Behind me, I can hear my grandmother Bianca yelling. Usually it's my dad and mom, along with my little sister, but my mom, along with her friends are in the Bahamas for the week, taking a much-needed vacation. It's a toss-up between my grandma and my mom being the team's biggest fans. Both of them insist that they sit behind the bench while my dad prefers to sit in the luxury suite. I get where he's coming from. He gets tired of the security always around him. He wants to enjoy the game and not be hounded by fans all the time.

But my mom wants to be where the action is, and since they're ridiculously in love, my father does whatever she wants. In turn, he tries to please my grandmother as well. They had a rocky relationship right up until my sister was born, but now they're close and she's making up for lost time.

My sister, Betty Paige, sits in between my dad and grandma with her nose tucked into a book. She has no desire to be a football fan, but my parents are adamant that she comes each weekend to support me.

Sometimes Nick and Aubrey, along with their two kids Mack and Amelie make the trip to Portland. It's usually when the high school football team has a bye weekend. He's still coaching and often asks my dad to help, especially with Mack playing now too. Nick and my dad are friendly, but will never be best friends. He saves that title for Harrison James and Jimmy Davis, his two band mates, both of whom are living in Los Angeles, far away from Beaumont.

Jimmy and Jenna, along with their daughter Eden chose to move to California after Harrison's sister got married there one winter. Jenna fell in love with the beach and didn't hesitate to pack up and move. Eden is some junior surfing champion or something like that and from what Quinn tells me, it drives Jimmy crazy.

With Quinn going to college in California and Elle following him, Katelyn wanted to be there even though Peyton decided that Northwestern in Chicago was more her speed. She's making a name for herself while in school being a sports reporter and apparently has job offers pending from every sports channel out there.

Once I left for college, I came home as much as my schedule would allow. Most of the time my parents came to Indiana for the holidays and sometimes Peyton would come with them. I think, deep down, my parents knew that I needed to see Peyton more than Elle or Quinn. She's my best friend, my confidant and there isn't anything I wouldn't do for her. When I was able to go home, it was rare that I would run into Quinn. After he graduated high school, he took off to Los Angeles and immersed himself in the music scene. I do, however, have every single song of his and am probably his biggest fan, minus the large contingent of women that he has following him around. It's been a few years since we were all together and truthfully, I miss the group. I miss having everyone around. When we're together, we're inseparable, a tight-knit group and right now we're spread all over the place.

I suppose the next big gathering will be someone's wedding and if my girlfriend, Dessie, has her way about it, it'll be ours. I'm not there yet, but she is. She's all about what everyone thinks and her fellow Victoria Secret models are telling her that she should have a ring already. Personally, I don't see anything wrong with waiting, with making sure that marriage is the right step.

I stand on the sideline with my hands gripping the neck of my jersey while I watch our defense give up yard after yard. The closer the opponent gets to the end zone the more my ass is puckering. If they score, the game is over. Their quarterback is seasoned and knows how to bleed the clock making sure that we'll have no time left.

We hold them on the forty and I groan when they send their kicker out. He's one of the best in the business and hasn't missed this year. Still, I stand there next to Bud and watch as he lines up and prepares to kick.

The ball is hiked, he starts his motion and his foot connects with the ball. Sure enough, it flies through the uprights as the clock expires. I hang my head as people pat me on my shoulders and tell me good game.

Good isn't enough. Not in my book. I want to win. I want the city to be proud of their football team. I want players to want to come here, to play here and make our team stronger and that isn't going to happen if we don't start winning.

After giving the other team congratulations, I head to the bleachers where my family is waiting.

"Good game," Paige says, even though she doesn't mean it.

"Did you watch, Little B?"

She shakes her head and shrugs sheepishly. At twelve she'd rather read, shop, and pretend that she isn't crushing on Mack Ashford.

"Tough loss," my dad says as he reaches out to shake my hand. "The clock—"

"Yeah, coach said the same thing. I'll work on it."

"Well, I thought you were great," my grandmother says.

15

My dad and I look at her and shake our heads. "You're supposed to say that because you're my grandmother."

She waves her hand dismissing both of us. That's one thing Bianca Westbury doesn't do, she doesn't sugarcoat. I love her, but she has no filter. I think that is why she and my mom get along so well. My mom doesn't hold back either.

We like to give my mom a hard time about how she reacts. During the game, she cusses like a sailor and threatens bodily harm if she feels like I'm not being protected. But when she's talking to me, she's sweet and syrupy, telling me that everything is okay. My dad calls her the Jekyll and Hyde of sports mothers. My grandmother is the same.

"I'll meet you guys at the hotel. I need to shower and go pick up Dessie."

After a quick team meeting and a shower, I'm home and walking into the arms of Dessie. She's usually at my games unless she has to work. She spent the last week in Costa Rica shooting a spread for a swimsuit catalog that will be out this spring.

"Sorry about the loss," she says into my shoulder. I breathe her in and am instantly relaxed. "Was it because I wasn't there?"

Oh how easy that would be. I laugh and pull away from her. "No, just wasn't our game to win," I tell her. "Are you ready to go to dinner with my family?"

She nods, but her enthusiasm doesn't exactly meet her eyes. Dessie is convinced that my mother doesn't like her. I tell her that she's just being silly and that my mom loves everyone. I have never asked my mom if she likes Dessie or not and figured that if she has a problem with her, she'd say something. I don't bother telling her that my mom isn't here today because that might give her a false sense of security.

Bianca Westbury's wrath is ten times worse than my mom's.

The hotel that everyone is at is only two blocks away from my apartment, allowing us to walk over. If it isn't my name being called by the people we pass, it's Dessie's. Rarely can we go out around town without someone noticing either of us. I guess it's a good thing when you think about it, and honestly, it's something I've been used to since I was about ten.

When we arrive, Paige opens the door. She's crying and one look at my dad tells me something is really wrong.

"What's going on?" I ask, causing my father to stop his frantic packing.

"It's Peyton."

"What about her?" I ask, reaching for my grandmother as she brushes past me with Betty Paige's bag.

"She was in a car accident, Noah. Harrison says they don't expect her to make it. We have to go to Chicago."

"Wh-what?" I ask, swallowing hard. My tongue feels thick and foreign in my mouth, while my stomach rumbles.

My dad shakes his head. "I've called for a chartered flight. Your mom... they're on their way from the Bahamas now on the band's plane."

"Harrison?"

"Chartered a flight with Elle, Quinn, JD and Eden. They're all coming."

"I'm coming with you," I say. My dad doesn't say anything because he already knows that is where I need to be.

"Noah?" Dessie says my name quietly. I look at her and she shakes her head. "We have plans."

I close my eyes and process what she's saying. "My best friend has been in an accident. I have to go to her." I look

17

deep into Dessie's eyes, looking for any sign that she understands what I'm saying.

"...It's always about Peyton."

She's right. It is. Peyton's all I'm going to think about because this can't be happening to her. I storm out of the suite and my thought go straight back to when I was ten and my uncle Mason was killed. This can't happen to Elle and Katelyn, not again.

3

PEYTON

*T*here I am, on a gurney with eight, nine or maybe it's ten people working frantically to save my life. They yell loudly and demand things that don't make sense to me all while machines constantly beep and my blood pools on the floor as someone screams that they have a bleeder. I have a tube coming out of my mouth and my eyes are taped shut, except I can see everything that is happening and I seem to be breathing okay. The clothes I wore are tattered and some pieces lay haphazardly on the floor with shards of glass embedded in the fabric while my chest is open and exposing my organs, yet I seem to be dressed. My brown hair is now jet-black and half my scalp's missing. Consciously, I reach up to feel my hair, but everything seems to be normal. So why am I there on the table, bleeding, broken and dying when I'm standing here watching everything happening.

"She's crashing!" the doctor yells as someone hands him two wands. They look like drumsticks with small symbols on the end. If my dad saw them, he would have a fit. He would never allow me to play his drums with something like those. His drums are precious to him, at least the ones that stay in the spare bedroom at my parents' house, that I'm allowed to play when I visit. When they moved to Los Angeles, I cried. I felt like I no longer belonged anywhere. My brother Quinn was already there and Elle was far too excited to leave me by myself in Chicago.

But they're not drumsticks because the doctor puts them into that gaping hole where my breasts used to be. Whatever he does, they cause me to jerk off the table. My body on the table feels it, but I don't. He does it again and again, barking out orders as if he's in charge. After each jerk, everyone pauses and watches one of the monitors.

"She's back," one of the nurses says. Where do they think I went? Do they not realize that I am on the table, waiting for them to fix me up so I can go to dinner with Kyle?

Where is Kyle? He was with me in the car, smiling at me as we pulled out of the parking lot. But where did he go. I look at the door and see people running by and I'm curious to know where Kyle is.

Out in the hall, the noise is different and the lights seem brighter. There is more yelling and alarms continue to beep. In the room next to mine, someone lays on the table with a sheet pulled over their face. I hate sleeping like that because I feel like I can't breathe.

The nurses are all wearing blue and green, but none of them stop and ask me what I'm doing or ask me if I'm hungry. I am, hungry that is because Kyle promised me dinner but somehow we're here. I don't think this was his idea of a good time. It's definitely not mine.

The room across from me is empty, but there's blood on the floor. A man brushes by me, whistling and pushing a mop bucket. He slops the wet threads onto the floor and pushes the puddles around, repeating the process until all the blood is gone then he's breezing by me again.

I go back to my room and now there are fewer people by me. A few of them leave the room with their hands and gowns covered in my blood, while the others filter around me.

"Let's stitch her up and get her to ICU. Has anyone contacted her parents?"

"They're on their way."

They are? My parents are coming to Chicago? But it's cold and snowing. My parents hate the snow. I can't imagine that they would want to come here when I could easily go see them at the beach house.

A big burly man comes in and the nurses pile wires on top of my bed as the man pushes me out of the room. I follow behind because I need to know where they're taking me. The room is small but with a very large window. After the nurse plugs everything back in, she pauses at my bedside and runs her hands through my hair, picking out more shards of glass. Each piece tings as it hits the stainless pan that is resting on my chest.

"You're going to be okay, sweet girl," she says.

"How do you know?" I ask, but she doesn't respond. She doesn't even look at me. She just keeps running her hand through my hair.

"Your parents will be here soon. As soon as they get here, we'll let them right in so they can see you. I bet your mom will spend the night because if you were my daughter, that is what I'd do. I'll make sure she has a blanket and pillow."

"Do you know my mom?"

She still doesn't answer me.

"What about my dad? He's famous, ya know. I bet if

you ask him, he'll give you his autograph."

She still doesn't respond. I wave my hand in front of her face, but she's focused on my body that lies in the bed being kept alive by the machines that beep incessantly. She continues to talk, telling my body about her family and how she doesn't have any children but wants to have a daughter with brown hair.

"What color eyes do you have, sweetie?" she asks.

"Noah says I have blue eyes like the ocean, but sometimes they change when I'm angry," I tell her but she doesn't acknowledge me.

A man enters my room and opens the binder that rests on the counter near my bed. "How's she doing?"

"I think she's waiting for her parents to get here. I don't know how she's alive," she says.

I look from her to my body and wonder the same thing. If I die, I can be with my father. I miss him, he has missed so much of my life that I would love to talk to him, to tell him everything.

But I would miss my sister. She's my best friend even though she's living in California I talk to her every day. Except I didn't tell her about Kyle and I need to. Elle would like him. He's cute, seems smart and was very polite when he escorted me out of the stadium.

And I'd miss my mom. She's already been through so much but has Harrison to take care of her. He sure does love her and us. He's always treated Elle and I like his daughters. It was like he was meant to come into our lives after my father passed away. He and Quinn saved us, made us whole.

"Does anyone know what time her parents will be here?" the doctor asks.

"They're flying in from California. I don't know if

anyone knows what time they got a flight."

"I'll stay until they arrive so I can talk to them," he says before writing something down in the book. I try to see what it is, but the words are blurry.

"I'm not leaving her," the nurse says. "I want to be here with her, just in case... so I can tell her mom that she didn't die alone."

Wait, I am dying? What if I don't want to? I mean I want to see my father, but I don't want to leave my mom. And there are things that I want to do, like be on television and be there when Noah wins the Super Bowl. That's his dream, and mine for him. We've spent countless hours talking about what it'll be like for his family to run onto the field and for him to raise the Lombardi trophy for all the fans of the Portland Pioneers to see. I plan to be there as a broadcaster even though I'd be biased during my reporting. Maybe that would have to be a game I skip so I can yell at him from the fifty-yard line. Either way, Noah will want me there, so I can't die.

The doctor leaves and another nurse walks in and stands by my other side. "Jenna, do you want me to sit with her while you eat?"

Jenna? I have an aunt named Jenna. She has beautiful red hair and looks nothing like the nurse who is holding my hand.

"No, I'm not leaving her."

"I'll bring you something then."

Jenna nods but keeps her eyes focused on my body. It's weird. Usually I can tell when someone is staring at me, but I can't seem to make my eyes open.

She leaves my side and goes to the sink, wetting a towel and filling another pan with water. When she returns, she picks up my hand and starts cleaning the blood that has dried around my nails and along my arm, cleaning around the cuts carefully. Every so often she dips the cloth into the water and it turns light pink. When Jenna has finished both arms, she starts on my hair, careful not to touch the area where my scalp is missing.

Jenna pulls a brush out of a bag and runs its bristles under the faucet. She runs it through the ends of my hair, working her way up until almost every strand is wet and then she braids what she can.

I wait for her to move the blanket that covers my chest so I can see what they did to my chest, but she never does.

"Your mom should be here soon, sweetheart. Then you can go and you won't be in pain anymore," she says, but she doesn't realize that I don't want to go, at least not yet. And I'm not in pain.

"I feel great," I say as I look down at my body. I'm still in the outfit that I wore to the game. My arms aren't cut up, my hair is still perfectly styled and I'm happy.

Her friend returns with some food and that reminds me that Kyle still owes me dinner. "Where's Kyle? Do you know? He was supposed to take me out to dinner."

Neither lady answers me and it's starting to make me mad that they're ignoring me. Why can't they see me standing here next to them? I can see them and hear everything they're saying yet they act like I'm not even in the room.

"Did you give her a bath?"

"Not really," Jenna says. "I cleaned up the blood and braided her hair. I don't want that to be the first thing her mom sees, ya know."

"You're a good nurse, Jenna."

She smiles at her friend with tears in her eyes. The other nurse goes to the book that lies on the counter and makes a note. Again, I try to see what it says, but everything is blurry. It doesn't make sense because I have perfect eyesight.

My dad, Elle, and Quinn walk by the large window of my room. I go to them, desperate to feel their arms around me, but my dad looks right through me.

"Dad... Elle... Quinn...?" but they don't say anything. In fact, they ignore me like everyone else has been doing this entire time.

I stand in front of Elle and look at my twin. She's so beautiful. Tears stream down her face and her hand covers her heart. Does she know that I'm not in pain?

There's an audible gasp and I turn to see my dad in the doorway. Elle now stands next to him with her hand covering her mouth. She almost falls to her knees but my dad holds her upright.

"Mr. James," the doctor stops speaking when he looks at Elle.

"This is Peyton's twin."

He nods. "I'm Dr. Stevens. I operated on your daughter when she was brought in by ambulance."

"Is she going to be okay?" my dad asks, but the doctor shakes his head.

"As we said on the phone, we don't expect her to make it through the night. She suffered severe trauma when the truck collided with her side of the car. We've operated, but the damage was extensive. I'm sorry," he says, resting his hand on my dad's shoulder.

My sister collapses even though Quinn tries to catch her, he's unable to. She cries loudly while my brother tries to console her.

"Just like our father," she screams loudly in between sobs. "Just like our father."

4

NOAH

From the moment I was told that Peyton had been in a car accident until now, everything has moved in incredibly slow motion. The details are fuzzy and each time my dad tries to reach Harrison, his calls are going to voicemail. The worry in my dad and Grandma's eyes is evident.

All I can think about is the time we lost Mason. His death changed everything. My father returned to Beaumont after learning Mason had died. They were best friends growing up until my dad made a life-changing decision. I suppose that you can say his decision was for the best or maybe it was wrong, depending on how you look at it, but it was right for my parents. They needed the separation to grow and find themselves individually. Everyday since my dad's return, I have witnessed his undying love for my mom. They have the type of relationship I want, the kind where it doesn't matter how your day is going, the moment you see that person, you know everything is going to be better.

My problem is that I don't know when I'll know. It's like I'm waiting for a flash of lightning or for the sky to open up and cast a rainbow that leads me to the one. My mom speaks of soul mates and one true loves, and why wouldn't she? One look and you can see that my parents are smitten with each other. They're ridiculous, acting like teenagers all the time, always embarrassing Paige.

Paige, or Little B as I like to call her, is nestled into my side, fast asleep. The tears she cried earlier were for Peyton. Paige loves Elle and Peyton. They used to babysit her.

Telling my coach that I was leaving didn't go well with him or Dessie for that matter. I promised coach I wouldn't miss practice and I intend to keep that promise. If it meant I had to travel back and forth between Portland and Chicago, I would do it. There was no way I wouldn't be there when Peyton woke up... because for me there is no other alternative.

Dessie, on the other hand, didn't understand why I needed to go in the first place. The problem is that this conversation took place in front of my dad, sister, and grand-mother. I don't think she meant to sound rude or insensitive, but that's how her words came off and what Bianca heard. If Dessie thought my grandmother didn't like her before, she can pretty much guarantee that's the case now.

We left my dad's hotel almost as soon as we arrived and I all but ran back to our apartment to pack a bag. The entire way, Dessie whined about me leaving, saying she just got home and it wasn't fair.

No, what wasn't fair was that my friend had been in an accident and the words "not expected to make it" had been said. That sentence alone should've prompted Dessie to encourage me to go, not complain. I would expect Dessie to do the same for her friends, except she doesn't have a connection with anyone like I do with Peyton.

For Dessie, she grew up in a sheltered environment and

started modeling at a young age. None of her "friends" are truly her friends and are more like acquaintances who wouldn't think twice about stabbing her in the back. Her friends have hit on me one too many times, and while I tell her not to trust them, she doesn't necessarily believe they would do anything to hurt her.

What she doesn't understand is the connection that I have with Peyton. No one really does and in the past, it has scared women away. This one time in college, I was dating a girl and Peyton came to visit for Homecoming. Peyton stayed in my room, sleeping in my roommate's bed, but that was far too much for my girlfriend at the time and she issued an ultimatum—her or Peyton—I chose Peyton. I always have and always will. We have a bond that is hard to describe.

And that's why I'm on this plane, traveling to Chicago. Peyton is hurt and she needs me. She needs to know that I'm there for her during her crisis, just as I would be if she picked up the phone and called me. I'd drop everything for her.

We don't know what to expect when we land in Chicago and I'm trying not to fear the worst. My memories of my uncle Mason have all but faded except for the night everything happened. I barely remember him showing me how to tackle properly or teaching me to learn the game of football and not just play it. But I do remember my mom getting the late-night phone call and her leaving me with Nick so she could go be with Peyton and Elle. Nick paced the living room while he chatted on his phone, trying to get whatever information he could about Mason. Being a doctor, he had privileges at the hospital, not to mention Beaumont is a pretty small town and everyone pretty much knows everyone.

It was Nick who told me that Mason didn't make it, and I remember wondering what was going to happen next. Mason was a teacher at the high school and the football coach. Katelyn would babysit me after school or be the one to pick me up if I were sick so I know she didn't work. I was worried that she would move away, but then Liam Page rode into town like a bad ass knight in shining armor and saved her. Financially that is. My dad never let on about all the things he did for Katelyn until much later. He paid for Mason's funeral, paid off all the Powell's debt and started trust funds for Peyton and Elle. And he brought Harrison to town, and his arrival changed everything.

Needing something to distract my mind I press the button that brings the small television to life and go through the channels until I am on ESPN, and because I forgot to pack my headphones, I can only read the ticker at the bottom. *__BREAKING NEWS__* is scrolling along the bottom and I catch the tail end of it, waiting for it to start again. Whenever I see this I always fear it's about me, or someone I know with a reported trade, although that wouldn't warrant a headline like this.

Chicago Bears quarterback, Kyle Zimmerman was involved in a fatal accident.

That's all the ticker says, nothing about who died or where the accident was. I find it ironic that he and Peyton were in an accident on the same day...unless he's the reason she's in the hospital. Did he hit her with his car?

I press the call button to signal the flight attendant. Considering this is a chartered plane it only takes her seconds before she's at my side. "What can I do for you, Mr. Westbury?"

"Do you happen to have any headphones?"

"Sure, one moment."

In a flash, she's back with a pair and already has the bag opened for me, making it easy for me to pull them out. Once the jack is inserted, I'm pressing the volume button so I can hear the report.

"...erman was leaving Soldier Field after the Bears loss this afternoon when he pulled out in front of a semi-truck that was unable to stop before colliding with the passenger side of his Porsche 911. Zimmerman was taken to Northwestern Memorial with unknown injuries while the driver of the truck was treated on scene. Zimmerman's unknown female occupant did not survive."

The segment cuts to clips of Zimmerman's career and highlights from today's game. He has been in the league one year longer than I have, but our games are similar and the media has compared us against one another. He excels in places that I'm weak and vice versa. He also has a better team than I do at the moment.

Still, I wouldn't wish an accident like this on anyone. It's tough on your psyche to lose a game and then to have this happen. I feel sorry for him, losing his girlfriend like this. I can't imagine what he's going through.

When Peyton announced that she was heading to Northwestern, I acted happy for her. Truthfully, I wanted her to go to UCLA with Elle because selfishly I liked the idea of them being together, but Peyton wanted to spread her wings and be on her own. I understood her reasoning, wanting to break away from being a twin. It was the same reason I chose to stay away from the University of Texas... my dad. Not that they wanted me to play football for them.

Deep down I was nervous that Peyton would be in Chicago by herself and when I was drafted I was praying that the Bears would take me. It was a long shot considering they didn't need a quarterback, but I had hoped. Moving from Beaumont to Chicago is life changing. The fast-paced world of a major city is vastly different from the ho-hum life that we were used to living. But Northwestern has the best sports broadcasting program in the country and that's what Peyton wanted.

Watching ESPN, I kept waiting for them to announce the name of Zimmerman's girlfriend. There was a growing pit in my stomach that this accident and Peyton's were somehow related, but I can't put much stock into it because if she had a boyfriend, she would've told me, even if the guy she was seeing was someone in the league. Honestly, I expected Peyton to marry a pro baller. He'd be the only one who could keep up with her and keep her on her toes.

The flight attendant walks by, telling us we're about to land. I rouse Betty Paige so she had a chance to be alert when we hurry off the plane and into the waiting car. I half expect a media frenzy at the hospital, but I'm hoping that word hasn't gone out that Harrison's daughter is in the hospital. It's bad enough when we have to deal with the media on a normal day.

"Are we there?"

"Almost, Little B," I tell her as she rights herself in her seat. She looks out of her window at the cityscape below. She's used to traveling and being on tour with the band and has long gotten over the thrill of arriving in a new town.

"Do you think Eden will be here?"

I hadn't thought about Jimmy and Jenna arriving, but I would imagine they would be. We're a close-knit family and when one is in trouble, we all come together for support.

"I'm sure she will be soon if she isn't already."

"Do you think Mack and Amelie will be here as well?" she asks.

I groan like any big brother should do. When I look at Nick, I see a father figure, but Paige doesn't. She sees the Ashfords as family friends who happen to have a son her age and a daughter a few years younger than her. Mack is a great kid, a lot like me in many ways, but a boy nonetheless and Paige is at that age where she has a crush. I suppose in the grand scheme of things it could be worse, although my dad vows that a Westbury will never marry an Ashford. I suppose there are some things you never get over and for my dad, that would be Nick hitting on my mom while they were dating. Never mind that shortly after I was born, Nick and my mom actually started dating. But we don't talk about that much.

The plane touches down and taxis right to a private hangar where an SUV is waiting. Pleasantries are exchanged as we pile in and within seconds we're on our way to the hospital. The closer we get, the worse I feel. I try not to let my father's words from earlier seep too far into my subconscious. I figure if I keep telling myself that the words "they don't expect her to make it" are overly dramatic then when I see her, she'll be sitting up and smiling. Except Katelyn would never allow a sentence like that to be muttered about her children.

I don't know if my dad paid the driver to break the law or if this is how he drives on a normal basis, but we're weaving in and out of traffic with our hazards on while he presses the horn every few seconds. By the time we pull up to the hospital entrance, I have never been more relieved to get out of a car.

With Paige's hand in mine, we follow my dad into the hospital and into the critical care unit. Grandma, Little B, and I sit in the waiting room while he checks in at the front desk. I could probably go with him, but I don't want to leave my sister out here by herself.

I'm not sure how much time passes, but when my dad comes back I can tell he's been crying and he motions for me to follow him. He takes me away from the waiting room.

"Go in and say goodbye," he says, choking up.

"Excuse me?"

He shakes his head and tears fall down his cheeks. I've seen my dad cry before, but not since Paige was born. "It's not good, Noah." He pats me on the shoulder, sidesteps me and heads toward the waiting room.

I turn and head toward the automatic doors that will take me to Peyton. I don't bother asking what room she's in because it's easy to tell with the half a dozen people cramming into the small room.

Quinn and Harrison smile gravely at me as I step into the room. I don't have a clear shot of Peyton because her mom and mine, along with her sister and a nurse are hovering over her. It takes me a few more steps until I can fully see the little girl turned woman, who used to follow me around carrying a football—the same one I took to her senior prom, taught how to drive, and used to picture myself with—lying on a bed connected to wires that are keeping her alive.

5

PEYTON

I suppose there comes a time in everyone's life when they die. For me, I've died and come back; at least that's what the doctor has told my parents. I was so excited to see them, but they can't see or hear me. Even now I'm trying to hold my mom's hand, but she doesn't feel me squeezing her back, even though she's begging me to. In fact, she's asking me to do all sorts of things like open my eyes or wiggle my toes. I *am* doing everything she asks. She just can't see me. It's like I'm in another realm where I can see and hear them, but everything I do, every question I respond to or comment I make lingers in the air.

Everyone is crying, and that's saying a lot because I have never seen my dad cry until today. Sure, he's had misty eyes like when Quinn left for college or when he came home and showed us the Oscar that *4225 West* had won for best song in a movie, but never have I been witness to seeing him cry like he is now. I tried to comfort him, to put my arms around him like I used to when I was little, but it didn't do anything to help ease his pain.

The same can be said about Quinn. He's always been

the big brother to us, our protector. We had Noah for that as well, but the age difference made it so we were rarely in school together. Quinn fell right in the middle of our group. Friends with Noah and brother to Elle and me, and until today I have never seen him cry. Not even when he was in trouble or when he was given his first drum set. But now he is. He's sobbing and holding onto Elle as if I've died already.

Maybe I have died and this is me as a ghost, standing on the outside and watching as my family falls apart. We've always been a strong unit, supporting each other's goals and aspirations. Growing up, our parents encouraged us to find ourselves and to follow what we love. It's how I ended up in Chicago while the rest of my family lived in Los Angeles. Elle wanted the sun, the sand, and surfers. Quinn wanted the music scene. My parents wanted solitude and quiet. I wanted the crazy, hectic life of a sports reporter.

There's no doubt in my mind that my time to shine was about to happen. Being on the sideline, even for one game, was going to be enough to catapult me into something amazing. I had big plans for that article even if my professor was the only one to see it. I would've used it as a reference when I applied at ESPN or Fox Sports. I suppose meeting Kyle changed all that.

Speaking of, I still don't know where he is. In my current state, it seems that I can roam the halls freely. I've tried to converse with the nurses and other staff members, but it's as if they can see right through me.

The hall is quiet, except for the annoying beeping sound coming from every room on this floor. I peek in each one, most patients are sleeping and only a few have people in them. My room by far is the most packed with bodies, all here to say goodbye according to the doctor that stuck those odd drumsticks into my chest.

Yet, I'm not ready to go. I'm not done being me. I continue to visit each room, looking for someone like me that can tell me what I'm going through. Is this common for people who have died? The only other person I know is my father and I was far too young to remember anything other than his funeral. Sure, I can recall bits and pieces of my life with him, but his funeral is vivid and often plays like a movie when I'm not sleeping well.

The double doors open when I approach. This hall is far quieter than the one I was just in, with the only sound coming from the television. The noise is easy to follow and I'm surprised to find the room empty when I arrive. Whoever left it on would be in trouble and on dish duty for a week in our house. That thought makes me giggle a little bit because it was always Quinn who left something on and was stuck with that horrible chore.

As I approach the elevator, it opens for me. I'm alone and the number for the fifth floor is lit up but once the doors close they open again and I'm left wondering if I even moved. There are a lot of people waiting to get on so I step off quickly, not wanting to be the reason they're held up any longer.

This floor is busy with nurses walking up and down the hall, patients being wheeled in their chairs to their next destination and a police officer standing outside one of the rooms. That's the one I go in, curious as to what they did to warrant a policeman to stand guard at their door.

It's Kyle! I rush to his bed only to realize that he can't see me either. His leg is in a cast that extends up his thigh and his arm is bandaged. He'll surely be done for the season with an injury like that, and he's probably very upset about it.

There's another officer in the room talking to Kyle. It's only after I hear my name that I start to pay attention.

"Tell me again how you met Peyton James?"

"It's Powell-James," I tell him, but he doesn't seem to repeat the change. My dad has always insisted that we hyphenate even though it can get a bit tedious.

"I met her before warm-ups. I thought she was beautiful and she knew her stuff about football. That was an instant turn-on so I asked her out."

"Kyle that's so sweet," I say.

"You said thought?" the officer says to Kyle, which confuses me.

"She was dead... I mean..." Kyle shakes his head and looks out the window. I wish he'd look at me so he could see that I'm not dead. I'm alive and standing right next to him.

"Did she have her seatbelt on?"

Kyle nods.

"Were you speeding?"

He shakes his head. "The truck... I didn't see it until it was too late. I couldn't do anything to move my car out of its way."

"It's okay, Kyle," I tell him as I run my fingers over his hair. He seems to like that since he closes his eyes and leans his head toward me.

"Were you angry that you lost tonight?"

I look at the officer and say, "What kind of question is that?"

"I was, but I was looking forward to spending some time with her."

"Me too, Kyle."

"When they run your toxicology screen will they find anything?"

Kyle shakes his head again. "I'm clean."

"Kyle stop answering his questions."

I turn to find a man walking in the room and handing the officer a card. He seems angry and quickly tosses his briefcase and jacket into the chair that rests by the window.

"From this point forward if you need to speak to my client, you will do so when I'm present."

"Have a good day, Mr. Zimmerman."

"Asshole," the man mutters to the officer's back. "What the hell happened, Kyle?"

Once again he's shaking his head. "I don't even know. One minute I'm talking to Peyton and the next the roof of my car is flying away and she's in my lap. There was so much blood and screaming."

"She was screaming? That's good. That means she was alive when they transported her."

"No, I was screaming. She didn't make a sound. She just laid there like she was sleeping," he tells the man.

Kyle's friend leans down and peers into his eyes. I do the same, wanting to know what he's looking for or what he's seeing. "Any drugs in your system?"

"No, I swear to God I'm clean."

The man nods and stands back up, but I'm still looking. I like Kyle's eyes. They're green, but look lifeless right now.

"This doesn't look good, Kyle. If she dies—"

"She's still alive?" he asks.

"Yeah, but they don't expect her to make it through the night. Her family is with her now."

"I want to see her," Kyle says, but his friend is shaking his head. Why can't he go see me? Maybe Kyle is the reason I'm not awake yet. Maybe I'm waiting for him. This man should help Kyle to my room so he can see me.

"Kyle..." his friend sighs and looks out the window. "Her dad is pretty famous and I'm afraid there will be a lawsuit. I don't want you going up there to see her to be seen as a sign of guilt."

I don't understand what the man means about my dad being famous and a lawsuit. It was an accident and not something Kyle could've prevented.

"I am guilty. I should've seen the truck. I should've looked again before pulling out. She's up there dying because of me. Her family needs to know that I'm sorry, that I was taking her to dinner after the game because I like her, they need to know that I thought she was beautiful and loved that in the few minutes we spoke she had me in awe of her football knowledge. They should know that I never wanted to hurt her and that I wanted to spend time with her and get to know her better."

"Oh, Kyle," I say wishing he could hear me. He turns his head away from me as if he doesn't want me to see his tears, but it's too late.

"I'll talk to their lawyer and see what the family wants to do, but don't get your hopes up." The man grabs his coat and briefcase and hastily leaves the room. Kyle punches his bed with his free hand and slams his head back into his pillow. His tears flow more heavily now and he turns away from me to face the window.

I take that as my sign to leave and return to the hallway, which is still busy. Nurses run down the hall toward the elevator and I follow, curious as to what is happening. They run through a set of double doors, but I'm unable to keep up. I try to return to Kyle's room, but can't find my way back. The only things visible to me are the elevators. I step back on and the number seven is illuminated taking me back to the floor where I am.

In the waiting room, I see my uncle Liam, holding my cousin Betty Paige. He's singing to her while he rocks her back and forth. Paige was such a cute and fun baby, although anytime uncle Liam was around, he was holding her. I heard aunt Josie tell my mom one time that Liam was making up for lost time because he wasn't there for Noah. The doors open and my dad and Quinn are standing outside the room I'm staying in. They look lost and in pain. I step back into my room to find my sister, mom, my nurse and aunt Josie flanking my sides. But that isn't who catches my attention.

It's Noah.

My Noah.

He's come to see me. To be here when I wake up. I stand in front of him, looking up so I can see his eyes and let my fingers ghost over the worry lines that have seemed to appear on his forehead. The normal vibrancy, the happiness that is usually there is missing. He peers down at my body and chokes on a sob. My instincts tell me to reach out to him, to catch him before he falls, but instead, it's Elle. She's there to break his fall and to hold him as he makes the most agonizing cry I have ever heard.

6

NOAH

The gut-wrenching sob that gets everyone's attention comes from me. I can't recall a time in my life when I have ever emitted another a sound like this, not even when I thought I tore my ACL in high school. My reaction then was purely out of fear and frustration. My response now is all out of heartbreak. I grip the end of her bed to steady myself, to keep my legs upright when all they want to do is collapse, but Elle's arms wrap around me and I sag into her.

My mother is there too, helping Elle hold me up so I don't fall on top of her. She whispers that everything is okay, but I know it's not. Peyton looks nothing like the girl I watched grow up into a beautiful woman. Her face is swollen and bruised. Her long brunette hair is missing on one side. And arms that have held me more times than I can count are bandaged and laying at her side, unmoving.

"What happened to her?" The words are barely spoken but heard loud and clear by everyone.

"The truck hit her head on, Noah. You need to tell her goodbye," my mom says as her tears dampen the side of my cheek, at least I thought they were hers until she wipes my face, clearing mine away.

I shake my head. "I won't. That was a promise we made to each other years ago."

"She's leaving us, Noah. You have to tell her it's okay to go be with our father," Elle begs me to do the unthinkable, but I still refuse. It's a long-standing thing between us. We never say goodbye unless we're singing Bon Jovi's song. I don't remember how it started, but I remember the last time she tried to say it and I wouldn't let her.

Seeing Peyton's number flash on my screen shouldn't surprise me, but it does. We haven't spoken in months, not because we're mad at each other, but because I've been busy and she's been trying to give me the space I need to get acclimatized to the NFL. I'm in my second year, and there are times when I still find myself shaking in my cleats. I'm getting better, but... well, I'm always going to have doubts that I'm not good enough.

"Noah," Alex Moore calls my name, taking my attention away from my ringing phone. I send Peyton to voicemail and rush over to where Alex is standing with two women. Dread washes over me the closer I get. Since the Portland Pioneers drafted me, he has been trying to set me up with anything that crosses his path. Of course it only works if the babe he's interested in has a friend, otherwise he's not willing to share.

"What's up," I say to Alex as we shake hands and the two women stand there watching. I try not to look at either of them. It's not that I'm playing hard to get or that I'm not interested, it's because more often than not, they're only interested in one thing. This was something I witnessed first hand when it came to my dad and his career. There was always someone who didn't give a shit that he was married or that Betty Paige and I were with him. They'd hit on him,

throw themselves at him or proposition him, always promising him something better than what he had at home. How my mom could put up with that, I never knew or understood until my senior year in college.

The team was really good that year and suddenly I was the most popular guy on campus, at least during the fall. It was as if I was an overnight sensation. Not only was I the starting quarterback, but also Liam Page's son and that made me the most eligible man on campus, meaning women were throwing themselves at me. I entertained a few, but none that I wanted to bring home to my parents.

When I was drafted, the attention from the opposite sex grew exponentially. It's everywhere I go. If I'm at the store, the gas station, walking down the street or even running out onto the field, I can hear them calling my name, telling me that they love me.

My father always told me to never say it back unless I meant it. He said that while fans love you because you bring a certain amount of joy to their lives, you appreciate them. The word love is to be saved for the people that mean the most in your life. I have always heeded his words and aside from my parents, sister, and grandparents I haven't told anyone that I loved them. Not even my high school girlfriends.

Alex introduces me to his new friends, Sabrina and Sadie, both of whom are models. He suggests that we go out on the town and before I can respond, my phone rings again.

"I'm sorry, I have to take this," I say as I step away from Alex and the women. I can hear him grumbling as I walk away, but that's par for the course with him. He's all about one thing and usually has no problem achieving his goal.

Looking quickly down at my phone, Peyton's name and number are there. She usually leaves a message, knowing I'll call her back, but not this time. I don't know whether I should be concerned or not.

"Hey."

"Did I catch you at a bad time?" she asks. That is how she normally starts our conversation, always conscious that I might be in the middle of something or about to become busy. There was a time in college when I would drop everything to talk to her, often pissing off whatever girlfriend I had at the time. They were jealous of her and it didn't matter that I told them they had nothing to worry about, they never believed me., but those days quickly faded when I was drafted.

"Just got done working out. What's up?"

"My prom is this week."

"Ah, joyous time. Remember to smile nice and bright for your mom."

"I don't have a date," she says, rendering me speechless. It's not that guys don't ask her out, they do all the time because Quinn fills me in, so I'm a little flabbergasted by her statement.

"How is that possible?"

She sighs and I swear I hear her sniffle. "Stupid Diana told everyone that you're taking me to prom and even though I told everyone that wasn't the case, no one asked me and now everyone has a date."

Diana Jenkins has been a thorn in our sides for as long as I can remember. Her mother moved to town after she became infatuated with my dad's band. Diana immediately tried to submerge herself into our tight-knit group. It didn't go so well and she's been a pain ever since.

"When is prom?"

When she gives me the date, I cringe. It's at the end of the week. I pull my phone away and open the calendar app to check and see what I have going on this weekend. Thankfully, I'm free and can't believe what I'm about to do.

"Do you have a dress?"

"Yes, why?" she asks.

"I need to know the color so I can match my bow tie."

"Noah," she drags my name out. "I didn't call and tell you this because I need you to take me to prom. I need to know how to handle my mom because when I tell her, she isn't going to be very happy. In fact, she may cry and you know how I am when she cries."

It's how we all are. Growing up I never knew Katelyn to be a crier until Quinn started high school then she went on this mom kick where everything was documented and he, along with the twins, had to partake in every rite of passage. Thankfully, the age difference between us meant I got off free of having to do anything I didn't want to, not that my mother didn't try and force me.

"Peyton, I want to take you to prom. In fact, I'd be honored."

"No, Noah. People will bug you for your autograph. I don't want that for you."

"It's too late, I already ordered my tux." It's a lie, but one that she'll buy.

"Noah," she whines. I already know what's going on in her head. She has held our friendship close to her heart and more so since she arrived at high school and I was in college.

"I want to do this, Peyton."

"You won't be mad?" she asks.

"At you? Never in a million years. Be ready for the time of your life."

"I gotta run."

"Okay, well goo—"

"Don't say it, Peyton. It's our deal, remember?"

"Only because of that stupid song."

"You love it and we'll dance to it at prom. See you soon."

As soon as I hang up I text my mom and tell her I need a tuxedo and to have it at the house for Saturday. Like any other mother, she asks me why and I tell her that I'm coming home to take Peyton to prom. I know for a fact that Peyton won't tell anyone because she feels like she's bothering me. Someday, I hope that she realizes that she never is.

I go back to Alex and the two ladies, who I thought would've left by now and try to engage in a conversation with them. My mom, dad, and Katelyn are all texting me and instead of being rude and answering them, I toss my phone into my bag so I can't feel it vibrating.

Alex suggests we all go out and grab dinner, I agree and offer to drive until Alex pulls me aside.

"You take Sabrina. I'm getting vibes from Sadie."

Of course he is. I pat him on the shoulder. "No problem."

"Sabrina, looks like you're riding with me," I say, much to Alex's dismay.

"Real smooth, Westbury."

I flip him off before motioning for Sabrina to follow me out to my SUV. I thought about getting a sports car like a few of my teammates but didn't feel secure enough in one, plus there is never enough room to carry my stuff. I open the door for her and wait for her to climb in before shutting it and going to the back to put my bag back there. I'm hoping that she's far enough away that the stench of my gym clothes won't make her sick.

"Sorry about earlier," I tell her. "I had to take a call from home."

"Girlfriend?" she asks, rather unabashedly.

I shake my head. "Not exactly." It was hard to explain what Peyton was to me because I always felt in limbo with *her. We were friends, best friends in fact, but there were times when I wanted more but was too afraid to proceed. It's not that I thought she'd turn me down, but more so of how Katelyn and Harrison would feel. Our age difference as of right now is a bit much I think socially. I know my agent would have a field day if I started dating an eighteen-year-old so I tell myself I'm going to wait until she's twenty-one.*

"What does that mean?" she asks as I pull out onto the road behind Alex.

"I don't know. I have always had feelings for this girl I grew up with. They started when I was about fifteen, but she's much younger than I am and the timing isn't right."

"Are you waiting for her?"

I shake my head. "No, I've dated and had semi-steady relationships, but those women didn't like her or like that I'm there whenever she needs me. She's my best friend." I don't know why, but I find myself telling this poor woman everything.

"Wow, she must be some girl."

"She is."

And she still is. Deep down I think she's the reason why I haven't asked Dessie to marry me yet because I'm holding out hope that Peyton is going to tell me someday that she wants to be with me.

But looking at her now, I don't know if we'll ever get the chance. My heart breaks thinking that we've wasted two years when we could've been together. The night of her prom, the night everything really changed for us, is when I should've asked her to be mine, but she was so excited about college and finally being away from everything in Beaumont that I couldn't bring myself to put the pressure of a long distance relationship on her. And now it may be too late.

7

PEYTON

I'm in front of Noah, trying to push my sister away. She's consoling him when it should be me. It's always been *me* that he's come to when he's felt like the world was crashing around him. It was *my* window that he snuck into at night when he had a major test in the morning and couldn't fall asleep. Not Elle's. Not even Dessie's. He used to tell me about their relationship. He *used* to confide in me until they became serious. Most of the time I've wanted to scream at him, to tell him that I don't care, and that I hate her, but I don't. I listened. I pretended I care about her when I don't.

I glance back at the bed where my body lies. My mom's head is rested on my shoulder. She strokes my hair, careful to stay away from the wound on the other side. Aunt Josie now holds my mom and they both cry, but my sister, she's still here, stuck to Noah's side. It makes me wonder if she will become his confidant when I'm no longer here.

Noah finally sits down but hangs onto the edge of my bed. His knuckles turn white and his jaw clenches. He's angry. I know this look from anywhere. I've seen him lash out at people before, especially when he thinks they've wronged me. I have no doubt if he finds out about Kyle, he'll... well I don't know what he'll do. I'm not sure if I want him to know about Kyle. It's stupid really because he has Dessie. It's only fair that I have someone. Even if the one I want doesn't want me.

Noah hasn't stopped looking at me. I hate it. This isn't how he's supposed to see me. He's supposed to see me smiling, laughing and running to embrace him because we haven't seen each other in such a long time. I'm trying to hold his face, but his tears make my hands slip away. Noah doesn't like to cry, not when people are around him. He's only done it once and that was when he was hit so badly during a game that his leg buckled and everyone thought he tore his ACL. He didn't. He was lucky according to the doctor.

He closes his eyes and mutters something unintelligible. "Please say it again?" I beg, but he doesn't hear me. Honestly, I'm getting rather pissed that no one can hear me. Am I dead, because if I am, shouldn't I be able to throw things around to get attention? That's what Patrick Swayze did in Ghost. And where's my father or his mother? I would like to think at least my father would be here, watching everything transpire. Isn't he always supposed to be watching over Elle and I? That's what everyone told us at his funeral. I may have been five, but I remember that day and those surrounding his death very clearly.

Death is nothing like they show you in the movies, aside from your family sitting by your bedside, crying and praying, which I don't get because my family has never been religious. We've been to church, but mostly for special occasions. But where's the bright light directing me to where I need to go? Where's my father? Shouldn't he be here to guide me, hold my hand while I crossover?

"Noah, you need to tell her. We think she's waiting for you." I hear my sister mutter into Noah's ear.

"Don't listen to her, Noah," I plead. "Tell me to hang on. Tell me to fight."

But he says nothing. He leans forward, and his tall frame causes his knees to crash into the metal bars at the end of my bed. His hand touches my foot. I can see it, but I can't feel him. "May I have a minute with her?" he asks.

Everyone looks at him with sad, blood-shot eyes. Elle is the first one to leave, followed by Josie. When my mom staggers away, Noah stands and pulls her into his arms. He's like his father in a lot of ways, but he's also different from the stories I've heard over the years about Liam. My uncle hasn't been shy about his actions when he was eighteen, telling all of us about the mistakes that nearly cost him everything. I asked him once if he regretted anything and he said no. I thought he would say yes because he missed so much, but he said that he wouldn't have been a very good husband or father to Noah, that he needed to leave so he could grow up. He only hates that he waited so long to return.

"She loves you, Noah," my mom says. I do. I do love Noah. I always have, but... well, I don't know. There was a time when I thought we'd be together, when I was fairly certain he was going to ask me to be his girlfriend, but he didn't.

I know it was because of our age difference and our families. While some may not think five years is much of a gap, it is when you've grown up with them. People often comment that Noah and I are like brother and sister. The thought makes me shudder. I will never consider him like my brother. Ever.

After my mom leaves, Noah sits in the chair next to my bed. He slides his hand under mine and rests his head on my torso. If he knew what I looked like under that blanket, he wouldn't touch me. My chest is battered. It's bloody, scarred and beyond damaged.

The beeping of the machine gets my attention. Red numbers flash and move upward. Noah laughs. "You know I'm here, right Peyton?"

"Yes," I tell him.

"I wish this were a nightmare, that we were talking on the phone right now so you could tell me everything I did wrong in my game."

"I didn't watch it," I say. "I was on the sidelines with the Bears. It was the most amazing feeling ever. I'm sorry I missed your game though."

"I need you in my life, Peyton. You can't leave me. I don't care what my mom and Elle tell me. I won't tell you it's okay to go. I'm selfish. I know." Noah stops talking and runs his free hand through my hair. There have been times when I thought I'd cut it, but he likes it.

"Everything will be okay, Noah." I go to him, wrapping my arms around his shoulders. His body shakes and he mutters my name over and over again. I can't console him, not the way I want to. He can't feel me, only the lifeless version that lies on the bed with tubes coming out of her mouth and arm, and machines keeping her alive.

"I refuse to give up," he tells my body. "Please find the will to live."

"I'm trying!" I want to scream at him. What does he think I'm doing? Throwing a party someplace between here and there, wherever there may be. I decide to sit on my bed, facing Noah and take his hand in mine, as much as I can. "Do you remember your first college game? I do. You were amazing and set the record for most passes completed by a freshman in Irish history, but that isn't what stood out the most. What is still clear to this day is the excitement in your voice when you called me the second you got into the locker room. I knew you had violated the rules, but you didn't care that you would have to run the snake twice at practice. Hearing your voice that day, it made me feel like I was there with you, cheering you on from the stands. I may have been thirteen at the time, but I was so in love with you.

"What about the time when I surprised you on campus by showing up at that frat party? You were so pissed off at me. I thought for sure you were going to call my parents, but you didn't. You put your arm around me and held me to your side all night long. I knew you were only protecting me, but deep down I kept telling myself that it was because you were in love with me. It's not like you could've told your friends because I was only sixteen, and you had a girlfriend. That night she told you to choose me or over her, and you chose me. You have every time and then you met Dessie. I can't compete with her, Noah. She's beautiful and exactly who any starting NFL quarterback needs to have on his arm.

"Deep down, I know you're going to ask her to marry you, to be your wife and have your children. All things that I've wanted for myself, but know that I can never have. I'm going to cry when you do. My heart will break more so than any other time you've dated someone, and I don't know if I'll be able to recover. Maybe I *should* let go, and be free from the pain my body is in now and prevent the devastation that will come later. If I'm not here, it can't hurt, right? Haunting her seems more fun to me right now because I hate her, Noah. I hate the way she makes me feel when she's in the room. I detest that she commands your attention and you give it to her. I know you love her though, which is why when Kyle asked me out, I said yes.

"I could've easily liked him if given the chance, but that truck... Kyle didn't see it. He's here, in the hospital. He wants to come see me but his lawyer won't let him. He's not you though, Noah." I run my hand through his hair, wishing I could feel it move between my fingers. It's been so long since I've held him the way I've wanted. He closes his eyes and for a moment I think he's leaning into my touch.

"It's like I can feel you here, Peyton." Noah laughs and shakes his head.

"What's so funny, Noah?"

He doesn't answer. Not that I expected him to.

"I feel like I should confess my sins to you or remind you of the things we've done together so you don't leave. I have so many memories of us, but the most important one has always been the night of your prom. Even though you don't think so, I was so happy to take you. You were the most beautiful girl in the room that night and every guy wanted to dance with you, but for one moment, you were mine.

"That night," Noah pauses and I lean forward, waiting for him to finish. "You asked me to rent a hotel room and I did, knowing exactly what you wanted. What you gave me that night, Peyton, I'll never forget it. I thought that things would change for us, but days after you were so excited about college that there was no way I could burden you with being with me. I wanted you to experience everything that I had, and now I fear it's too late. If you can hear me, I'm begging you, please don't leave me. I don't know what I can give you in return for staying, but I'll do anything, just stay."

"I love you, Noah. That night we spent together was the most magical night of my life. I want to stay. I want to be here with you, I don't want you to marry Dessie."

Noah turns toward the door at the sound of my uncle Liam clearing his throat. He stands there with his arms crossed over his chest. He's glaring at his son. Tension fills the room, but neither of them moves from their positions.

"What'd she give you?"

"Um..." Noah doesn't answer. Instead, he turns his attention back to me.

"You took her virginity, didn't you?" he asks, and even though I'm not technically here, I feel the scrutiny under his gaze.

"She was eighteen, Dad."

"That's very noble of you to wait until she was an adult."

Noah turns back and looks at me. "You wouldn't understand."

Liam comes into my room. He towers over Noah and I. "There isn't any justification, Noah. You've known her all her life. You're supposed to protect her. She's a sister to you."

Noah stands, the force of his movement pushes the chair into the wall of my cramped room. "Don't," he says, pointing his finger at his dad. "For as long as I can remember everyone has said Peyton is my sister, but I have never seen her like that. Ever. No one understands the relationship that we have except for us."

"Noah..."

He holds his hand up. "Please, I asked for a few minutes

alone with her. Unlike everyone else, I won't tell her it's okay to go. I'm going to remind her why she needs to stay."

Liam leaves, but not before taking one more look at me. I can tell that this particular conversation isn't over yet though. As soon as Noah sits back down, his face morphs back into the sad smile he's been sporting.

"Sorry about that, Peyton. Now where were we?"

"You were about to tell me that you won't marry Dessie," I say as loud as my voice will carry, but still he doesn't hear me.

8

NOAH

*T*he smile I wear is forced. There isn't a single thing I'm happy about right now. Be it, my best friend lies motionless in her bed or the fact my father heard me admit to something only Peyton and I are aware of. I'm assuming she hasn't told her sister although I've often wondered whether Peyton told Elle about prom night or if Elle asked where we ran off to.

"I can't believe you came home to take her to prom," Mom says as she straightens my bow tie. When I called to tell her, she thought I was joking, but quickly realized I was serious. Thing is, there isn't anything I wouldn't do for Peyton. I likely would've done the same for Elle, but she's never had a problem getting a date. My friendship with Peyton has always put a damper on her dating life, not that I'm complaining.

"She's a senior and needs to experience everything." If I were living back in Beaumont, this wouldn't even be an issue, but I've made Portland my home. It's easier to stay there, especially with my off-season regimen. After my first year in the league, I felt that I was lacking the right speed and strength to compete at the highest level. My coach was thrilled I recognized I needed improvement and set me up with one of the best trainers in the business. The constant work makes it nearly impossible to visit my parents.

My manager wasn't very happy when I called and told him that I was traveling home, mainly for the fact that I wouldn't be readily available for a benefit dinner this weekend. Even with most of the team living in town, many vacationed or went back to their hometowns. Plus, the bigger draw for attendance is always the quarterback. I didn't even tell him what I was doing while at home, just I wouldn't be around this weekend.

"Well, Peyton will have the best looking date there." My mom is biased. But what parent isn't? For me, escorting Peyton to prom is something I wanted to do five years ago, but with her being thirteen at the time, it wouldn't have gone over well at all. I hate our age difference. I don't see her as being five years younger, but everyone else does and they're none too shy about reminding me of it. And if it's not her age, they're commenting about how she's my sister. I have never looked at her like a sister. Elle, yes, but never Peyton.

When we were younger, we were always together. But it wasn't until her father died, did I realize that her pain was my pain. She was losing her dad, while I was gaining mine. What should've been a happy time for me was confusing. At first, I was jealous that she attached herself to my dad, but I had done the same thing. While I had Nick, Mason and I were very close, and when he died, Peyton had no one and I knew she needed someone.

I became that someone. I became her protector. Her confidant. She became my best friend. She was, and still is, the one person I will drop everything for, without question, with the exception of Betty Paige. Not even my parents get that sort of attention from me.

And I developed feelings for her, feelings that I've had to hide and will continue to hide out of respect for our families, and for Peyton. She has a bright future waiting for her. The last thing she needs is my muddled thoughts deterring her path.

"You look handsome, Noah." The sound of my little sister's voice rings out from behind me.

"Yes he does," my mom says as she stands behind me and straightens my tuxedo jacket, brushing her hands along my shoulders. She's trying to stay out of the mirror, knowing her reflection will show she's tearing up. She was a mess when I went to prom back in high school, and deep down I want to believe she understands why taking Peyton is so important to me.

"Come here, Little B." She does as I ask, making sure to jump when she gets to the bottom step. My mother rolls her eyes and mutters something about breaking a leg before leaving us alone in the foyer. From the day my father bought this house, I've always jumped off the last few steps and so far I haven't broken anything. Well, except for the vase that my grandma Bianca had set down. I may have kicked that, but still to this day I plead the fifth.

With my phone in my hand, I crouch down next to my sister and wrap my arm around her waist. She nestles into my side and all but hides her face in the crook of my neck. Paige is a bit camera shy, not that I blame her, but I want to capture this moment. "Smile, Little B." She does, but most of her face is hidden. Honestly, I don't mind. Fear of the paparazzi has been ingrained into her mind, and rarely has anyone ever truly photographed her. For the longest time, my dad would make her wear a hood whenever she was out and *about. He wanted her to have as much anonymity as she could.*

"Are you putting that on Instagram?"

"I am." *Paige leans closer and watches me upload the photo and add the caption,* "My perfect girl." *I add various hashtags and wait a few seconds for the comments and likes to start. Most often, everything is positive. But occasionally, someone will post something that I have to delete. Thing is, I know what my mom, Aunt Katelyn and Aunt Jenna go through when it comes to the band. The last thing they need is to see sexual comments about me as well. And as far as Paige is concerned, I don't want her seeing the nastiness of social media.*

"Look, everyone says I'm cute."

"That's because you are." *She wraps her arms around me, giving me the strongest hug she can.*

"Tell me all about the dance and what Peyton is wearing when you get home, okay?"

"You bet." *I stand and shake out my pant legs. Taking one last look in the mirror, I head for the door where my mom meets me with Peyton's corsage in hand. The three champagne colored roses are nestled in baby's breath and tied together with a pink ribbon. The fact that I know anything about flowers has really upped my dating game. Chicks dig random knowledge.*

As if on cue, the limousine I rented for the night is idling in the driveway. Technically, it's easier for me to pick Peyton up, but I want her to have the full experience. Also, Elle and her date will join us for the ride over. That is one thing I've learned about living in a massive city like Portland – the teens really go out of their way to make prom something spectacular. In little ole Beaumont, it's held at the school gym with paper streamers and balloon arches. That's how it was when my parents went, and it was the same way when I went. I can't imagine much has changed.

The black limo stops in front of the Powell-James home, and I'm out of the car with Peyton's corsage in my hand before the driver can do his job by opening my door. I'll let him focus on the girls and let them feel like a million dollars. One would think considering how famous their dad is, boys would flock to them, but they don't. When Quinn and I were in high school, it was the other way around, and we learned early on our popularity had a lot to do with our fathers. Believe me, Quinn and I don't mind if the girls are left alone.

Harrison opens the front door before I reach the final step. Even though I've known him for half my life, I extend my right hand to shake his. "Good evening, Mr. Powell-James." Harrison tries to hide his smile but accepts my hand firmly.

"Evening, Noah. Peyton is almost ready."

I follow him into the house and am immediately introduced to a tall lanky kid in a tuxedo. "Noah, this is Ben. He's Elle's best guy friend."

We shake hands, but it's awkward. "You're Noah Westbury."

No shit.

"Man, this is surreal. I mean, Peyton said you were taking her, but most of us thought she was bullshitting us."

I shake my head slightly. "Nope, no bullshitting here. I'm happy to take her to prom."

"Man, the guys at school are going to flip," Ben says. He turns his back toward me and from what I can gather is pulling out this phone. There isn't a doubt in my mind he's informing everyone of my presence. Unfortunately for him and his "guys" I won't sign autographs or pose for pictures tonight unless Peyton instructs me to. This is her night.

The sound of heels coming down the hardwood steps grabs my attention. I step out into the entryway in time to see Katelyn leading her twin daughters down the stairs.

"Thank you," she whispers into my ear before giving me a kiss on my cheek. I don't tell her that it's my pleasure, but I should.

When Peyton comes into view, all wind is knocked out of my proverbial sail. She's gorgeous with her long tresses curled and pinned to the top of her head, and her dress... I swallow hard and chance a look at Harrison. His eyes are hard and there's a noticeable tick in his jaw.

"The night of your prom, you wore that pink dress. Do you remember it, Peyton? When you were coming down the stairs I thought Harrison was going to make you go change. I can't even tell you what Elle was wearing because I couldn't take my eyes off you. Everything changed for us that night. I thought things were going to turn out differently, but I was wrong."

I stand up and stretch. A quick glance out of her window shows my father and Harrison talking. I'd like to think my father won't sell me out, but who knows at this point. The fact that Peyton and I have been intimate shouldn't matter, and won't if she doesn't make it. It was her choice, and I was too enamored with her to tell her no. I thought we'd be together afterward, but I was mistaken.

My dad glances toward me or at least at the room. I'm not ready to leave Peyton. It's selfish of me, I know. There are others out there that want their time with her, but I can't bring myself to walk out the door or even invite them back in.

The hard plastic chair is as inviting as being sacked in an outdoor stadium. Both suck beyond words. Yet, I find myself sitting down and picking her hand back up. Her body temperature is questionable, and probably a bit on the cold side. I refuse to believe she's dying. Peyton wouldn't do that to me.

"Okay, you're going to let up on the break, but do so gently."

It's midnight and Peyton's birthday. Legally, I'm not allowed to teach her to drive, but she asked me to. She's nervous about her permit test in the morning and thinks that a crash course behind the wheel of my Wrangler is the way to pass. She's not fooling me though. I know she's been waiting for this day since I got my Jeep for my eighteenth birthday. Peyton is often hanging out in my dad's garage, taking pictures of herself in it, so who am I to deny her this late night or early morning ride.

For good measure, I grab hold of the 'oh shit' handle and hold my breath. Peyton eases my prized possession out of my parents' driveway and onto the darkened street.

"Which way do I go?"

"Where do you want to go?" I ask, sitting up straighter so I can be more attentive to her. "If you turn left, we can drive toward the school. Right and we go by your house."

Peyton looks in both directions, and honestly, neither seems appealing. For the longest time, the twins refused to drive on the road in front of the school where their father died. Over the years it's gotten easier, but most of us detour when they're in the car to prevent any uneasiness for them. However, going by her house probably isn't the best option either.

"Want me to drive us out of town?"

She nods and puts the car in park. We quickly switch seats and within seconds I have us speeding out of town. I drive us to Greenfield High, one of Beaumont's rivals and strongest nearby competition.

"This is where you're going to teach me to drive?" she asks, as we meet in front of my Jeep. The headlights give off a strong enough glow that I can see her face clearly. Her lips are pursed and kissable. There have been many nights, alone in my dorm room, where I have dreamed of kissing her. No one, not even Quinn, knows about my fantasies. No one ever will.

I never cared when she followed me around with her football or wanted to scrimmage with the rest of the guys. I always knew she was in the stands, watching and cheering me on, ready to tell me about my game. If she were like a sister, I would've been annoyed. I would've pushed her away, but I didn't. I found excuses to keep her close.

"Sure, why not?" I look around the deserted parking lot, which are the best places to learn the basics. "You'll be fine, Peyton. I promise."

"Remember when you took your permit test? You aced it while Elle missed four. That was the last time I was home for your birthday because I was drafted a year later. Sure, we celebrated when we'd see each other, but it's not the same. Don't forget we have big plans for your twenty-first. You remember the plan right? We're going to live the high life and use our names to get us everything we want. You just have to wake up, Peyton, or we can't celebrate."

"Noah?"

Elle's voice is soft as she calls my name. I turn in the chair to find her resting against the doorjamb. She comes to me, wrapping her arms around my neck and cries softly into my shoulder. I hold her and find myself quickly following suit. My tears are hot and streaming fast down my cheeks.

"You have to tell her," Elle mumbles, but I'm shaking my head.

"No. I can't. I won't."

9

PEYTON

y mom stands in the doorway watching Noah and Elle comfort each other. Her stance mimics the way Elle was standing earlier. She and my mother are clones of each other. We may be identical twins, Elle and I, but we're nothing alike. From early on, I favored our father, while Elle took after our mother, or so we've been told. Elle was the cheerleader in high school. I preferred football, choosing to stand on the sidelines until I joined the school paper. She liked to dress up, making sure her clothes were perfect. I didn't care as long as I was comfortable. The one thing that's the same, well was until now, is our hair. Neither of us has cut it without the other doing the same, and we've never dyed it.

Elle and I changed when we went away to college. I started dressing more like her, while she took on the grunge rocker look. I had never seen my sister wear flannel before until she moved to Los Angeles. Now she owns combat boots, nylons with holes and wears black nail polish. Our dad calls it a phase.

"Noah... Elle... may I have a few moments with Peyton?"

My sister removes herself from Noah's lap and goes to our mom. They hug each other and by the shaking of Elle's shoulders, I'm assuming she's crying. My attention is on Noah though. He clears his throat before standing. He hovers over me, his thumb brushing lightly along my forehead and finally, he leans down to kiss me. I wish I could feel him. Feel the warmth of his lips against my tepid skin. I try to move my arms, wiggle my fingers, open my eyes and even grunt, but no amount of straining produces the results I'm seeking. Noah seems to be the only one who hasn't given up on me.

Is that a sign that I'm supposed to find my way out of here? Have I been lingering in this 'in between' because I'm waiting for something more meaningful to show me that I need to leave this realm? Everyone except for Noah is hell bent on saying goodbye to me. He's the only one refusing to give up. Why is that? Since when do we not pray or have hope?

Noah stops and gives my mother a hug. She's short and has to stand on her tippy toes to get her arms around his broad shoulders. I'm jealous that she and Elle get to hug him and I can't. I'd give anything to feel his arms around me, at least one more time.

Mom waits until Noah and Elle are out of sight before she comes in and sits down. She picks up my hand and holds it to her face. The ring that my dad gave her when our adoptions were final doesn't sparkle inside this drab room. It's almost as if the ring has died a bit because I'm in here. I remember, after he gave it to her, I used to try it on. It's always been my favorite piece of jewelry and I think it's because it represents my family.

"My sweet baby girl," she whispers against the back of my hand. I'd give anything to tell her how much I love her, to make sure she knows she is the best mother I could've asked for, but I can't, and I don't know if I'll ever get the chance.

I vaguely remember speaking to her yesterday. Or was it the day before? My memory before the accident is fuzzy. Did I interrupt her time with my aunts? Would she have told me if I did? No, I can't imagine she would've. My mom has always put Elle, Quinn and I first, over my dad and the band. Even though I can't remember my conversation with her, I'm telling myself that she was happy for me. I hope I told her I love her and miss her.

I wish she had come to visit me instead. If she did, maybe I wouldn't be here right now. There is no way I would miss time with my mom to go out to dinner with a handsome quarterback, although she probably would've encouraged me to.

"There are so many things I want to say to you, Peyton, but I don't know where to start. I hope you know that you have been the best daughter. You remind me so much of your father. I see him in your eyes, your smile and the way you command a room when you walk in. You've always been noticeable, even when you thought Elle was stealing the spotlight."

"That's because she was," I blurt out. Elle has always had an indescribable air about her. When she walked into a room, people flocked to her. We were both popular in school, but Elle seemed to hold herself higher than I did. I suppose there isn't anything wrong with being that way.

"When you see—"

A gut-wrenching sob takes over my mom's voice. Her head falls to my leg as she cries. I'm there to comfort her, wishing with all my might she could feel my hand rubbing through her hair. I rest my body on top of hers, holding her as tightly as I can. "It'll be okay, Mama." But I'm not sure I even believe what I'm saying.

She cries louder, hiccupping and muttering words that I can't make out. In a flash, she's out of my arms and being held by my dad. It's as if he knew she needed him. He's always known. He sits on the floor with her on his lap, holding her to his chest as he rocks her back and forth.

"I know it hurts, baby. Our girl is strong though, we have to have a little hope."

"She's so cold, Harrison."

"I can feel her slipping away from me," Elle says, causing my mom to cry louder. I glance at the door to find my sister and Quinn. They both descend on our parents, arms all tangled within a tight circle, one that I'm not a part of. "I haven't felt right since before we got the call. And now I'm starting to feel numb in certain places." The freaky twin connection is real, at least it is between us. We can sense things about each other. It's weird and most of the time I don't like it.

I especially didn't like it the morning after Noah and I... well, the morning after prom. Elle knew something had happened and even though I smiled and acted like nothing was amiss, she hounded me for days, wanting to know why she felt odd. When she lost her virginity, I didn't have to say anything because she told me about it. Every. Last. Detail. We're sisters. We share. Except when we don't. Any and everything I feel about Noah is off limits. As far as Elle and the rest of my family is concerned, Noah's my best friend. To me, he's the man I'm desperately in love with.

Being in love with Noah is difficult. It's like chasing a butterfly without a net. He's there, looking catchable and when I think I can get close enough, he flutters away and is out of reach. I know being with him is a stupid fantasy, but part of me wishes it'd come true. And now it's probably too late.

Quinn starts humming. The sound is soothing. Not only to me but our mother as well. She finally stands with the help of our dad and returns to the chair that seems to be glued to the floor next to my bed. He stands behind her with his hands resting on her shoulders and his eyes staring down at me. Elle and Quinn are on the other side of my bed. She holds my hand, while his hand rests on my leg.

I'm at the end of my bed, wondering if this is my moment. Is Elle right? Can she feel me dying? I don't feel any different now than I have since I've been here.

"How's our girl?" Jenna the nurse walks in and immediately squeezes by Quinn and Elle to access the machines I'm plugged into. She pushes a few buttons, writes notes in my chart, and studies the printout, which spits out of one of the monitors. I stand next to her, trying to decipher whatever it is she's looking at. "No change," she mumbles.

That's good, right?

I look at my family with an expectant smile, but either they didn't hear her or they don't believe her.

"You're a fighter." My nurse brushes my hair. "If you'd like, I can redress her wounds." Mom nods and Dad helps her out of the chair. My siblings follow, leaving me alone with Jenna. "You have a lot of family waiting for you out in the waiting room. I can't imagine they'll leave here tonight, not knowing... just like I'm not leaving. I know I said I would once your mom arrived, but I can't."

Jenna cleans and redresses the wound on my scalp before she pulls the blankets down that have been keeping my chest hidden from everyone.

"You'll have a scar," she says this as if it's something I don't already know. "But surviving what you did... well, I think you'd be okay with it like this."

Once she has it cleaned and covered my wounds, she dresses me in a new nightgown. It's my second one, and I haven't been here very long.

"I've watched your family. They love you. Your dad pulled a lot of strings to make sure everyone was allowed in the waiting room. Everyone out there is waiting for you to wake up, for you to defy what the doctors say. What a miracle you'd be."

Once I'm dressed, she pulls the blankets back up and makes sure the wires protruding from my body aren't constricted in any way. I sit, crossed legged on the bed, watching her care for me as if she's known me her whole life and not hours. I hope that I get the chance to thank her... if I remember any of this when I wake.

"All the nurses are going crazy because of your family. Who knew you were rock star royalty? I think more nurses are pulling overtime so they can sit and stare at your dad and uncles. What was it like growing up with them?"

"The best." It's true. Many think that we're spoiled, Noah, Quinn, Elle and I, even Eden and Paige. It's so far from the truth. Sure, our mothers could've sent us to private school. We could've been chauffeured around like brats. Had a maid service, landscapers, everything else our peers have, but our parents refused to let money dictate our lives. Quinn and Noah mowed lawns. I worked at an ice cream shop until I graduated. Elle worked at the mall. I don't know much about what Eden does, aside from the surfing career she's building, because she lives in California, and Betty Paige... well, she's still too young to work.

I look at some of my friends in the entertainment circle

and realize that they had everything handed to them. They don't know the value of hard work or what it's like to earn money from doing a job. Sure, we have our trust funds, but that doesn't mean we're idly waiting for the day to come so we can cash them in.

"The young man you were with. He's been asking about you, but is afraid to come see you," she says as her hands brush down over the blanket, tucking me in.

"It's because of his lawyer. I was there, listening to them talk. I'd like to see Kyle. He seemed really nice and I was excited for dinner."

"Maybe your parents will let him in."

"Let who in?"

I turn to find my dad stepping into my room. He stands at the end of my bed and rests his hands on the edge. "Who do we need to let in?" he asks again.

Jenna clears her throat. "The man she was in the car with. He'd like to see her."

Dad nods but otherwise, doesn't say anything. If I could tell him that Kyle isn't at fault, maybe I could see him, but the expression on my dad's face tells me otherwise. I'm willing to bet Kyle is being blamed for everything.

I go to my dad and hug him, even though he can't wrap his arms around me. The drumsticks he always carries around are in his pocket and while they would normally jab me in the stomach. I can't feel anything.

Maybe my time is up and I'm delaying the inevitable. The doctor did say I wouldn't make it through the night, and well, it's night.

10

NOAH

$\mathcal{I}$ wait for Quinn to come out of Peyton's room. It's an avoidance tactic so I don't have to speak to my father. I hate lingering, but I need some time to think things through. It's not that I plan to tell Quinn about what my dad overheard. It's more that I need a friend right now, and being near Elle is rather hard. As soon as he comes out we're hugging because we're both hurting and for the life of me I can't remember a time when we've ever been like this.

Our hands are squeezing the back of each other's necks, making sure neither of us moves until the other is ready. Both of our faces are buried, away from eyes that are trying not to pry, but can't help themselves. Quinn grew up with people always staring. I had ten years before it became an issue. I can't really say it bothers me because look at my profession. I could've easily gone into business or gone to work at the mill, but I chose a career in football. In fact, none of us, with the exception of Betty Paige, has gone down the path of anonymity. Deep down, maybe we like the limelight.

When we finally part, we don't look around to see who's

watching. We stare at each other and while this may look awkward to people around us, it's almost as if we're having a silent conversation. I imagine he's feeling like his walls are closing in, and nothing makes sense right now.

"I'm about to go down to the cafeteria and see what I can scrounge up for food. Wanna come?" Quinn motions with his head toward the door. I quickly spot my father who makes eye contact with me. I should've never brought up Peyton's prom night, but I thought I was doing something right by bringing up memories that are important. I thought by telling her that night meant everything to me would help her wake up.

"Yeah, I need some air."

We bypass everyone who is in the waiting room, almost acting as if they're not there. I'm not lying when I say I need air. I need to clear my thoughts and make sure when my dad broaches the subject of Peyton and I, I know what I'm going to say.

Downstairs, the cafeteria is quiet. It's late and there are very few items out for us to purchase. Quinn picks up two pieces of pie and I pour us some coffee. He pays while I find us a corner to sit in.

"Thanks," I tell him as he pushes the dessert toward me. I take a bite of the apple pie and close my eyes. It probably tastes like garbage, but right now it feels like anything but. It has to be because my emotions are a mess and it's comfort food. Everything else, though, is no different than high school cafeteria food.

The coffee is sludge, but I drink it anyway. I need the caffeine to keep me awake and alert. The normal aches and pains that I get after a game are starting to set in, and without going through my routine of stretching and soaking in the tub, I know I'm going to pay the price in the morning.

Not to mention I plan to sleep in one of those waiting room chairs. There is no way I'm leaving this hospital.

It's been so long since Quinn and I have been able to sit and chill, I want to ask him how things are going, but under the circumstances, the question seems insensitive and completely wrong. Upstairs, the woman we love, for different reasons, is fighting for her life. This isn't the time to play catch up.

We eat in silence, well as much as possible with the television blaring and the two older men sitting not far from us. They came in shortly after we did, and while they had the entire cafeteria to pick seats, they chose to sit close to us.

"Do you think they know who you are?" Quinn mumbles through his sentence.

I glance over at them and one of the men makes eye contact with me quickly before turning his attention to his phone. I don't need to be a betting man to know he's texting someone that he's spotted me. I don't even know why he would do that. It's not like it's front page news unless he thinks I'm here to meet with the Bears since Zimmerman was in an accident, but even that wouldn't make sense since I'm sitting in a hospital cafeteria.

Nodding slightly to Quinn, I adjust the way I'm sitting so the men don't have a clear angle of my face. Any other time, I wouldn't care. I don't mind signing autographs or posing for pictures, a habit that Dessie hates. She didn't grow up with the cameras always around and doesn't realize if you give the media what they want, they're less likely to be dicks to you.

Quinn finishes his coffee and sets the porcelain mug down with a thud. "Elle said it was only going to be a matter of time before someone alerted social media that the band was here."

"I'm sure someone already has. It's big news."

"Dad says they're going to hold a press conference in the morning."

"Why then?" I ask, picking up my mug and finishing off the black tar. I'm going to need more, but am tempted to call for delivery. I don't think I can stomach this shit.

Quinn sighs and pushes the crumbs left over from his pie into his fork. "Doctor says she's not going to make it through the night."

"But she is." I sit upright and lean closer to Quinn so we can keep our voices down. "You know Peyton, Quinn. She's the most resilient one out of all of us. When she's told she can't do something, she proves to everyone that not only is she able, but she does it better than anyone else. If everyone would encourage her to fight instead of giving up, she'd stand a damn chance at surviving." By the time I'm done, I'm gritting my teeth. I'm frustrated and hurt because everyone's giving up on her. "She's not going to die."

I push away from the table and head for the exit. "Noah," Quinn yells my name. I stop and realize my mistake. If the two men weren't positive about my identity, they are now. Quinn catches up to me, putting his hand on the back of my shoulder to guide me out.

"Sorry, I wasn't thinking."

"It's fine. You'll be back in the spotlight soon."

Quinn doesn't say anything as he follows me down the hall. I bypass the elevators and head toward the stairs, taking them two at a time until we've reached the main floor of the hospital. I'm back to needing air and quickly move toward the courtyard.

Breathing in the cold Chicago air does nothing to calm the anxiety I'm feeling right now. I'm numb all over and the heartbreak is starting to turn to anger. My hands are clenched into fists and the roar I let out comes from somewhere deep within. I finally collapse onto the bench and bend over to hide my face.

Quinn sits down next to me. "You've known her longer."

"You know her better, differently."

"I've never known death," he says. "I don't know what I'm supposed to do. She's my sister and I..."

I pull Quinn to my chest, forgetting about my feelings and hold my friend. We didn't run in the same circles at school, but he's always been a part of my life. The only death that is vivid in my mind is Mason's. I remember being at his funeral. My dad standing up there in front of everyone, speaking to people that he turned his back on. He was there for Katelyn, Peyton and Elle, as they were for him. Forgiving him when others wanted him to leave town.

"Most would say we're supposed to pray, but I don't know if that works. I mean, my team prays before each game and we still lose."

Quinn laughs as he pulls away from me. He hides his face, likely embarrassed that he's crying. He shouldn't be. I can barely keep my tears at bay and can feel another round of them coming on. I'm so angry, crying seems to be the only way to relieve the tension. Shit like this isn't supposed to happen to us or to people like Peyton. We're supposed to live our lives, be happy, and not worry about whether or not we're going to survive a car crash.

"Losing her will kill my mom. I don't think—"

"Well, why don't we start thinking about Peyton surviving. Then we don't have to worry about Katelyn." I've seen her at her worst, and he's right. If she loses her daughter, I think we lose her. Especially if it's the same way we lost Mason.

"What do you say we order some takeout and feed the family? I have yet to really see my mom, and I'm sure I can convince my grandma to take Eden and Paige to a hotel. The girls really shouldn't be here." I stop short of finishing my sentence. My grandma and the girls would honestly be happier at a hotel for a while, rather than hanging out in the waiting room. I'm sure everyone is tired and our emotions are starting to take over.

"You're probably right."

I pull out my cell phone only to realize I haven't turned it on since I arrived in Chicago. I stare at it for a good minute before pushing the button. Once it's through the startup cycle, messages come flooding in. Most are from Dessie, but a few are from Allen Lowe, my agent/manager, asking me how everything is.

"This may take a bit. Can we use your phone?" I hold my phone up and shake it as if this is supposed to alert him to what's going on. He looks at me strangely and rightly so.

"Pizza?"

I nod and turn my attention back to my notifications. The number of text messages increases, along with the voicemails. I'm starting to think that something is wrong until I open Dessie's texts and see that she's being overly excessive with wanting to know what I'm doing and why I'm not responding to her. Scrolling through her messages, they're whiny and coming off as self-centered. Demanding that I call her back immediately or else. Yet, there is not one mention of Peyton. Nothing asking me how she's doing or how I'm doing.

I'd like to know what she's going to do if I don't call her back. I can't even stomach reading through the barrage of messages nor do I want to talk to her right now. Powering it off, I slip my phone back into my pocket and try to forget what I saw. I'm used to former girlfriends being jealous of Peyton, but with Dessie, I have really tried to put her first. I love her, but it's different from the way I feel about Peyton. It's hard to explain. I would give anything to show Peyton how I feel about her and prove to our families that we should be together, but she rebuffed me the day after prom. I thought our friendship was over, that I screwed up beyond repair. I paced the floor of my bedroom waiting for her to call me before I had to fly back to Portland. When she finally did, the words were on the tip of my tongue, me telling her how I feel yet she reminded me about Chicago and how she was so excited to start school. I couldn't bring myself to say the words. But this side of Dessie is something I've never seen before and I'm not sure I like it.

Quinn gets the food ordered while I try to calm down. Part of me wants to call her and ask what her problem is, but the other half doesn't really care right now because my best friend is fighting for her life and Dessie should know it's more important that I be there for Peyton. I'm grateful I never turned my phone on otherwise, I likely would've busted it in half by now.

I look up and watch as snowflakes start to fall and stick my tongue out to try and catch them. Quinn does the same and before I know it, we're laughing, our faces are wet and I'm not sure we've caught anything.

"I hate the snow."

"Me too. It doesn't snow in California," Quinn points out the obvious. It's funny, I never thought Quinn would go back there, but it makes sense. It's where he's from and only moved to Beaumont because his dad fell in love.

"Portland sometimes gets snow."

"Do you like it there?"

I shrug. "I do. It's a great city, but it's not home."

"Do you miss Indiana?"

This time I laugh and shake my head. "No, not at all. School, yes, but not the weather."

Quinn looks down at his phone. "The food should be here in a few minutes." Thanks to technology we can now time when our delivery will show up. No more 'old fashioned' waiting by the window for headlights to appear.

The delivery driver arrives just as we step out into the front of the hospital. Thankfully, we seem to have lost the two men from downstairs, at least for the time being. When we get back to the ICU, we ignore the glared looks from the staff as we step into the waiting room where food is clearly not allowed.

"Eat up," Quinn says, depositing his armload onto the small table. I use one of the vacant chairs, and as soon as my arms are free, my mom pulls me into an embrace. She doesn't say anything as I wrap my arms around her. I hold her tightly, knowing that she's drudging up memories of years gone by.

"I've missed you." She holds my face between her hands and smiles, except it's forced.

"Season is almost over and then I'll be home." There's a small glint of happiness in her eyes. My mom kisses me on the cheek before being shoved out of the way so Paige can jump into my arms.

"Hey, Little B." She's far from little, but will always seem that way to me. "There's a cheese pizza over there with your name on it."

"I'm not hungry."

"Of course you are." I take her over to where the make-shift dining room table has formed and set her down. Elle hands her a paper plate with a slice of plain pizza on it.

Honestly, I'm surprised Elle is functioning right now. I don't know if I would be if the tables were turned.

The waiting room is small. We're crammed in here like sardines, but everyone feels miles away. "Where's Grandma?" I ask Paige.

"She went to make some calls about getting a suite. Daddy is with her."

I hadn't noticed that my father wasn't around, but am sort of thankful that he's not glaring at me right now. Eden sits down next to me and sighs. I can't imagine she likes being here much either.

"You can probably go with Bianca when she takes Paige to the hotel."

"My mum already said I should. Do you think Peyton would be mad?"

"Not at all, Eden. She'll understand."

Paige and Eden continue to pick at their food, while I stare at mine. I thought I was hungry, but now that I have a pile of slices stacked onto my plate, my stomach is telling me otherwise.

As I look around, everyone is here except for Harrison. My mom and Jenna are huddled by Katelyn, and Jimmy is on the phone, likely handling band business or possibly setting up the press conference.

"I'm looking for Mr. and Mrs. James."

The voice comes from one of the three police officers standing at the end of the waiting area.

"It's Powell-James," Katelyn says, correcting the officer in regards to her last name. "Is this about my daughter?"

"Yes, ma'am. We have the information you and your husband requested." This time she doesn't correct him regarding her marital status, although I think by law they're considered married. I never understood, but always respected why she and Harrison never got married.

Harrison comes around the corner in time to hear what the policeman said. He extends his hand and shakes each one of theirs. "You have news about the accident?"

"Yes, would you like to go someplace and discuss?"

"No, we're all family," Harrison says.

"Very well. We've spoken with Mr. Zimmerman. He states that he met your daughter earlier before his game and asked her to dinner, which is why she was in his car."

"She had a date," Katelyn cries out, covering her mouth before burying her face into Harrison's chest.

"Zimmerman?" I say out loud. All eyes turn on me, but I'm focused on the police officer. "Son of a bitch," I say as I stand abruptly, causing my pizza to go flying. "Is that bastard in the hospital now?"

11

PEYTON

*M*y dad stares down at my body. I stand there next to him, looking at myself. Nothing has changed, except maybe my hair because Jenna brushed it, but everything else looks the same.

"Before you go," Dad says to Jenna. "What's the tape for on her eyes?"

Jenna rushes back to me and removes the tape. I touch my eyes, waiting for the sting that always follows when you pull a bandage or something sticky off your body, but it never comes. "It was placed there during surgery. There's no need for it now."

"Thank you," he says. Jenna pauses and smiles at him.

"In my head, she's this amazing young woman with a bright future."

"You're right. She is."

"She's very lucky to have you."

Dad shakes his head. "I'm the lucky one."

Jenna doesn't say anything else. She exits the room, leaving the two of us alone. He reaches out and touches my foot. The still me doesn't move, but I pretend that I can feel him and wiggle my toes. I don't like to think that I will never see my parents again or my sister and Quinn or any of my other family members. I don't want to know a place where they don't exist. Where I'm whatever this is now, watching them go on with their lives.

How long does it take until you forget someone? I barely remember my father. Being five when he died, the memories faded rather quickly, except for the stuff I've made up about him in my mind. At what point do your loved ones become only a date that you remember? When do you start talking about them in past tense? Telling stories to make others remember?

Dying isn't what I want. I want to live. I want to work in television and commentate one of Noah's games. I'd be impartial and not afraid to tell the viewers when he's done something bad. It's what he'd expect from me.

I want to stand next to my sister when she marries Ben because we all know it's going to happen. Elle can deny it as much as she wants, but I see it in her eyes when she looks at him. It's the same way I look at Noah, except Noah and I will never have that sort of future.

And when Quinn finally brings a woman home, I want to be there when he introduces her to our mom, knowing that this woman will have to move mountains in order to impress her. Never mind the fact Elle and I are related to her by blood. When it comes to Quinn, he's her world. It's okay that he is because he didn't have a mom, and Elle and I got a double bonus when Harrison came into our lives.

My dad finally sits down in the same chair everyone else has been using. He picks up my hand and presses his lips to it. I can see that he's crying, but can't feel the wetness as his tears land on my skin. I want to though.

I desperately want to feel his arms wrapped around

mine. From the day he taught me to play the drums, I knew he'd be my knight in shining armor. He encouraged me to do everything, nothing was ever off limits and he rarely told me no, except for the time I asked if I could have a motocross bike. I had seen it on television one day, the X-Games, and I wanted to do it. My mom freaked out. My dad said no, but took me to the nearest store and asked me to pick out a bike. Next came the gear, and by the time I was all set to start riding, he told me that I'd have to have years of training. I gave up immediately and went back to playing the drums and dissecting game film with Noah.

My dad reaches for his drumsticks, sliding them into my grasp and clutches our hands together. "Use these, sweet pea. Beat off whoever is trying to take you away from me. I know you can do it. You're a strong girl, Peyton. Tell them no. Tell whoever it is you're not ready. And if it's your..." he chokes up and takes a few shuddering breaths. "If it's your father... if it's Mason, you tell him you love him, but you're not ready. I'm not ready, baby girl. I haven't had enough time to be your dad yet."

His head falls to my side and he sobs. I curl into him and tell him that everything is going to be okay. I will fight if I can figure out how. There wasn't exactly someone waiting for me when I arrived at the hospital, handing out instructions on how to avoid the afterlife. I'm a good student. I would've read or listened to whatever they had to say because I don't want to die. I don't want to leave my family.

My name's being called, but when I look up there isn't anyone else in the room and my dad still has his head resting next to me. Yet, I follow the sound of the voice until I find myself standing in front of a large window. There are babies, wrapped in various color blankets with either blue or pink beanies on their heads.

Inside, a woman dressed in a yellow gown is holding a baby girl, rocking her to sleep. I go in and see that the baby is tiny and she has cords coming out of her blanket, much like I do upstairs.

"Please, God," the mother cries over and over again. Her eyes are closed and she's muttering words I can't understand. Is her baby sick? I try to get a better look, but her face is hidden.

Another baby cries, and I follow the sound until I'm standing in front of a bassinet. She too is wearing a pink hat, but something is wrong. There are two cards in her cradle, and the others only have one.

She's a twin, but where's her... I look back at the woman and again at the baby who is crying. Did she have twins? And what's wrong with her baby?

A man walks in wearing the same yellow gown that the woman is. He rests his on the back of her chair and leans down, whispering something into her ear.

"I will not," she yells at him.

Suddenly, I don't want to be here, but I can't leave. I try to picture another room, anywhere else but here, but I'm stuck.

"You have to let her go. You have another child that needs you."

"NO! That child killed my baby."

"That child is our daughter. She needs us, and we need her." The man looks frustrated. He has tears in his eyes as he comes closer to me. I move out of way even though I'm not really here. He picks up the crying baby and holds her to his chest.

"It's okay," he tells her.

"None of this is okay. That thing killed our baby."

The man shakes his head. "She didn't. There was

nothing that could've been done to save her." He points at the baby in his wife's arms. He moves toward the woman, but she's vehemently shaking her head.

"Get that thing away from me. I hate it."

The man pauses and looks down at the bundle in his arms and nods. He doesn't say anything else, but goes to the other side of the room and starts to rock the baby. It's not long until he starts crying.

My name is called again and it's like I'm being teleported to another part of the hospital. I wish I had some say in where I was going, but I don't seem to be in control.

Now, I'm outside. It's dark and while it's winter, I should be cold, but I'm not.

"Peyton?"

I look to my left and on the bench is a woman with long dark hair like mine. She motions for me to come sit with her, but it's hearing a familiar voice that's keeping me grounded. "Noah," I say, but he doesn't look over. He's talking to a homeless man and they're deep in conversation. He laughs, heartedly, causing me to smile. I love his laugh. It's one of his best features.

"Peyton," she calls my name again and this time I go to her. She pats the spot next to her on the bench and I sit.

"How can you see me?"

"You don't know who I am?"

I study her, trying to pull her face up in my mind. I shake my head. "No, I don't."

"I'm your grandmother, Grace."

Now that she's said as much, yes, I can see it now. "I'm sorry I didn't know. The pictures my grandpa has up of you are old and..."

"It's fine. I'm so happy to meet you."

I don't want to be happy to meet her because she's dead

and that would mean I'm... I can't bring myself to say the word, fearing that doing so would put some finality into my situation. I'm not ready. I haven't had the chance to tell everyone how I feel or do the things I've wanted to do.

I'm almost afraid to ask, but I have to know. "Am I dead?"

"No, you seem to be taking your time crossing over. Your dad and I have been waiting."

"My dad? He's here?"

She nods. "He's with your mom right now. He's been here the entire time, watching over you and your sister."

"Why can't I see him?"

"He'll make his presence known when the time is right, but for now, he's comforting your mother so she doesn't feel lost."

But that's Harrison's job.

I look back at Noah and wonder what he's doing with that man. They seem friendly, like they've known each other for years, yet I've never seen him before in my life.

"Is he a good man to you?"

"He's a friend," I say, shaking my head.

"But you're in love with him."

"Doesn't matter how I feel anymore." I look at him one last time before turning my attention back to my grandmother. "What's it like? Dying?"

"It's different for everyone. For me, it was peaceful. I was ready to stop the pain."

"And for my father?"

"He had a harder time with it. He was young and had his whole life ahead of him. Mason fought hard to stay, but the damage was extensive."

"Like mine. I'm not supposed to make it through the night."

She doesn't say anything. She doesn't have to. I gather she's here to help me cross over or whatever it's called. Just follow the light or so they say on television.

"If I go, will my mom be okay?"

"In time."

"And what about my sister?"

"She's strong, like you."

"And my brother?"

She doesn't answer, only nods. I get the impression she's not fond of my family.

"My grandpa Powell, he loves Quinn. And Harrison."

"As he should. They're good men, but I'm not tied to them like I am to your sister. I only speak about your mother because she survived when her husband passed away. That's a testament to her character. But you, your sister and I are linked."

"And if I'm not ready to go? How do I fight? How do I wake up from whatever this is? Everyone is hurting and I want the pain and tears to stop. I want to open my eyes and see my mom, my sister, and Noah."

My grandma adjusts. "You'll have to ask your dad because I don't know."

"Didn't you fight?"

"I did, with everything I had. I wasn't ready to leave my life behind. To leave my husband and son, but after awhile, the cancer became too much for me and by the time I realized I was dying, it was too late."

"My grandpa misses you."

"I know, sweetie. I miss him too. But I'll see him soon."

I don't ask her how she's going to see him because I don't want to know. There are only two options that I can think of, and neither is acceptable. I turn back to Noah, only to watch him leave. He goes through the double doors, walking as if he's on a mission. "I'll be right back," I say, but when I glance over my shoulder, she's gone.

Going over to the man, I find him staring down at his hand. In it, is a wad of money and I have a feeling that Noah put it there. That seems like something he'd do. I lean into him and whisper, "Wait for him. He's going to need a friend."

I stand back and watch as the man looks around. I try not to laugh, but I can't help myself. If I can talk to him, maybe I can talk to the others and let them know that I'm fighting. Let them know that I'm here and can feel their love and that I'm trying to wake up.

The man finally looks up and smiles.

NOAH

*N*o one answers my question. They all stare, probably wondering what my problem is. I make eye contact with the adult members of my family and when Elle touches my arm, I brush her off as I head toward the double doors that lock us in or keep everyone out.

"Noah." My father's voice is stern. I don't turn around to look at him. I don't need to see the disappointment in his eyes right now. I push through the doors and hightail it to the stairs. My feet pound the concrete, taking them two at a time until I've reached the top. My hands are clenched into fists as I pound on the wall.

Why of all people is it Zimmerman? He's not my foe, but he's a football player and I stayed away from her purposely so she could have a life, and yet she's with him and now... No, I can't say it. I can't bring myself even think it. Peyton is going to survive. She's going to wake up and I'm going to tell her how I feel and put the ball in her court and hope that she feels the same. For all I know, she's in love with him.

"No, she would've told me," I say out loud as I start to

pace. Would she have told me? There's a good chance that she would've kept this to herself. Maybe she felt like it wasn't my business. But no, Katelyn said, "she had a date" that means something.

I open the door and step out into the hallway. It's fairly dark and eerily quiet. I find myself tiptoeing down the hall, pausing when I come to open hospital room doors, looking to see if the rooms are occupied. I don't know why, it's a morbid curiosity I suppose. As far as I can tell this floor is empty. I don't know whether to breathe a sigh of relief or turn and run back to the stairs.

My heart is pounding and my palms are sweating. With each step I take, the fear builds. How is it possible that a hospital in Chicago has an empty floor?

"Can I help you?"

I turn to find a short older woman, dressed in white standing behind me. I won't go as far to say she's creepy, but the thought is crossing my mind.

"I... uh..."

"Are you looking for someone?"

Am I?

I nod. "Zimmerman. Kyle Zimmerman. I thought I was told he was on floor..." I look at the stark white walls for any indication of what floor I'm on but there are none.

"He's not on this floor," she deadpans and turns to the side as if that's my indication to leave. Don't need to tell me twice.

"Thanks." I walk by her as fast as I can, not stopping until I'm at the elevators. I turn back and she's watching me. Everything about this situation seems like a scene from a horror movie and I'm determined to believe that I'm making it all up. Nonetheless, I push the heavy metal door open and hustle down the stairs as fast as I can.

When I get to Peyton's floor, my hand rests on the handle, but I don't tug it open. My mind goes back to her and Zimmerman. He's somewhere in this hospital and I intend to find him. Another flight down, I exit the stairwell and hop in the elevator. I figure my best chance at finding out which room he's in will be from my agent.

The temperature must've dropped a few degrees in the last hour. I shiver as I stand outside, waiting for my phone to boot up. Once it does, the notifications start coming in again. There are a few from my teammates asking if I'm heading out with them tonight, but most are from Dessie, and I can't stomach to look at those right now. I tap the green Phone icon, press Allen's name and bring the handset to my ear. It rings twice before he's answering.

"Westbury?" Allen became my agent the day my college football career ended. He was one of the few who didn't come after me early, which earned a lot of respect from me. "Everything okay?"

"My friend was in a really bad accident and isn't expected to make it through the night." My heart seizes as I say those words. I want to take them back and tell Allen that she *is* going to make it, but it's too late. This entire time I've been telling myself that Peyton will pull through, refusing to believe what the doctor has said or what everyone around me believes.

"Let me know what I can do for you." He doesn't have a clue who Peyton is, but cares anyway. Not because it's his job, but because that's the type of man he is. I've heard the horror stories about my dad's manager, Sam, so I'm thankful Allen is a stand-up guy.

I nod even though he can't see me and kick a pile of snow away from me. "There is one thing if you don't mind."

"Anything."

"Kyle Zimmerman was also in an accident this evening and is rumored to be at the same hospital. I'd like to pay him a visit." I tell him which hospital I'm at, but nothing more. Allen doesn't need to know why I have to go see Kyle. Something tells me that he'll find out soon enough. Undoubtedly there will be a reporter that will put two and two together after Harrison holds a press conference tomorrow and Peyton's love affair with Kyle will be all over the news.

"Sure, sure. I'll find out what room and text you."

"Thanks." We hang up, and I decide to sit on a bench near the entrance. The whooshing of the sliding doors is somewhat calming. It oddly reminds me of the machines that are helping keep Peyton alive.

An elderly man, who has seen better days, sits down next to me. I'm trying not to stare, but I can't help it. It's cold here and this gentleman is wearing tattered clothing and a light jacket.

"Hey Mister, I know you," he says. My head snaps toward him and I smile, recalling those exact same words that I said to my dad before I knew who he was.

I extend my hand and shake his rather frail one. "Noah Westbury."

"Leonard Ramsey. My friends call me Leo."

"Well, I hope to some day call you Leo, Mr. Ramsey." He smiles an almost toothless grin.

"What brings you to Chicago?"

"My friend is here," I say, motioning with my head toward the hospital.

"Oh, and here I was hoping you were coming to play for a real team." He laughs and as much as I don't want to, I do as well.

"I like Portland. We're young. We'll be good soon."

"If you say so." Again, he's laughing at his own joke.

I don't know how long Leonard and I sit there talking about football. He has a plethora of knowledge and all I can think is that Peyton would love to be out here with us. When Allen finally texts, I'm torn on what to do. The urge to go see Kyle is stronger than ever, but hanging with Leonard is nice. It's peaceful and keeps my mind off what's going on one floor above me.

"How long are you in town for?" he asks, tearing my gaze away from my phone.

"Few days. I have to go back."

"Practice... it's just practice." He smiles, and this time I find myself laughing.

"Allen Iverson. I remember that press conference." Allen Iverson could've been one of the greatest in the NBA, but his attitude got him into trouble a lot. "You know Leonard, you've really turned the last hour or so around for me. Thank you."

He waves me off as if it's no big deal. I'd like to do something for him and normally, the guys and I walk up and down the streets of Portland with bags of food feeding the homeless, but with the cafeteria closed there isn't much I can do. I take my wallet out of my back pocket and open it. There's a couple hundred in there, which is now his.

"I have to run, but thank you, Mr. Ramsey," I say as I shake his hand. I don't know if he can feel the cash being pressed into his palm or not, either way, it's his.

"Please call me Leo."

I smile and nod. "Leo. Thank you!"

He calls after me once he realizes what I've done, but I don't stop. He doesn't need to thank me for anything because what he's done for me in the little time we've spent together, is worth more than anything.

I take the elevator to Kyle's floor. When I pass the nurse's station, she hollers out that visiting hours are over. I ignore her. What I have to say won't take long. I don't bother knocking when I enter his room. He's watching television, Sports Center to be exact, and his leg is suspended in the air.

"Westbury?" Of course he looks surprised to see me. He reaches forward to shake my hand, but I don't budge. His surprised expression quickly morphs into something upsetting. "They're already replacing me?" Kyle slams his head back onto his pillow and sighs. "I figured they'd at least wait until the morning. You're here to take my job, huh?"

"No, I'm here because you've about killed the woman I'm in love with." The words are out of my mouth before I can stop them. I wasn't intending to tell him that I love Peyton, only that she's close to me.

Zimmerman's eyes go wide but quickly turn to confusion. "Aren't you with some model? I don't understand."

"I'm referring to Peyton."

"Peyton?"

"Yes, the one who you somehow conned to get into your car, then tried to kill."

Kyle shakes his head. "No. I was taking her out to dinner. I saw her earlier, at the game, and we clicked."

My jaw clenches. I don't want to hear that they hit it off. That she would choose him over me. I look down at my wet shoes to avoid eye contact with Kyle. I'm so stupid for not telling her years ago how I felt.

"Can I see her?"

"No!" I blurt out.

"Yeah, my lawyer says the same thing. I didn't..." he pauses and turns his attention to the window. "That truck came out of nowhere."

Just like the one that killed her father.

"Please tell her I'm sorry, that I'll make it up to her. I don't know how or when, but I will."

"Right. Well, if she survives I'll be sure to let her know how sorry you are." I stand and head toward the door.

"Westbury?" he calls out. "I didn't know she was seeing someone, let alone you. I'm not the kind of guy who moves in on another man's woman. I didn't know. But if she is yours and you're messing around on her..." he shakes his head. "She seems like too good a woman to have a man treat her like that."

I don't bother correcting or telling him that I agree as I leave his room. He doesn't need to know that I'm battling demons right now. Instead of heading back to Peyton's floor to spend more time with her, I go back down to the main entrance, hoping that my new friend is there. Luckily for me, he is.

"Why are you still here, Leo?" I'm thankful he is but expected him to be at the nearest diner eating his weight in meatloaf.

He shrugs. "Someone told me that I should wait for you, that you need a friend."

I look around, wondering if my mom or Elle is outside. "Who?"

"Dunno. Couldn't get a good look at her, but she told me she loves you and asked that I stay until you came back. So here I am."

"Yeah, here you are. Why don't we go inside? The cafeteria isn't serving food right now, but they have disgusting coffee with our names on it."

"Sounds good to me," he says as he gets up and follows me inside. He walks with a slight hunch and shuffles his feet as fast as he can to keep up with my long stride. The receptionist gives me a look, but I ignore her. A hospital is supposed to be a safe haven for people like Leo.

"I'm really glad you were still out there," I say to him as we enter the elevator.

"Me too. Now I can tell you what's wrong with your team." He laughs, and deep down I'm laughing too. It has to be the first time since I heard the news about Peyton, and it feels pretty good.

13

PEYTON

*I*n my room, my mom and dad are asleep in the hard plastic chairs. Each of them has an arm across my stomach and they're holding hands while my sister lies next to me. Quinn is propped up against the wall, staring at me intently. I wish I could ask him what he's thinking or how he's feeling, much like I told Noah's friend to wait for him, but I don't want to give Quinn false hope that I'm going to make it.

They're waiting for me to die. They want to be in here so I'm not alone. *"She won't make it through the night."* Those are the words that play on repeat. There are a few who have hope, but I think most are resigned to the fact that I'm not supposed to live.

Death is coming. I can feel it, and I don't know how to fight it. It would be one thing if death were an inanimate object that I could touch, but it's not. It's a pull I've been ignoring since the truck slammed into me. I wasn't ready then, but maybe I am now.

I know I don't want to die because I would miss every-one, although it's a thought that I'm finding hard to understand. How will I know? Is everyone guaranteed to keep an eye on his or her family as time goes on? What if I die and never have the ability to see them again?

Out in the hall, it's quiet for the most part. The other rooms are dark, but you can hear the beeping of machines, notifying all those who are listening that the person in the room is still here. There is one nurse at the large desk, her head is bent and she looks like she's reading or maybe studying. The other two nurses are moving from room to room, checking the patients. Only three nurses to maintain a section where everyone is likely dying.

It's odd. Now I can think of a place where I want to be and I'm there. I expect to find a waiting room full of people, but only my aunts Josie and Jenna are there, along with my uncle Jimmy. Everyone is sleeping, but the television is on with no sound. The bright colors of the TV show they are watching casts shadows around the small room.

Josie stirs. She opens her eyes and smiles. Can she see me? Does that mean my time is getting closer to the end? Why isn't there a rulebook or some manual for us to read so we know what to do? I watch her for a second, studying her features,watching as they morph from a smile to a frown. Her forehead is pinched as if her dream changed from happy to something sad.

Jenna sleeps on Jimmy as much as the chairs will allow. They can't be comfortable, yet they both look very peaceful. Every few seconds, Jimmy sighs and adjusts his arms, pulling Jenna closer. When Eden was born, Elle and I were so excited to have a baby around. Eden was the first child we babysat. The age difference meant we could really play with Eden while Jenna ran to the store or Jimmy had band practice. It didn't matter though because we were always together and had plenty of opportunities to play with her when she was a baby.

It hits me that the next time everyone likely comes together is for the birth of a baby, unless of course, I can't fight my way back to the living. It'll probably be Noah's because he's going to end up marrying Dessie, and they'll have children. Maybe it's good that I won't be around to witness the birth of his children because I don't know how I'd take it. I guess I'll always have my dreams unless those go away when I die.

Elle though, she's going to make a good mom. She's always been more caring than me, always wanting to bring in stray cats, saving bugs from an untimely death and volunteering wherever she can. I'm going to miss it though, the day she becomes a mom. Maybe I'll be able to watch from wherever it is I'm going, and be there when my niece or nephew is born.

And Quinn. He'd be the best uncle and dad too. He'd teach everyone how to play the guitar, piano and drums. Although for him to have children, he'd actually have to admit to having a girlfriend. All through high school, the girls would come around but they were never anything more than friends according to him. Maybe it's because Elle and I always made fun of him when a girl would come over to study. It's what little sisters do, right?

If I could cry, tears would be streaming down my cheeks right now. I'm not ready to die. Up until the accident I had my whole life ahead of me. My dream of reporting from the NFL sideline was happening, and even if it were only for one game, it was still my moment. And Kyle Zimmerman asked me out. I was excited for our dinner date, but when I looked into his eyes... he knew the truck was going to hit me but there wasn't anything he could do about it. He saw it coming, and so did I. I turned in time see the grill in front of my face. There was nothing stopping the collision.

Missing from the waiting room is my uncle Liam. I thought he would've been in to visit me, but he has yet to do so. I shouldn't be sad about it, Jenna and Jimmy have visited, and Nick and Aubrey aren't here. Liam's my uncle and while we may not be related by blood, he's been there for me since my father passed away. Even though I have Harrison, Liam is different. He's the one connection I have to my dad when it came to our love of football.

I start to search the halls, thinking about him, hoping that if I do, I'll somehow find where he is. There are so many voices saying my name, though. It's hard to tell who is alive and who may be trying to get me to follow them toward the path of least resistance. That's what I'm going to call it because I don't want to go there. I feel like I'm back in school and my guidance counselor is talking to me about peer pressure. How it's easy to fall into the trap of drugs and alcohol if someone you like is doing it as well. The speech fell on deaf ears. I grew up in Beaumont. Drinking at the water tower is a rite of passage, even one Harrison understood.

I find myself staring at the chapel. The door is slightly ajar, making the voice easier to hear. My name is said, and I step inside. The only light in the room comes from the various candles that are burning, and even with his back to me, I know it's my uncle. He's on his knees, praying, doing something I've never seen him do before. I slip into the pews behind him, knowing I shouldn't eavesdrop, but I can't help it. I want to see him. I've missed him and was so excited to tell him about the assignment, and I want the chance to tell him about the game.

"I let you down, my brother. I told you I'd protect your

daughters and I feel like I've failed," Liam says. "The girls... oh, how I wish you could see them. They're beautiful and smart. They're kind and humble. Peyton... she's a special girl, Mason. I don't know if you can hear me, but if you're with her, tell her to fight. I have no doubt in my mind you miss her, but we love her and need her here. We're not ready to let her go."

"I don't want to go either, Uncle Liam, but I don't know how to stay and fight. No one is helping me. They keep calling my name and it's like I'm being pulled to them."

Liam sighs and takes a seat next to me. I lean into him, but can't feel his presence. What I wouldn't give to be held, by anyone, one more time. To feel the warmth of their body press against mine, to hear their heartbeat sound in my ear as I rest my cheek on their chest. Liam has always told me that if he likes you, he hugs you with one arm, and two means he loves you. From the day I met him, it's always been two. His love for me has never wavered.

"Do you remember the first time we met?" I ask, knowing full well he can't hear me. "You sat next to me at my father's funeral and promised to watch football with me. Every weekend, for as long as I can remember, and you were home, we would make party food and invite whoever wanted to watch over to your house. Most of the time it was only us, and it was perfect. I have learned so much from you, not only where the game is concerned, but about life and my father. Hearing stories about you and him, growing up, it made me feel like I knew him better."

"Oh Peyton," Liam says, his voice shuddering. "You gotta pull through this, baby girl. Losing you will destroy everyone." He bends over and continues to sob. I can't comfort him the way Josie or Noah can. He would at least tell his dad that he's encouraging me to fight and not giving up. It's the others who are choosing to listen to the doctor, who I might add hasn't come back to check on me.

Liam gets up and kneels at the altar again. "I'm not ready to say goodbye to her."

I gasp and quickly cover my mouth as my father appears next to Liam. He's kneeling down, with his arm draped across Liam's back and his head resting on his shoulder. After a long beat, he turns, making eye contact with me. My father looks the same as he does in the picture I have on my bedside table, the one with his infectious smile.

"Daddy..." I whisper as I rush to him. He meets me half way and pulls me into his arms. I wish I could feel him. I wish we were both alive and able to hold each other. I have long forgotten what it feels like to be held by him.

"You're so beautiful and grown up."

I laugh, but it sounds more like a cry. "And you... you look like the man I remember."

"That's because I am. Call it a luxury."

He sits us down, keeping his arm resting on my shoulder. He nods toward Liam. "He feels guilty."

"Why?"

"Because he's afraid to go see you, afraid that he's let me down."

"Has he?"

My father shakes his head. "Never. There was a time, back when we were teens, but I long forgave him. I don't blame him for what he did, only wish he had confided in me before he had done it or kept in touch."

"Things would've been different. You could've—"

"That accident was going to happen whether Liam was home or not. Thing is, he could've easily been in the truck with me. And then where would everyone be?"

His question gives me pause. It's almost as if Liam

leaving Josie has been the catalyst for our lives. Who knows what would have happened if he didn't leave, where would he be right now? Or if he took Josie with him, would we have Harrison?

"Everything happens for a reason," I mutter.

"It does. But now, you have a decision to make, Peyton. You can come with me or stay."

"What if I want both? What if I *need* both?"

My father presses his lips to my forehead and sighs. "It's only a decision you can make, but know this. I'm always here, watching over you and your sister. Missing you every day. I can't always make my presence known, but when I do, know it's me holding your hand or giving you a hug."

"If I stay, how will I know you're there with me?"

"The wind will blow around when you least expect it. The sun may shine on you brighter than it had before. A door will open when you least expect it and one will close when you need it to."

The last time I felt a random gust of wind was my graduation day. Elle's and my gowns went flying as we crossed the stage to receive our diplomas. I never thought it was my father doing that.

"If I go, will you be there to meet me? To make sure I get to wherever it is I'm supposed to be?"

"I wouldn't have it any other way, Peyton."

I open my mouth to thank him, but Noah's voice interrupts me when he calls out for Liam. "Dad," he says. "I thought now would be a good time to have that talk."

I turn back to my father, but he's already gone. Part of me is thankful that he won't be sitting here, listening to Liam and Noah discuss my prom night, but knowing that my father's here... well, I don't like that either.

14

NOAH

*T*he scenery of downtown Portland passes by in a blur. I haven't been able to focus on anything since I left Chicago. Leaving Peyton, lying there and still unresponsive, was the hardest thing I've ever had to do. In fact, I don't even know if I'll stay in Portland. I know I made a commitment to the team, but my head is not in the game right now. Not when my heart is thousands of miles away, begging the one I'm in love with to stay with us.

When she made it through the first night, I thought for sure she was going to wake up. Her vitals improved, and finally, everyone jumped on my train and started encouraging her to open her eyes. She hadn't by the time Tuesday afternoon rolled around and I was left with the decision to get fined by the team or head back home. I figure if I tell the coach what's going on, he'll understand and let me skip practice because like my friend Leo says, "it's only practice." And as much as I wanted to agree with Leo, we need the practice.

I was in two minds when I arrived back in Portland. Go directly to my coach's house or go home. Neither seemed pleasant, but I chose the latter and now that I'm standing in front of the door to the apartment I share with Dessie, I'm preparing for the worst. I deserve whatever I'm about to walk into. I've ignored her for the past few days, choosing to focus on Peyton instead. No one, except for maybe my father now, understands my feelings for her.

I find my dad kneeling in front of the altar, praying. We're not religious by any means and have spent our Sunday's praying in front of the television by watching football. But it seems that you become religious when a loved one is suffering.

Searching him out to discuss what he heard isn't my idea of a good time, but while we were drinking the nasty coffee downstairs, Leo said something about how we should never leave doubt or speculation when it comes to a loved one. His words hit home hard. I've always been honest with my dad about everything, except when it comes to Peyton because I fear his reaction. I wasn't honest with her, even though I've had plenty times where I could've been and now I may never get the chance to tell her exactly how I feel.

"Dad?" *I feel horrible for interrupting him. He has his own demons he's been dealing with for years, and I imagine being alone in a chapel is what he needs. Even though he wasn't here when Mason died, he carries a tremendous amount of guilt over his best friends death.*

"Noah?"

"I thought now would be a good time to have that talk."

He stands and motions for me to sit down. My steps are slow as I walk toward the altar, eyeing the burning candles. The pew is hard and does nothing to comfort the aches and pains I'm feeling.

"I don't know where to start."

"Your mom always tells me to start at the beginning because I'm less likely to get into trouble." He smiles.

"I can't be in trouble for what I've done, so maybe you'll listen and understand where I'm coming from."

"I'll try," he tells me.

I suppose trying is all I can ask for. Clearing my throat, I stare straight down at the ground. "For as long as I can remember, Peyton has been in my life. Everywhere I went she was there. Every holiday. Birthday parties, a family get-together, you name it, and she was there."

"She's family."

I shake my head. "Not to me. When I was about fifteen, I started to notice her differently. I couldn't stop thinking about her in ways that I shouldn't. I'd cry at night because I thought I was going to go to hell for having those thoughts about her and hoped they would go away, but they didn't. They grew stronger.

"I hoped that once I started dating, things would be different. But they weren't. Every girl I dated, I compared to Peyton. No one has ever been good enough and it's caused a lot of drama in my life, but I wouldn't change it. Anytime Peyton would call, I'd drop whatever I was doing and pick up the phone. I'd talk to her for hours, ignoring whomever my girlfriend was at the time because Peyton made me feel that much better. When she called and told me she didn't have a prom date, I told her I'd take her. She didn't ask me, I asked her. Well, I pretty much told her it was happening. Prom gave me a full night of being next to her and I desperately needed it.

"We had been dancing all night when she asked me to get a room. I did, and did it without hesitating because I thought this would be the night that I get to finally tell her that I'm in love with her, and have been for years."

"So because you were in love with her, you took her virginity?"

"Am."

"Excuse me?"

"I am in love with her, Dad. And that night, I thought things were going to change for us, but I was wrong. I drove her out to the cliffs the next morning, preparing to tell her everything and she kept going on and on about college and how excited she was to start. I started evaluating my life, the craziness, and figured I didn't want to burden her and kept my mouth shut."

Dad shakes his head. "Man, you're not too bright."

"What?"

He looks at me and laughs. "You take a girl you just slept with to the cliffs... Peyton probably thought you were going to tell her that what happened between you should've never happened. She was saving face."

My dad's words hit me like a ton of bricks. Is that what happened?

"Do Katelyn and Harrison know?"

"I don't think so." I shake my head. "Maybe Elle, if anyone."

"You're lucky she didn't end up pregnant."

I grimace. He may see it as luck, but I don't. She'd be mine if that were the case and wouldn't have been in Kyle Zimmerman's car.

"What are you going to do about Dessie?"

I tilt my head and take in a deep breath. "I'm going to break up with her."

"Whether Peyton makes it or not?"

I nod. "I love Dessie, but it's not the same. Whether Peyton makes it or not, my heart isn't whole without her, and Dessie deserves better."

The music is blaring when I step inside. There are a few girls, other models I presume, lounged out on my couch, and the place is trashed. They scramble to clean up whatever is in front of them and it doesn't take a genius to figure out they've been doing drugs. I try to keep my temper in check as I head toward my bedroom door. I'm not prepared for what I might find behind it but open it nonetheless.

Dessie is standing there, with her tiny bathrobe on, looking at me. Her eyes narrow as her fist flies toward my head. She's slow and easily blocked. "What the fuck are you doing?"

"Get out," she screams, coming at me again, but I'm able to pin her hands down and hold her to my chest. She squirms and tries to kick her way out, but I'm too strong for her. "I want you out."

"It's my apartment, Dessie."

"Fine, I'll go then." This time I let her go and she starts pulling her clothes from our closet. All I can do is stand there and watch. I told my dad I was going to break up with her and the cowardly thing to do would be to let her go without saying anything, but I can't.

"Dessie, we need to talk."

"Why, so you can tell me you screwed that bitch?"

Rubbing my hands over my face, I sigh heavily. "She's in a coma and she's not a bitch."

"Do you think I care, Noah?" she asks, getting into my face. "You've been gone for days and haven't bothered to return a single one of my text messages or calls." She comes over to me. I purposely avoid touching her, knowing I'm ending our relationship tonight. I should've known better than to assume we could be adults about this.

"I know, and I'm sorry, but I was dealing with a lot

while I was in Chicago. She's my best friend, and seeing her like that..."

"Yeah, well I've been dealing with a lot too while you've been gone." She steps closer, backing me into the wall.

I scoff. "Like what, getting high?"

This time her open palm connects as she slaps me across the face. I deserve it, but not for calling her out for her drug use. I pull my lower lip in, sigh and shake my head. "I told you before I wouldn't tolerate the drugs. At any given time, my place could be inspected, and yet you brought your trashy ass friends into my house and did who knows what while I've been holding a vigil for my best friend?"

"I told you, I don't care."

"Same."

I storm out of the bedroom and take one look at her friends. "Get out," I yell at them. They go scrambling as fast as they can, making sure they have all their paraphernalia with them. I look down at my coke-smeared coffee table. The sight of it disgusts me. It's the piece of furniture that goes flying against the wall. Followed by my two end tables. I bend over at my waist to catch my breath, only to feel her hands on my shoulders.

"Noah... Noah, stop," Dessie yells, but the damage is done. My living room is a wreck with shattered furniture everywhere. "It's okay, baby." The switch in Dessie's tone doesn't take me by surprise. I've been with her on enough photo shoots to be familiar with her Jekyll and Hyde routine. Although this is the first time she's used it on me.

Righting myself, I move out from her under touch and look at her. "I'm in love with Peyton, Dessie."

"What?"

My body sighs, almost as if saying those words out loud

to her is some sort of relief. I suppose in a sense, it is. "I love her."

"For how long?"

Shaking my head, I stare down at the ground, too cowardly to look her in the eyes. I was wrong to ever pursue anything with Dessie, but the pressure of looking a certain way for the league has weighed heavily on me.

When I finally find an ounce of courage to look at her, she steps back and shakes her head. "Have you slept with her?" she asks, her voice barely above a whisper.

I nod, knowing that by admitting this, I've lied to her about my relationship with Peyton. "It was before you and I met."

"Doesn't matter, Noah. You told me you hadn't, that nothing had ever happened between the two of you."

"I know."

"So how many times, huh? Are you sleeping with her when you're at away games? Do you fly her there because she certainly doesn't come to your home games or is she here when I'm on location? Do you screw her in our bed?"

"I've been with her one time, Dessie. Like I said, it was before I met you."

"I don't believe you," she scoffs. I knew she wouldn't, which is why I never told her the truth. "Was the accident a ruse by your parents to get you away from me? Is that why you've been in Chicago to see her?"

"You really think that little of my parents?"

She shrugs. "It's not like they like me. Your father didn't even invite me to come with you to Chicago."

Shaking my head. "The last words you said to me were something like, 'It's always about Peyton.'"

"Well, isn't it?"

I nod without reservation.

"Fuck off, Noah." Dessie rushes back toward the bedroom and slams the door. I do the same, except I leave the apartment and head to the basement garage where my car is parked. It feels good to be in control of the car, telling it when to turn, speed up or slow down. It's the only thing in my life that I can tell what to do. I'd like to tell Peyton to wake up and have her listen, but she isn't.

I find myself in the driveway of my coach's house. As luck would have it, his wife is outside tending to her rose bushes on this rare warm winter day and waves, although I have a feeling she has no idea who she's waving to.

"Hi, Noah. How are you?" she says as soon as I make my presence known.

"I'm good, just here to see Coach."

"Go on in, you know where to find him."

I do as she says and head toward his basement where he has a massive media room set up. Our last game is being shown and most of the coaches are here, watching it.

"Westbury, to what do we owe the pleasure?"

"Um..." I run my hand through my hair and motion for him to join me in his home office. He follows me in and takes a seat behind his desk. "Sunday afternoon, my best friend was in a car accident. You may have heard about it, Kyle Zimmerman was driving."

"Oh, Noah. Yes, I had heard. I'm sorry. When is the funeral?"

I shake my head, understanding that ESPN had inaccurately reported the passenger in Zimmerman's car died. "She's hanging on by a thread. Peyton, that's her name, she's in a coma, and honestly Coach, my head and heart is in Chicago with her."

"What are you saying?"

"I'm not asking for time off, but I am asking that after

the game this week I be excused from practice so I can be with her."

"It's a mighty big request."

"I know, but until she wakes up I'm really not going to be of any use to you, physically or mentally."

He nods but doesn't answer my question. "Let's see how this week goes, shall we?"

I shake his hand and excuse myself. I don't know where I'm going to go, but the idea of heading back to my apartment doesn't sit well with me right now, although I have a strong feeling things aren't over between Dessie and I just yet.

15

PEYTON

*T*he soft sounds of a guitar filters through my mind, but it's coupled with a strange beeping. The intermittent noise is annoying and ruining the melody. I can't understand why my dad, Liam or Jimmy would allow this to happen. I want it to stop but can't seem to move my hand. It feels heavy and my skin feels tight.

In fact, everything feels... off. My head hurts and when I try to touch the pain, neither of my arms will move. My chest burns, and yet I can't rub the spot either. The more I start to access my body, the more I realize I'm in agony. What the hell did I do?

I struggle to move my fingers, toes... my leg. My right side feels like it's burning, like someone is jabbing me with a thousand fire rods. Something clicks and the pain subsides. It's there, but not as forceful as before.

But there's something in my throat, and it's cutting off my airway. I can't swallow. Taking a deep breath is near impossible. Panic ensues as I struggle to get air. I gasp and cry out in pain, except it's a deep throaty moan that makes me sound like a zombie. I need help but am stuck. I can't move. I can't talk. I open my eyes and see the faint outline of a person, but nothing else because tears cloud my vision. I try to scream for help, but I'm only able to groan. The guitar has stopped, but the beeping increases. *Someone help me!*

"Hey, hey, hey, it's okay, Peyton."

Quinn appears almost as if he's hovering over me. He's smiling and I think there are tears falling down his cheeks, but I can't be sure. He gently holds my shoulders down and says, "It's okay, it's okay. Just hold tight." As if repeating himself is reassurance. It's not.

I do the exact opposite and try to find where the noises are coming from. I look to my left and find a machine, the more I study it, the higher the numbers climb. Paper is printing out of it like crazy and now something is squeezing my arm. Frantically, I look back at Quinn. He's still smiling and I don't understand why. Can't he see that I'm in desperate need of assistance?

"Well, would you look at those beautiful blue eyes," some lady in a Pepto pink shirt with flowers on it says. She presses a few buttons and thank God the beeping stops but that doesn't help the fact that I can't breathe. I grunt, getting her attention and she smiles softly at me. She seems familiar, but I don't know her. "Okay, Peyton. I know you're scared, but I need you to relax."

Easier said than done, lady.

She starts checking my vitals, but I'm still unaware of what's going on or where I am. And why is Quinn here, but no one else? I look to him for answers, but still he's smiling, almost like he's done something bad and is waiting for me to figure it out.

"Peyton, can you hear me okay?"

I nod, and she focuses her attention on Quinn. "I've given her a sedative to keep her calm. She's a little too alert after the traumatic experience she's had. She'll start to drift in and out of consciousness. Don't be alarmed. It's her body's way of healing, but until she can sit up, we're going to leave her tube in a bit longer and let her body stabilize on its own."

"Okay, I'll tell my parents when they come back."

I try to follow the conversation, but everything is fuzzy and out of focus. Once the nurse leaves, I grunt at Quinn to get his attention.

"Hey." He holds my hand, but not in the way you normally would. He's slid his under mine. It's odd, yet comforting. "I know you're scared, but everything is going to be okay. I texted Mom and Dad, and they're on their way back."

I grunt again, which translates to me asking him where am I?

"They're going to be so happy."

Another grunt. Why can't I move my arms? Why can't I feel my leg? Give me something, Quinn.

Quinn starts playing his guitar. He begins to sing to me softly. This was the sound that woke me up from wherever I was. As much as I want to turn my head toward him, I can't. My eyes start to droop. I fight to keep them open, but after each blink, it's harder to open them the next time.

Except, I'm not sleeping. I can hear everything around me. The beeping is back, but so are voices. My parents, Elle and Quinn's voices are distinct. Others, I'm not so sure about. People come in and out of my room, and for the most part, they seem happy. They're talking quietly, but I can hear a few of the things they're saying.

As much as I want to, I can't open my eyes. Even though I attempt to each time someone asks, I fail. And whoever is sitting around me at the time gets unbelievably upset when I can't accomplish what they're asking. I want to tell them I'm trying, but that's near impossible. My body feels like it's detached from my nervous system and no matter what my brain says, my body is rejecting the notion, except for the twitching.

Every few seconds my right arm jerks, which causes an obscene amount of pain. Each internal scream is nothing more than a grunt. After the sensation dies down, I'm numb again. I've gathered that one of these machines I'm hooked up to is keeping me doped up because right now I'm pain free.

By sheer luck, my eyes open. Someone notices. I don't know who but there's a mad rush to my bedside with everyone jockeying for position. They say my name repeatedly, asking if I can hear them. They do know I have something stuck in my mouth and can't answer them, right?

Frantically, I look around trying to focus on one face, but my vision is blurry and the people clamoring around are nothing more than blobs making noise. It's easier when I'm asleep or pretending to be so I close my eyes and the commotion around me stops. Now it's peaceful even though I can hear the people in my room talking. My mom is worried there's something wrong because I won't wake up. Maybe if they'd leave me alone, I'd open my eyes and greet them, but the instant onslaught isn't helping my brain cope with whatever is going on.

My room is quiet, with the exception of the machines and the sound of someone talking. The voice is muffled though and I'm having a hard time placing who they might be. I open my eyes again and find Quinn next to me. This time, he's not focused on me, but a small television, which is sitting on a cart. He's staring at it intently, completely unaware that I'm watching him.

At some point, someone elevated my bed. I have the urge to cough but am afraid to with this tube down my throat. I can't kick him because my leg won't move and each time I try to move my arm, I feel like I'm being stabbed so I grunt, hoping I'm loud enough he'll be able to hear me over the television.

He looks at me from over his shoulder. I try to smile and his eyes go wide. "Welcome back." He reaches over the top of me and fiddles with something and within seconds the Petpo pink shirt-wearing lady is back.

"Hello, we look a little more awake this time."

Nodding is really the only thing I can do, and the action brings a smile to her face. She busies herself with setting various other tubes.

"What are you doing?" Thankfully Quinn asks because I'm wondering the same thing.

"I'm going to suction out her tube before I remove it. She's going to be very sore and with her chest wound the last thing we want is for her to have to cough excessively."

Chest wound? I glance at Quinn and wait for him to look at me, but his attention is solely on my nurse. I don't have to do anything while she completes her task, but that doesn't mean I'm not scared. Quinn leans toward me, careful as to where he touches me.

"Okay, sweetie. I need you to open your mouth." I do as she says and she suctions out my mouth, making me feel like I'm at the dentist. "Now, I'm going to remove the tube. If you feel like you need to cough, go ahead."

The process seems slow. I can feel the tube moving inside of me. The tickling sensation causes me to cough, but the pain is almost too much to handle. My eyes go wide as I gasp for air. Quinn is in my ear, telling me that everything is going to be okay, but I'm not so sure I believe him right now.

"One second and you'll feel fine," the nurse says, and she is right. Just like that, I'm numb again. She places an oxygen mask over my mouth and nose, tightening the straps on the side. "You'll need to wear this for a while, but feel free to talk if you're up to it. Okay?"

I close my eyes and nod.

"How long will she be on the morphine?" Quinn asks.

"It's hard to say. The doctor will be in to discuss everything with your parents as soon as they return."

"Hey, can you hear me?"

I turn my head slightly toward Quinn. I smile at him.

"You don't know how good it feels to see your eyes, Peyton. Everyone is here: Mom, Dad, and Elle, Liam and Josie, Jimmy and Jenna. They've all been waiting for this moment and I've gotten to see you open your eyes twice. I think that means you like me the most."

"Love," I whisper, but I don't think he can hear me with this mask on or the fact that my voice is barely audible. I want to ask where Noah is, but I'm not surprised he's not here. He has a life away from us now, one led by someone I can't stand.

"Everyone is about to be on TV. Do you want to watch?"

Quinn doesn't wait for my answer. He pulls the cart closer so I can see. As far as televisions go, this one is fairly small and looks extremely outdated, but on the screen is the band's manager, Mira, with my dad and uncles standing behind her. I love Mira. She really takes care of the band and has increased their staying power. My dad says there was a time when they struggled with a manager, but since hiring Mira, they've been very happy.

"Good afternoon. I want to thank you all for coming out. I know it's a bit chilly, but I promise to keep this short and sweet. Over the past week, there has been a lot of speculation about 4225 West. I can assure, as you can see behind me, everyone is okay. However, Harrison James' daughter, Peyton, was involved in a near fatal accident last Sunday. As many of you will recall, Chicago Bears quarterback, Kyle Zimmerman, was also involved in an accident. His passenger was Peyton. As erroneously reported by ESPN, the passenger in Mr. Zimmerman's car did not pass away on the scene."

My eyes go wide and according to one of the machines I'm hooked up to, my heart must be racing. I don't know how I didn't realize I was in an accident... is that why I can't move? Mira continues to talk, and I try to focus on what she's saying, but my mind is wild with questions.

"It is also with great pleasure I can report that Ms. Powell-James is conscious and her status has been upgraded to critical but stable. I will give you my normal spiel and tell you the family requests their privacy during this time, but we all know there is no such thing anymore. We are willing to answer any questions you may have."

"*Will Zimmerman face any charges?*" The camera person doesn't pan to the media gathered, making it impossible to find out who is asking.

"From the family, no. We are unaware if the authorities are pursuing anything. Next?"

"*What about the driver of the truck?*"

"Yes, he was cited. His charges are pending. Next?"

"*How long is Ms. Powell-James expected to remain in the hospital?*"

"Her injuries are significant."

I grunt to get Quinn's attention. He turns the television down and scoots over to me. "Do you need the nurse?"

I shake my head and point my eyes toward my mask. He removes it slowly. "What happened? Why can't I move?"

Quinn returns the oxygen mask. "You were in a really bad accident, Peyton. We thought you were going to die."

I close my eyes and try to turn away but my body is a prisoner to my injuries and I can barely move. Either way, I don't want to look at Quinn right now. I don't want to see what his eyes will tell me... I'm not the same person as I was before.

16

NOAH

"*A*gain, Westbury, and maybe this time you'll try hitting Cunningham," Coach yells, even though he's standing right next to me. Standing behind the center, Alex Moore, I call out my cadence.

"Louder!"

I start over, increasing the octave of my voice per Coach's instructions. "Set, set, hike," I holler. With the ball in my hand, I step back and stumble over my own feet before falling to the ground.

"Goddammit, Westbury." Coach picks me up off the ground by my facemask. He's yelling so hard, spit is flying into my face. He's asking me what's wrong. He wants to know if I've suddenly forgotten how to play.

"No, sir."

"Get out of my sight." He pushes me toward the side-lines. Normally I would stay and prove to him I'm exactly the player he drafted, but my mind is not on the game. Every part of me is in Chicago, and he knows this. I don't know if this is some mental tough love thing or what. If it is, it's not working.

I forgo the sideline and head right to the locker room. I need the quiet so I can think and reflect on my on-field performance. Mentally, I should be stronger. I should be able to block what's going on with Peyton out of my mind and focus on my job, but I can't get over the fact that I want to be there with her.

My phone sits on the top shelf of my locker. I pick it up and press the home button. Each notification is from Dessie. Since our fight and subsequent break-up, she's been calling and texting non-stop. Most of them I ignore, especially because it's easy to tell when she's angry, which usually means she's been drinking. Her messages range from being sorry to offering to share me with Peyton, telling me that she doesn't care whether or not I used her to pass time. Where she came up with that idea, I'm not so sure. Subconsciously, I think that's exactly what I've done.

When I first met Dessie, I was attracted to her. There's no doubt she's beautiful. She was wild though, and I've never been one to play around in the party scene. My body is my temple sort of thing. I caught her once snorting coke, and threatened to leave. Dessie promised it would never happen again, and to my knowledge, it hadn't until I left for Chicago. Thinking back though, we're not with each other when we travel, so how the hell do I know if she's doing it or not. Either way, I can't tolerate it. I refuse to.

I undress as quickly as I can and hit the shower. I'd love to go home, but leaving before Coach has another opportunity to ream me out wouldn't be wise. I deserve the ass chewing, but he knows where my mind is right now. I warned him.

As soon as I'm out of the shower, I hit the trainer's room. He motions for me to hop up on the table, and once I do, he starts giving my aching muscles a rub down.

"I heard what happened out there," he says as he works the kinks out of my calf.

"I have a lot of shit going on right now."

"You know I used to be a bartender so I think there's some underlying rule in place that allows you to open up."

I chuckle and sigh. "My best friend was the passenger in the car accident Zimmerman was in. She's in a coma back in Chicago and I'm stuck here."

He pauses and looks like he's about to tell me something important. Everyone knows about Zimmerman's accident, it's the talk of the league right now. "I saw a press conference, I think she's awake or improving."

I bolt upright, startling him. "What did you say? When?"

"Yesterday, I think it was. They said she's..."

He doesn't have a chance to finish his sentence because I'm running from his room back to the locker room. Grabbing my phone, it falls from my hand as my other one desperately tries to keep my towel cinched at my waist, which is near impossible. I drop the towel as I bend to scoop up my phone and sit on the cold leather chair.

I press my mother's number. Voicemail.

I try my father. Voicemail.

Quinn is next. Voicemail.

Pressing Elle's name, the phone rings on the other end. She answers on the fourth ring. "Hey, Noah."

"Hey, Noah? Is that what you have to say to me?" I ask her.

"Um..."

"How about, 'Oh shit, Noah we forgot to call and tell you Peyton is awake!'" I scream so loudly my body temperature rises. "How could you not call me?"

"I thought someone else would've called. I mean your parents—"

"Right. I'm sure it never crossed your mind to find out if I knew. Instead, I have to find out from my trainer."

Elle sighs. "You know what, Noah? Not everything is about you right now. Yes, someone should've called you, but our sister woke up and we've been trying to make her feel better about herself. When did you become so damn selfish?"

Tears drip down my face. Both out of excitement because Peyton is awake, and also out of anger because Elle is right. I *am* selfish. Everything going on with Peyton isn't about me. I'm not the only one who loves and cares about her. "You're right, I'm sorry, Elle. I'm just—"

"You're just like us. You're worried and scared, and I'm sorry no one called. But yes, Peyton is awake. She actually woke up twice yesterday and I missed both times. Once was the middle of the night and the other time was when I was picking Ben up from the airport." I'm not shocked Ben is there. He's been Elle's best friend since high school. They have a similar relationship to what Peyton and I have or had up until recently. It makes me wonder what's changed between us, aside from Dessie.

"Who was with her?"

"Quinn. He actually hasn't left her side."

I clear my throat. "How is she?"

Elle sighs. "Honestly, not good. It seems that the doctor was so sure she wasn't going to make it he didn't cast her leg or arm. We've been moving her arm so much that we've likely caused more damage. Her leg... well, he has to go in and re-break it so it can set right, same with her arm," Elle pauses and tells someone she's speaking with me. "He also has to fix her stitches. God, Noah, this asshole—"

"Your parents will take care of him, Elle, you focus on Peyton. Keep her spirits up. When's her surgery?"

"I don't know, they haven't said."

"Are my parents still there?"

"No, they left this morning. Along with Jimmy and Jenna. The girls have to get back to school."

"I'll be there on Sunday, after my game."

"Where exactly are you going now, Westbury?"

I turn to find Coach standing behind me. I half smile, half grimace and tell Elle I'll call her later. I stand up and my coach cocks his eyebrow at me. I quickly cover my junk with my hand, which is also holding my phone.

"My friend, she's awake. I need to go back to Chicago."

"My office, now," he says as he walks out the door. "Put some damn clothes on," he yells before the door shuts. I do as he says and hustle down to his office and take the seat in front of his desk.

"Look, Coach. I know my head isn't in the game. I told you this the other night, and I'm sorry. I'm letting you and the team down, but she's awake and I feel like a thousand pounds has been lifted off my shoulders."

"That's all fine and dandy, Westbury, but I need a committed and focused quarterback who can lead the charge not only on Sunday but every day in practice, on and off the field."

"I know, and I'm sorry. I need to be mentally stronger."

"You're not the only one who has lost someone in the league. Many athletes perform the same day as a tragic loss."

I nod. Normally, I think I would be okay if I didn't come to the harsh realization that I'm in love with Peyton and haven't been able to tell her. Not knowing whether or not

I'd ever be able to talk to her or feel her arms wrap around me again, really did something to my psyche.

"Your commitment is to this team, and if you can't be here—"

"I will be," I say before I realize I interrupted him. I shake my head and sit up straighter in the chair. "Sir, I know my actions these past couple of days haven't been up to standards."

"I feel a but coming on, Westbury." He leans onto his immaculate desk and glares at me.

I slink back as far as I can in the chair under his penetrating gaze, feeling about two feet tall. "After Sunday's game, I'm asking that I be allowed to miss practice until Friday."

Coach threads his fingers together and taps his lips with his clenched hands. "I'm in a position to say no, that after today's performance, you need all the extra reps you can get, but I'll make a deal with you. If we win on Sunday, you can have the week off."

I stand and extend my hand. He shakes mine, squeezing with enough force to remind me he can make or break my career. "I'll do my best." Sometimes my best isn't good enough, but I'm going to try. I leave his office and head back to the locker room. The guys give me shit about being in trouble. That's one thing about sports; the childish antics never change.

"I'm fine. Rough day."

"I heard Dessie left his sorry ass," Alex says.

I don't know how he would've heard, unless she's posted something on social media, but it's not her style to air dirty laundry.

Jessie McAvoy, our right tackle, slaps me on the back. "Don't worry, I'll take care of that fine woman of yours."

"She's too much for you, McAvoy." I move away from him and head toward my locker. Julius is standing there, looking confused. "I'm good."

"You sure?"

"Yeah, you wanna grab some dinner?"

"I do," Alex says, putting his arms around the both of us.

"Is this going to be a gossip session where we talk about our feelings and go to the bathroom together?" Julius asks.

"Pretty much," I tell him.

Alex claps his hands together. "Yes, Moore is gonna get him some tonight!"

I roll my eyes and finish putting my stuff in my bag. Alex thinks women flock to him when he's being emotional. Julius and I have told him repeatedly it's because when he walks into a place everyone suspects he's a pro athlete by his size.

Before leaving the locker room, I pull out my phone and send a text to Peyton. I have no idea if she even has her phone, is able to look at it or what, but I want her to know I'm thinking about her.

I'll be there in a few days. I miss you.

And against my better judgment, I look through the many messages from Dessie.

I love you

I'm sorry

Call me

Can I see you tonight?

We need to talk

They're endless and remain unanswered by me. I can't imagine what we have to talk about. I lied to her. She lied to me. That alone puts us in an unhealthy relationship neither of us needs right now. Dessie needs to focus on her career and getting clean if she has a drug habit. And I need to focus on what I'm going to do about Peyton and my feelings for her. Not only do I need to tell her, but also her parents. I think they have a right to know I plan to pursue Peyton if she'll allow me.

17

PEYTON

$\mathcal{M}$y room is a revolving door of visitors. Many times over the past few days the nurses have had to tell my family to keep their voices down. One went as far to threaten to remove them and reinstate the one person at a time visiting rule. I'm tempted to ask her. It's not that I don't appreciate them being here, but they're *always* here, and I'm in pain. A crap ton of pain to be exact. Sometimes I just wish I could just be left alone to suffer in silence, without them worrying about me.

They don't get it. By they, I mean my mom and sister. Every grimace and grunt has them rushing to my side. They're either petting my hair or running their hands over my blankets as if they need to be straightened. For whatever reason, they can't comprehend that my meds are on a timer and when they start to wear off, I start to hurt more.

I'm tired of the question, "how are you doing?" I mean seriously, look at me. I have no control over my body. My right arm is now taped to my side so I don't move it suddenly, and my leg... considering I can't feel anything, even when someone accidentally touches my toes, pretty much tells me I'll never walk again. Let's not forget the hole I have on the side of my head or my missing hair. And while I can breathe on my own, I have to wear a mask to sleep. So how do they think I'm doing? I'm not sure I can say the word "fine" anymore than I already have. I get that I almost died, but I'm awake now and it would be nice if people started treating me like Peyton, and not some fragile doll. I've always hated dolls.

No one is talking about what happened either, despite me asking. My uncle Liam came to visit, I asked him. He had this far off look about him and changed the subject. The same with my uncle Jimmy, he acted like he had no idea. My dad, mom and my good for nothing siblings haven't been any better. Quinn and Elle should at least be on my side, slipping me pudding and milkshakes, all while telling me how it is that I almost died. But they're all tight-lipped and pretending everything is sunshine and rainbows.

The last clear thing I remember Sunday is walking to Kyle Zimmerman's car. I wish they understood that my memory's fuzzy and it would be nice to have some recollection of what I was doing before the accident happened. If I had access to my phone, I'd be able to look up the media reports, but my parents are doing a stand-up job keeping me out of the loop. I don't even remember why I was at the Bears game even though everyone says I was there for an assignment.

My aunt Yvie walks in and stands at the end of my bed. It's like we're having a staring game, except she's winning because I'm still doped up on morphine. I have a feeling that once I'm out of this hospital, I'll be sent to another one to deal with the drug addiction I'm developing.

"Are you just going to stand there?" I ask. My voice is

groggy and hoarse. Side effects of the tube they stuffed down my windpipe to help me breathe.

"I'm afraid to touch you."

"No one said you had to, but you can come closer. I won't bite." I offer her a smile, but it doesn't feel like my lips are even moving.

Yvie floats over. I say float because she's as dainty as a butterfly. It comes from teaching dance and yoga. She and Xander own a state of the art facility in Los Angeles where they cater to the rich and famous. My uncle specializes in physical rehabilitation and is one of the most sought-after injury specialists in the country. Many sports teams hire him after their star athlete has been injured. Yvie expanded their mini-empire when she started posting videos on YouTube of her teaching yoga. Now she has a full line of DVDs out, plus there's a waiting list to take one of her classes.

"Promise not to bite?"

"I promise not to move," I tell her, straight-faced. I wish I were joking. I'd give anything to lunge out of this bed and tackle her, but any such movement would kill me or leave me wishing I had died.

She kisses my forehead and when she pulls away, she tries to hide the fact she's crying. "I'm so happy that you're okay."

"Thanks. Is Xander here?"

Yvie nods. "He's out in the hall with your parents and grandma."

"She's here too?"

"Of course. We wanted to be here earlier, but your dad..."

"It's okay. I know I wasn't supposed to make it."

"We should've come earlier," she says. Maybe they

should've or not. Honestly, if she hadn't said anything I probably wouldn't know the difference. According to one of the nurses, because of the people I've had here and who they are, they've had to change their policy around about letting multiple visitors in a room because they didn't want my dad, uncles and Noah harassed by the families of other patients.

"How's Los Angeles?" I ask, needing to change the subject. I don't want her to feel bad. Her and Xander have a busy life, and while they never had children, the gym and their clientele keep them occupied.

"L.A.'s great. Your dad says you'll be spending a lot of time there."

"What?"

"Peyton?"

My eyes glance toward the door where my dad has walked in. He looks like his normal self with his cargo shorts, thermal long-sleeved shirt with some random band on it from another group and a beanie.

"What's she talking about, Dad?"

"Hey, kiddo!" Xander bursts in behind my dad and rushes over to me. I brace myself for impact, but he stops in time and kisses my forehead just as Yvie did.

"Hey... someone want to tell me what's going on?"

Xander looks from Yvie to my dad and now to my mom who is standing in the doorway before he settles his gaze back to me. "So, long story short, your body is messed up and I'm going to fix it."

"Wh-what?" I swallow down the lump that's forming in my throat. I know I'm damaged, but I thought... well, I'm not sure exactly what I thought. That maybe I'd wake up and everything would be a dream.

"You gotta do some extensive rehab. Lucky for you, your uncle is the best in the country."

"My uncle is booked solid."

He waves me off as if he's not. "I'm always free for you, Peyton."

"Right, back to this rehab."

"Hi, Peyton, I'm Dr. Colby." A woman walks in carrying a clipboard. Behind her are two nurses who are flanking my bed. "I want to say you've surprised everyone in the hospital with your survival and I want to apologize for my colleague's behavior during surgery. He should've treated you better. With that said, because of the extent of your injuries we need to take you to surgery."

The lump I had earlier when Xander mentioned Los Angeles, is back only now it's ten times larger. I look at my parents for confirmation. My dad looks pissed off and my mom looks sad. "I don't understand."

"We need to reset your bones in your arm and leg. Flush the wounds on the right side of your body. Make sure your sutures are healing along your torso and head."

"And I have to have surgery to do this?"

"Yes, it's the safest way."

"But... but..." I don't get a chance to finish my sentence before one of the nurse's slips the oxygen mask over my face. The heart monitor starts beeping rapidly and my mother's face is masked with concern. Before I realize what's happening, my bed is yanked from the wall and portable machines are set down next to me. The doctor leads the way out of the room, and my parents are on either side of me. I desperately want to hold their hands, but it's all but impossible.

We come to a set of double doors, where Elle and Ben are standing. Ben leans down and kisses me on my forehead because it's literally the only spot that doesn't hurt on my body aside from having a headache.

"I'll be the first one to sign your cast," Elle says. I know she's trying to make me feel better, but I could honestly do without a cast, although I have a feeling the doctor was sugarcoating my injuries. I can't feel or move my leg. That's not normal.

My parents are by my side through the ride down in the elevator, until we get to another set of doors. "If you'll wait here, as soon as I'm done, I'll be out," the doctor says to my parents.

Mom removes my mask and kisses me on the lips. My dad opts for my cheek. He whispers, "Don't cry, baby girl." I hadn't realized I was until he mentioned it.

"I'm scared."

He cups my face and looks into my eyes. "Dr. Colby is the best. We brought her in from UCLA for you. She's going to take care of you. Mom, Elle and I will be right here."

"Where's Quinn?"

"He'll be here, I promise." Dad doesn't exactly answer my question. He and Mom both kiss me again and continue to tell me they love me as I'm pushed into an operating room. The staff filters around me, no one is talking or making eye contact with me. It makes me wonder if they're upset they have to work with a doctor who isn't on staff here. It also has me questioning how is this possible and what did my dad have to do to make this happen.

"I'm going to lay you back, Peyton." One of the nurses says. "Your dad told me you're a football fan. Why don't you give me a list of your favorite players?"

"Mason Powell," I say even though she has no idea who he is. "Noah..."

This time when I wake, there isn't any music to soothe the panic, but I can see the Chicago skyline from my room. My leg is suspended in the air and my arm is bent and resting on my chest, only I can't really feel my chest at the moment. I try to wiggle my toes, but the effort is too much. The soft sound of breathing catches my attention and when I look, there's a familiar head of hair and pressure on my hip I hadn't felt before.

I would know Noah's hair anywhere. When he lets it grow, which he always does for football season, there's a slight curl to the top. I run my fingers through it, praying that my IVs don't get caught. He moans softly and rolls his face into my non-injured leg. When his eyes open, he seems shocked.

"You're awake."

"For a few minutes now." I also notice my oxygen mask is off but can feel air being pumped into my nose. I'm tempted to touch whatever contraption is on my face, but that would mean taking my hand away from where it dropped next to Noah's.

"I should go wake your parents." He stands but stops at the sound of my voice.

"Please don't," I plead. "Just stay, for a while."

Noah turns and looks at me. Something is different, but I can't put my finger on it. He leans forward, bracing a hand on either side of my head and kisses me on the lips, lingering there longer than what would be considered friendly.

When he pulls away, he sits back down and takes my hand in his. "You don't know how long I've been waiting to do that."

Sure I do, two years since you kissed me goodbye. I

would never say those words to him so I let his statement hang in the air.

"I was here, before, when you were unconscious."

"You were?"

He nods. "I have so much to tell you, Peyton, but you really need your rest. I want you to be completely coherent when I say what I have to."

"Okay," I whisper.

I don't know how long Noah and I stare at each other before I fall asleep, but when I wake again, the sun is shining and the halls are much busier than before.

18

NOAH

*T*hank God we won because seeing her baby blues is worth the shit my coach is going to give me for bailing on the press conference after the game. When the clock hit zero, I rushed off the field as fast as I could. It was completely unprofessional of me, and I could've easily waited since I asked my dad if I could use the band's plane, but I wanted to get here. After the conversation with Quinn, this was where I needed to be.

"Sorry for not calling."

"It's fine. I get it." I don't, but the issues between Peyton and I are for us to figure out. Peyton and Dessie don't get along, and I foolishly tried to keep them both happy, when I really should've focused on Peyton.

"Nah, man. My phone died and these nurses are vicious. They have a strict no phone policy. But anyway, my parents are filing a lawsuit against the doctor who performed Peyton's surgery. A nurse came forward and backed the claim Peyton wasn't taken care of properly. Xander is here and he brought some doctor from Los Angeles. My parents

have been *fighting* with the board to give this doc hospital privileges so she can go in and fix everything."

"What do you mean everything?"

"Shit, Noah. Peyton's arm's shattered. Her leg is busted up. There's still glass in her side and the bastard didn't sew her up right after they cracked open her chest. Mom is really worried about infections because we haven't been wearing gowns and we touched her, and that's another thing. We kept moving her arm. Who knows how much pain we've caused or the damage we've done."

My mind goes blank, listening to Quinn. I definitely picked up her arm. I kissed the top of her hand and held it to my face. I didn't want to let her go.

"Son of a bitch."

Quinn sighs. "Anyway, she's heading back into surgery on Sunday. It's the only day the hospital would give the doctor."

Sunday, while I'm playing in a game. I push the palm of my hand into my forehead and groan. For the first time in my career, I wish I had chosen baseball. I'd be off right now. I could be sitting next to her, watching games on my iPad or filling in crossword puzzles. I don't care if we sit and stare at each other as long as I'm spending time with her. I feel like I have so much to make up for, but don't even know where to start, assuming that I can. The one thing I do know is I want my friend back, and with Dessie and I no longer together, it can happen.

"Do you know what time her surgery is?"

"I don't, but shit, Noah..."

"I know, Quinn. We have to think she'll be okay. Better than ever when she gets out. I'll be there after the game. Can you pick me up?"

"Yeah, of course. You gonna get into trouble?"

I sigh. "I have permission to miss practice if we win today."

"You better win."

"I will." We hang up and I send a text to my dad, asking if I can use the private plane. It would be one thing if it were a jet, but considering the size of our family, the band opted for a full-size aircraft to haul us around when we're all together. It's a complete waste of airspace and fuel to cart one person. He, of course, says yes, saving me from having to depend on an airline to get me to Chicago quickly.

Kissing her though, while completely unplanned, is worth it. It's been two years and some odd months since prom night. I was a nervous wreck while she was calm and collected. You would've thought I was the one about to lose my virginity, and part of me wishes I was, but I spent years fighting my attraction to her simply because our families wouldn't approve.

But now I don't care. I hate that it's taken her accident and the threat of her dying for me to admit my true feelings for her. Surely, I'm not the first man to have a moment of clarity when he's staring at the woman he's loved for as long as he can remember. Those feelings for her, the ones I've buried deep down, hit me like a ton of bricks when I saw her in bed, barely hanging on. Waiting is no longer an option for me unless Peyton doesn't feel the same way. If she tells me I'm crazy or we can never be together, I'll tuck my tail between my legs and move on.

As luck would have it, Peyton was still sleeping when I arrived. I somehow encouraged the Powell-James family to take the nurses up on their offer and use their lounge to get some sleep because even she knew they weren't leaving Peyton in this hospital by herself, especially under the circumstances and the likely soon-to-be lawsuit.

This time when I looked at her, I saw my future. I saw the woman I want to kiss after I win the Super Bowl, the one who will give me children, who will bear my name, lie next to me at night, listen to me complain about my aches and pains, and take every compliment I throw at her. I saw the woman who is going to keep me on my toes, call me out on my bullshit, and love me unconditionally. And I couldn't wait to tell her.

Except spilling my guts the moment she woke up, was not going to get me very far. She was groggy and could barely keep her eyes open, but she knew I was there, waiting for her. And waiting for her is exactly what I'm doing.

"Here," Harrison says, handing me a cup of coffee. "It's from the corner coffee shop, not that nasty shit you and Quinn have been making everyone drink."

I smile and thank him. "We didn't want to leave the hospital."

"I know. Me neither. But Ben's here so I make him do all my errands."

"When's Elle going to come clean and tell everyone they're dating?"

Harrison shrugs and motions for me to follow him. I glance into Peyton's room, relieved to find she's still sleeping. Katelyn is in there, reading to her, likely some sappy romance story about true love and second chances... a story about us more or less.

We sit down in the waiting room, where the television is on, but the sound is muted. I look quickly to see what's on, hoping it's ESPN, but it's some home makeover show that is probably all the rage right now.

"I don't think they're dating." Harrison takes a drink of

his coffee and sighs. "Which is a shame because I really like the kid. And if they are, she's hiding it really well."

"From the outside, it looks obvious. I mean, he's here, right? What friend would come spend time in the ICU of a hospital?"

"You," Harrison points out. I want to respond with, "it's because I love your daughter," but I don't.

"I think my relationship with Peyton is a bit beyond what Elle and Ben have going on. I've known Peyton since she was a baby."

"True. So... what's new?"

Nice change of subject, Harrison. "Not much. We won, but it won't be enough for the playoffs." I shrug. Harrison wasn't really into my sports scene when I was growing up. Sure, he came to games, but I think most of that was because Elle was a cheerleader and Peyton was on the sidelines. I know things would be different if Mason were across from me. We'd probably talk sports to pass the time, but Harrison's life is music.

"Your dad is really proud of you."

"Thanks, his support means a lot."

"I remember the day he came back from Beaumont. Hell, he didn't even tell JD or I he was leaving, but he comes back with these songs and I'm thinking 'this bastard went and fell in love.' It was days before I got it out of him, but man once your dad started talking he didn't shut up. Not about you or your mom."

"Is that why you came to Beaumont?"

Harrison finishes off his coffee and sets the paper cup down on the table. "Your dad invited Quinn and I to spend the holidays there. He thought that if you met Quinn, he could help you understand the lives we lead. What it's like to have your picture taken all the time or to have people follow your every move."

"You fell in love with Katelyn that day."

"Best damn day of my life."

"Mine too," I mutter. Quinn is one of my best friends and I can't imagine not knowing him. Even if Harrison and Katelyn weren't together, I'd know Quinn, but I don't know if we'd be as close as we are.

"What do you know about this Zimmerman kid?"

I shake my head and wonder if I should tell him about the conversation I had with Kyle or not. "Not much. I think he came into the league either a year before or after me. I don't really remember. Why?"

Harrison runs his hands down his legs. The dude is wearing shorts and it's freaking cold outside. Thinking back, I think the only time I've ever seen him in pants was for my parents' wedding. Even for Quinn and the twins' graduation, he wore shorts.

"Lawyer thinks we should sue him."

"Mira said no charges would be pressed, right?" I must've watched the news conference over and over again after I found out about it. I was shocked to find out the police weren't pursuing charges against Zimmerman, but they were against the other driver. Deeper research brought me to a few articles stating the driver was speeding.

"Yeah the police said he's not at fault, but—"

"But Peyton suffered."

"Exactly. So what about you? How are things with...? I'm sorry, I've spaced on her name."

"Dessie," I say, shaking my head. "We're not together anymore. It's pretty damn complicated," I tell him before he can ask why.

"Noah!" Elle comes in with Ben following behind. She gives me a hug, acting as if she hasn't seen me in months.

Ben stops and motions to the bags he's carrying. "Here, take one." I do, and as soon as I open it, my stomach growls.

"Thanks, Ben."

"No problem. It's what I'm good for."

Harrison grabs a bag and Ben sets the rest down on the small table. I watch as he takes a seat next to Elle and she leans into him. He kisses the top of her head and sighs and I find myself wondering again whether there's something going on between them.

"What are you up to these days, Ben?"

"School and work," he says.

"And being Elle's personal slave?" I ask.

Elle slaps me in the arm and gives me a dirty look. I can joke like this with her, but I can't with Peyton. I see them so differently. "That's rude, Noah."

"It's the truth. Right, Ben?"

Elle turns and looks at him. It's mushy as shit. If they're not dating, they're messing around between the sheets.

"I don't mind," he says, looking deep into her eyes. The sight makes me want to gag, but honestly, I'm probably not much better when it comes to Peyton.

"Noah!" I stand as my aunt Katelyn comes toward me. "Thank you so much for sitting with Peyton. We really needed a couple of hours of shut-eye."

"My pleasure." And fully for my benefit. I was there when she opened her eyes. I got to kiss her, and I'm praying she remembers it when she wakes fully.

"The nurse is with her now. They're going to try and wean her off the morphine a little, hoping she'll stay awake longer. I don't know though, I don't want her in pain."

"She'll be fine," Harrison says as he reaches for Katelyn. "She has her family to help and guide her."

And me. She'll have me because once the season's over, I'm not leaving her side.

"Quinn said Xander is going to take over her treatment?"

Katelyn nods. "I'm not sure if Peyton realizes this or not, but she'll be coming home with us when she's discharged."

Which means I'll be living in Los Angeles during the off-season, hopefully somewhere near where the Powell-James live because I need to be close to Peyton. I don't want to let her out of my sight, and if that means I have to work out with her everyday, so be it.

19

PEYTON

*W*hen I wake, sunlight beams through my window. I'm having a hard time recalling whether the window was there before or if I've switched rooms. Either way, I lay my head back and stare into the rays, pretending I'm outside basking in their warmth. Wishing I were outside, free of these casts and the constant pain I'm feeling.

Outside my room, the hall is busy. Busier than I can recollect from earlier, but mostly everything is fuzzy, and right now I'm having a hard time separating fact from fiction. Someone is singing. Another is whistling. And I remember someone playing guitar earlier. Or was it the other day? I'm starting to feel like I've imagined things, such as Noah being here and kissing me.

That I know is fiction. Not only would he not be here, but kissing me is definitely out of the question. He's with Dessie. And whether I'm hurt or not, there would be no way in hell she'd let him come to see me.

It doesn't escape my notice that my room is empty, and honestly, I sort of like it. I welcome the peace and quiet. I know my family is worried, but they're hovering. They ask me how I'm doing or if I'm okay every time I grimace. They want to touch me, hug me, coddle me, and when they realize they can't, the look of upset on their faces makes me feel like I've done something wrong.

I look at my casts. Long gone are the days of white plaster which could be decorated with an array of sharpies. A hard bandage looking material has taken its place, making it almost impossible to write on. Both my casts are pink, making me believe my mother and sister picked them out. I hate pink. I would've opted for black or something fun like orange.

The color orange makes my thoughts switch to Kyle. It took a day or two for my memory to come back but I'm still lacking the small details. From what I can remember, we met at the game and hit it off. Still, I'm going to ask my mom. At least, I'm hoping she knows. There's something in the back of my mind telling me that Kyle could be special though.

A nurse or an orderly, I don't know which or if that's even her title, comes in with my tray of food. I press the button that raises my bed until I'm somewhat comfortable and wait for her to push the mobile cart into place. Thing is, I can't recall doing this any other time, so how is it that I know?

"It's nothing fancy, but the toast is pretty good."

"Wait, is this my first meal?" She looks at me as if I have two heads. "What have I been eating?" I ask her, utterly confused.

"That machine over there."

"Oh, okay."

As soon as she leaves, I pick up my fork and stare at the over easy eggs, the slices of ham that need to be cut, and my left hand. "Yeah, not gonna work," I mutter to myself. In fact, the only possible thing I can eat are the slices of fruit, the toast, which is dry, and if I can get enough force behind it, I'll be able to stab the foil on my cup of juice so I can drink that. Everything else requires two hands. I have one working one, if you can call it that. The IVs pinch if I'm not careful.

Out of frustration, I push the tray away. My stomach protests. The couple pieces of fruit and dry toast aren't doing anything to curb my hunger. I'm also very uncomfortable. The pain in my chest is almost unbearable. I recline my bed and the ache starts to subside, but not enough. I push the button that delivers my painkillers and wait for the agonizing feeling to go away.

I'm on the verge of tears when my mother walks in. She's nothing but smiles when I'm nothing but anger.

"Sorry I wasn't here when you woke up."

"It's fine. You don't have to be here twenty-four seven."

"You know I'm going to be, Peyton. Did you eat your breakfast?"

"Nope."

"Are you not hungry?"

I look at her, then down at the cast on my arm, which extends over my fingers. "I have maybe the use of one hand. I can't eat unless it's finger foods. Speaking of which, how was I eating before I went into surgery?"

My mom pulls the tray over and starts cutting up the eggs. They're runny and considering I've already eaten the toast there isn't anything to sop the yolk up with. "You had a feeding tube, but Dr. Colby removed it when you went back into surgery."

I glance down at my chest, wondering what kind of monster I look like. "I'm ugly now."

"Open up," she says, feeding me like I'm a baby. "And please don't say that. You're alive, Peyton, and you're beautiful, inside and out. The scar on your chest is just a sign of how resilient and strong you are. When I look at you, I see my daughter, the fighter, who looks the same today, with her gorgeous brown hair and bright blue eyes as she did last month."

I do as she says, chewing and swallowing my food. This continues until everything on my tray is gone. She sits down and pulls out a book from somewhere under my bed or on the stand where the machines sit, still monitoring my life.

"I was reading to you earlier, do you remember?"

I shake my head. "Mom, what do you know about Kyle?"

She sets the book in her lap and folds her hands. So damn prim and proper all the time. "Honestly, not much. From what the police have said, you met him at the football game and he asked you out."

"How did I meet him?"

"What do you remember of that day, Peyton?"

"Not much, and I'm starting to wonder if the things I do remember actually happened."

"Like what?"

"First tell me about Kyle and how I met him," I plead.

"Professor Fowler gave you an assignment. You were to write an article about the game, but you had press credentials to be on the field. According to Kyle, he almost hit you with the football and you said some smart ass remark back to him."

I close my eyes and search my memory bank for any sign but come up blank. "I can't believe I don't remember being on the field. It must've been a dream come true."

"Peyton, honey, I'm sure it'll happen again. Once you've

recovered, you'll have another opportunity. Now, why don't you rest a little and let me read you some more of this story?" I lean my head back and start listening to the sound of her voice. The words she reads really aren't making much sense, but I love hearing her talk. Every so often, she pauses and looks up. Her smile is the widest I've seen in a long time. Mom places her hand on top of my fingers and squeezes them gently. We really can't hold hands because of all the tubes so this is as good as it's going to get.

The book she's reading is unfamiliar, but the story seems to trigger something in my mind. "I met Grandma Gracie."

Mom pauses, but she doesn't look up. "Grandma died before you were born, honey."

"I know, but I met her, while I was... I saw Dad too."

"Peyton, I'm sure you were dreaming. You're on some pretty heavy drugs and the nurses say they can cause hallucinations." She starts reading again, but I need her to believe me.

"I wasn't hallucinating. Dad and I were in the same room, and he looks exactly the same as the pictures I have."

"Of course he looks the same as the pictures, it's all you remember."

"He told me he'd be there to help me, that he's always watching over Elle and I."

"Peyton, that's enough." Mom slams her book shut and immediately pinches the bridge of her nose, a sign she has an impending headache. "It's the drugs, nothing more."

"I almost died, Mom."

"But you didn't. You survived and you're here, with us. Your family is here and I promise, we're not going to let anything happen to you." She doesn't say anything else as she opens her book again and starts reading. I close my eyes and think about the images of my grandmother and father. They seem so clear and present in my mind. I want my mom to believe me, but I'm not even sure myself.

At some point I must doze off because when I wake again, my dad is sitting in the chair, playing on his phone.

"I miss my phone," I say groggily.

He leans forward and kisses me on my cheek, careful not to get anywhere near my head wound. Most of the damage was done to my right side, except for the missing chunk of scalp I now have. My long hair has been sheared on one side, giving me some emo look that I'm not fond of.

"Nice nap?"

I smile and nod. "I guess. Although I'm always tired."

"It's the medicine."

"So I've heard. What am I missing in the world?" I ask, nodding toward his phone.

He turns it around and shows it to me. "I'm chatting with JD about the construction on the house."

"They're building?"

Dad shakes his head. "No, we're putting in a temporary ramp for when you come home."

"Oh." I look down at my leg and that's when it hits me. I don't get to return to my sorority or stay in Chicago. I can't walk because of my leg, and I can't use crutches because of my arm. I'll be in a wheelchair until who knows how long. Tears stream down my face and my dad is there to wipe them away.

"Don't cry, baby girl. It's going to be okay."

I shake my head. "But it's not. I'm damaged and broken. Nothing will ever be the same."

"You know that isn't true, sweet pea. Your uncle Xander is the best out there and he's going to make sure that you're back at school in the fall. Your mom and I have already met with your professors and because of the circumstances, they're letting you finish out the year this summer. You can take courses over the internet."

"It's not the same."

"You're right, but for us, it works because the alternative wasn't exactly going to." He smiles and doesn't need to tell me he's referring to the fact I almost died.

"What would you say if I told you I saw my father?"

My dad leans back and sighs. He shakes his head slightly before making eye contact with me. "First, I'd say it's likely the drugs you're on, but I have a feeling you'd try to convince me otherwise, so then I'd say it's probably likely. You were on the brink of death. I'm not naïve to think an afterlife doesn't exist and I would hope your father would be there to meet you."

More tears come as I nod my head. "He was. I called him daddy because—"

My dad comes forward and hugs me the best he can. "It's okay, baby girl."

"Mom doesn't believe me."

He nods into my shoulder. "She's in denial about a lot of things, right now. Be patient with her, she's struggling and having a hard time coping with the fact she almost lost you the same way she lost your father."

"I love you, Daddy."

"Not nearly as much as I love you. There are never going to be enough words, lyrics or songs to accurately describe what it feels like being your dad. You, your sister and Quinn, it's because of you, my life makes sense."

We stay like this until my machine starts to beep. Reluctantly, I let go of my dad so he can silence it quickly. "The nurse will be in to give you some antibiotics."

"Oh joy. Is anyone else here?"

"Yeah, Quinn, Elle, Ben, and Noah."

"Noah's here?"

"You don't remember? You woke up with him in your room during the night." My hand instantly goes to my lips and I smile.

"Can you tell him I want to see him?"

"Of course." He kisses me on the forehead and almost runs into the nurse as she comes in with some medicine.

"You look cheery. It's a nice look on you."

"Thanks. This won't put me to sleep, right?"

"Definitely not. Just going to give you a little dose to help ward off any infections."

"Perfect."

As soon as she leaves, I catch a glimpse of Noah walking by my window. The heart monitor machine spikes, causing the nurse to pause and look at me. When Noah steps into the doorway, she glances at him and smiles. "I'll just close the door behind you," she says as Noah walks into my room.

"Hey, Peyton," he says, stuffing his hands into his jeans. Words escape me as I look at him with his mop top hair, scruffy face and dazzling smile. He looks amazing.

20

NOAH

*P*eyton's leg is suspended in the air, putting her toes within my line of sight. I'm tempted to touch them, but knowing how ticklish she is, I think my fun attempt at making her laugh would likely cause more harm and the last thing I want is to see her in any sort of pain because of me.

And yet, as I stand here looking at her, with her disheveled hair and mangled body, all I can think about is how beautiful she is, and how she asked for me. Of course, now I'm wondering if she called me in here to tell me to take a flying leap because, for all I know, her and Zimmerman could be a couple. And if that's the case, I'll back away.

"Are you going to come sit down or stand at the foot of my bed?"

I shrug and run my hand through my hair. As soon as football season is over, I'll cut it but likely grow a beard. The grooming side of personal hygiene seems to take a backseat during both the regular and off-season. It's a cross between superstition and laziness.

My body groans as I sit in the plastic chair. One would think with the amount the hospital charges, especially in the intensive care unit, they'd put some better chairs in here for family. But no, they seem hell-bent on making us feel uncomfortable, maybe so we don't outstay the visiting hours, not that it's worked for us.

"Did you win?" she asks.

I smile and nod. It's been far too long since we've discussed football. "We did, otherwise I wouldn't be here."

She looks at me oddly.

"After last week's loss, we got the news about the accident. I came right here with my dad, Little B and Grandma."

"Did you miss practice or get fined?"

"Nope." I shake my head. "But I did screw up in practice. Peyton, you should've seen me. I was tripping over my own feet. Throwing the ball on routes that didn't exist. Coach was livid. He kicked me off the field, told me I disgusted him."

"Noah," she draws my name out.

"It's okay. He told me if we won, he'd excuse me from practice this week."

"Did you win?" she asks excitedly.

"We did. Beat 'em by twenty, although I'm probably in trouble because I ditched out on the press conference."

"Why would you do that?"

I shrug. "So I could see you."

Peyton leans back, resting her head on her pillow. Our eyes never leave each other. I find myself rising out of my seat about ready to kiss her.

"Tell me what I've missed. How did Chicago do this week?"

My ass hits the chair with a clunk. "Right. Chicago.

Zimmerman. Um..." I scratch the back of my head with one hand and pull my phone out with the other, avoiding eye contact with her. I've had it on 'do not disturb' since before my game, and by the sheer amount of notifications from Dessie, I'm glad that I have. I grow frustrated with my phone and her name each time a new text comes in. It's like she knows I'm on my phone and has decided to light it up with messages. "Come on, Dessie," I mumble under my breath, hoping Peyton doesn't hear me.

"She's probably upset you're here."

"Among other things," I say, waiting for the sports app to load. Right now I wish I had my iPad so we could look at the highlights and scores on there instead of my phone. Something tells me Dessie isn't going to stop texting until I speak with her. I hold the phone sideways and press play on the blooper reel from this past weekend. Hearing Peyton laugh has to be hands down the best sound in the world right now. Even thinking for a minute, I'd never hear it again has my throat seizing up.

Once the clip is done, I find the broadcast from ESPN and play it for her. The first thing they talk about is Zimmerman. I don't really know the guy, but I hate him right now, and I have no right to other than he was the one behind the wheel when Peyton was hurt. Throughout the time she's watching, Dessie continues to light up my phone.

"Maybe you should call her."

I lock my screen and slip it back into my pocket. "Tell me about Zimmerman," I say, avoiding Peyton's statement. "How long have you been dating."

"Kyle and I aren't dating, at least I don't think we are."

"Oh?"

"I don't remember much from that day, but from what

my mom says, I met Kyle at the game. He told the police he asked me out to dinner, and I guess I said yes."

"Do you like him?"

Peyton laughs. "I don't know. Why the interrogation?"

"No reason." I shake my head because it's not exactly true. I have a ton of reasons, but I don't know if the timing is right. Is it? It should be, but I don't want Peyton to think my feelings are only because she's had a near-death experience, and telling her now makes it seem that way.

My mind is a damn mess. Do this. Do that. Tell her. Don't tell her. Yet, I don't know which way to go. I want nothing more than to tell her that I'm in love with her and ask her for a chance, but what if it's not what she wants? Maybe Zimmerman is more her speed. Maybe Peyton looks at me like a brother, and that kiss... it could've freaked her out.

"You look like you're a million miles away, Noah."

"I am, I think. I don't know. I just..."

"You just what?"

I finally look at Peyton, sweet and caring, beautiful and perfect, and kissable. The kiss I gave her in the middle of the night meant everything to me. It's how I want to spend the rest of my days, kissing her, making her feel loved, showing her she means everything to me.

"You kissed me earlier," she blurts out, breaking my reverie.

"You remember?"

She nods and pulls her bottom lip in between her teeth as if she's meaning to torment me.

"Good. I'm glad. I meant that kiss, Peyton." I rise up and lean toward her, gripping the bed rail strongly to hold me up. I'm afraid to touch her. Scared I'll hurt her.

Peyton places her hand in front of me, halting my slow

progress toward her mouth. "I have a question, well it's more of a statement."

"Anything," I say, without moving.

"I don't want to be the side chick, someone you come and see when you're not playing or fly to tropical destinations. If you're going to kiss me, it's because you want me, and only me."

"Dessie and I broke up, Peyton, because I'm in love with you. Now before you say anything, hear me out. I have felt this way... well for as long as I can remember. Unfortunately, it took almost losing you for me to open my eyes. I realized I'm with Dessie for all the wrong reasons and the feelings I have for her, pale in comparison to what I feel for you. We have a ton of hurdles if we want to give us a chance. That is, if you want to try this."

Her ear-to-ear grin is all I need. I press my lips to hers. It's a chaste kiss at first until she opens her mouth and I slip my tongue inside. I keep it brief though, out of fear her parents may walk by. I need to do the right thing and talk to Katelyn and Harrison, ask for their permission to be with her. The last thing I want is to be the cause of a family rift, but I'm in love with their daughter and have been for a long time. I hope they can accept that and give us their blessing.

The clearing of a throat has me looking over my shoulder. My blood runs cold when I see Dessie standing in Peyton's doorway.

"What are you doing here?" I ask. I stay standing next to Peyton.

"Hi, Peyton," Dessie says instead of answering me. "I wasn't aware that you were awake." She cocks her eyebrow at me.

"Hey, Des—"

"Peyton's recovery is none of your business, Dessie. Again, what are you doing here?" I ask pointedly.

"We need to talk, Noah."

I shake my head. "We don't have anything to say to each other. I made myself pretty clear on where I stand." My hand dangles near Peyton's, desperate to feel connected to her. She locks her finger with mine as if she knew this is what I needed.

"But we do. If you would answer your phone, you'd know that we have something very important to discuss."

I honestly thought if I avoided her, she'd go away. I was wrong. I sigh heavily and look at Peyton. She's smiling, despite the awkwardness in the room.

"Fine, you don't want to come with me, I'll say what I have to say. I'm pregnant, Noah. Almost two months along."

With my eyes still focused on Peyton, I watch as the color drains from her face and the blood all but leaves my body. Her finger slips away despite my attempt to hold on, and her eyes break hold with mine.

"What'd you say?" I sound like a strangled man when I ask her to repeat herself.

"We're going to have a baby."

"Noah?" Peyton's voice is merely a pained whisper.

"I'll be right back," I tell her, kissing her on her forehead. I motion for Dessie to leave the room, glancing quickly at her, with her Cheshire Cat-like smile. I guide her down the hall, past the rest of my family, who conveniently stops talking as we pass, and through the doors. I keep pushing her toward the stairwell and as soon as we're behind the solid door, I scream out, "What the hell are you playing at?"

"What are you talking about?" The innocent act isn't

going to get her very far with me.

"Why would you barge into Peyton's room and announce something like this? Are you trying to hurt her? She's done nothing to you."

"Except steal you away."

I shake my head. "She hasn't stolen me, Dessie. I'm in love with her and I know it hurts you. Believe me, if I could go back to the day we met, I would've never pursued anything because it's not fair to you or her."

"So what now? I go home and play the single mother while you woo some college student? Is she going to play step-mommy to our child? Do I have to hammer out a visitation schedule around her school work?"

"Dessie..." I push the palms of my hands into my eyes. "You're messing with lives here. You can't do shit like this."

"Wait a minute, Noah. You think *I'm* messing with lives? I'm pregnant. With your child, no less. I have to tell my boss who might blacklist me for the next round of shoots." Dessie leans against the wall. "Look, I know we broke up, but this changes everything, I can't do this without you. I need your help. And you're right, I have a slight issue with drugs, but I need to be clean for this baby and I can't do it alone."

"Dessie..."

"Noah, I'm sorry for everything. For the way I acted, for accusing you of cheating on me. I haven't slept since we broke up. I've missed shoots. I've shown up late with bags under my eyes. I even went to your game so we could talk, and waited for you outside the locker room, only you never came out. Julius told me you already left. I had to track you down here. Do you know how hard this is for me? I know you don't love me, not like you love Peyton."

"I can't imagine it's been easy, but—"

Dessie steps closer to me. "Before you brush me off, give us a chance. We're going to have a family, Noah." She takes my hand and places it on her stomach. I feel nothing. "When this baby was created, you loved me, and I know you already love this baby growing inside of me."

Dessie doesn't give me a chance to respond, to tell her exactly why we broke up, before she steps back into the hallway. I chase after her, afraid of what she might say to Peyton, but when I get back to her room, she's lying on her left side, facing away from the door. Her broken arm rests in front of her face, elevated slightly on a pillow. She doesn't seem to flinch when I clear my throat. I go to her and press my lips to her ear. "I'm so sorry, Peyton."

Those are the last words I say to her before leaving. I need time to think, to figure out what I have to do. Honestly, I'm not worried about whether Dessie is embarrassed. I know I should be, but Peyton's happiness means more to me.

PEYTON

*I*t's been thirty days since my life changed. No, I'm not talking about the accident. I'm talking about Noah telling me he's in love with me and subsequently walking out the door to chase the woman carrying his baby. And in some twisted form of irony, this all happens in one freaking day, and I'm never given a chance to tell him how I feel or to say the words that were sitting on the tip of my tongue. Never mind the fact I couldn't chase him because of my mangled body and broken heart after he whispered in my ear he was sorry. He couldn't even be bothered to see if I was awake before he pushed me aside for Dessie.

She's pregnant. I get it. The baby comes first. But at what expense, your own happiness? Mine? I'm selfish because for one brief moment I thought I had my best friend back. I thought I was going to have the man of my dreams and we'd ride off into the sunset with our families cheering us on. When in reality, it's likely my accident that caused him to profess his love for me. The fear of losing someone can do that to a person.

Over the past month, everyone has asked how I'm doing. Fine. It's always the answer. I have nothing else to say. I'm cooped up. If I'm not in bed, I'm in a wheelchair. And my heart is broken. No one will ever know or understand the pain Noah Westbury has caused me. He gave me a glimmer of hope, only to rip it away and hand it to Dessie.

"Good morning," Jenna, my nurse says as she comes through my door, pushing a wheelchair, with an orderly right behind her. Normally, patients would leave intensive care, but my parents wanted the privacy so they paid who knows how much to keep me here. I don't mind because I do love my nurse. She's spent ample time in here, telling me about my first night and how she took care of me, waiting until my dad arrived. I'll be forever grateful to her, for staying by my side so I wasn't alone. "Are you dressed?" she asks.

"Yes, my mom and sister had the dubious task of helping me this morning. What's going on? Is it time to leave?"

"Not quite, but we're going to take you over to orthopedics and they're going swap out your casts."

"What? Are you serious? I'll be able to bend my arm and leg?"

She nods happily.

"Oh thank God. I'll be able to have a little independence."

Jenna lowers my bed and helps me move down so Bob, the orderly, can pick me up. The drawback to intensive care is that the rooms are small and it's hard to maneuver. As soon as I'm in the chair, Bob, who happens to be a former linebacker from Ohio State, pushes me down the hall. The nurses we pass tell me they want to sign my new cast when

I come back. I look down at my thigh-high one now and try to make out the names.

When Betty Paige and Eden visited, they both decorated my casts with different drawings. Eden drew a water scene with a surfer. It was a guy and I teased her, asking her if he was her boyfriend. She turned red and my uncle Jimmy muttered something about a bloody bloke. Paige drew an elaborate garden scene with roses and vines weaving in and out of everyone's signatures. I'm sad to be losing the artwork, but happy that the cast will be gone.

And finally, I get to choose my own colors. No more pink. When the physician's assistant asks me what I want, I tell him black on the bottom because it'll match most of the leggings I'll be living in until it's off, and blue for my arm.

When I'm done, only Bob is there to get me. Unfortunately, I still have to ride in the wheelchair. I haven't used my legs in almost six weeks and won't even be able to attempt doing so until I can get the cast off my arm, which according to the doctors won't be for another six weeks or so. "Let's detour for lunch," I suggest.

"Now, Miss Peyton, are you trying to get me into trouble?"

"I am," I tell him, laughing. This isn't the first time we've done this. In fact, anytime I have to leave my room, I request Bob take me. We bonded over our love of apple pie and eating nachos on Sunday while we watch the games.

Bob does what I ask and takes us down to the cafeteria. I've become a regular here, using this as an excuse to get out of my room as much as possible. The day Dr. Colby gave me the okay to move around, I've been bugging my family to get me out of my room. My mom all but freaked out though, afraid I'd catch an infection or something, but my chest is healed, if not still sore. I'm not sure the pain I feel there will ever subside.

"Hey Peyton, I see you conned Bob into bringing you down for lunch."

"It doesn't take much when I promise him some pie," I tell Susie, who hands me a tray. I set it on my lap and point to the things I want, making sure I have two of each item. Bob never picks up food he wants to eat. I think it goes against some hospital code or something, so I make sure to double up. I have no idea what he actually likes to eat, aside from nachos. Unless of course he's only eating those to appease me, which could very well be the case.

I tell the cashier to put everything on my tab, aka, my hospital bill, which I have no doubt has exceeded seven digits by now. I know my parents are looking forward to discharge day. No more taking turns sleeping in my room and living out of a hotel.

"So who do you think will win the Super Bowl?" I ask Bob, in between bites of chicken and some pasta dish we picked up.

"Patriots. The goat is just too good."

"Hmm, you're probably right. You know he's one of the lowest paid QB's in the league."

"That's because he cares about this team and keeps restructuring his contract so the Pats can spend money else-where," Bob says. Our first Sunday of football watching, he told me he was injured his senior year and couldn't recover in time for the Scouting Combine. His degree is in commu-nications, but it's rather difficult to get a job as a broadcaster when he has nothing to show for himself where his career is concerned.

"I'm getting sprung any day now. Are you going to miss me?"

He shakes his head. "Nope. Since meeting you I've gained fifteen pounds." For a minute I think he's serious until he starts laughing so hard, people around us are staring. "I'm only kidding. Yeah, I'm going to miss you. You're fun to hang out with. When are you getting discharged?"

"I don't know. I imagine any day now that my casts have been changed. I feel like I'm living here permanently."

"Back to L.A.?"

"My parents don't actually live in L.A. but on the outskirts, and I've never called it my home. We have a house on the beach, it's pretty cool, but it takes forever to get anywhere, so I normally hang out at home."

"Except you'll be going to rehab with the best therapist in the country."

When Bob met Xander, his eyes bugged out. Bob went on and on about how amazing and sought after my uncle is. "Only because he's my uncle."

"Your dad would've paid for him."

"Probably."

Bob and I finish up and he takes me back to my room. He helps me get settled and promises to come by before his shift ends. This is when the depression settles in. It's when I'm alone my thoughts run rampant about what Noah's doing right now. Part of me is happy we haven't spoken, but the emotional part is hurt and pissed off. He owes me an explanation, yet I don't want to hear what he has to say. I think if he were to tell me he chose Dessie, I'd lose it. He's right to be with her if she's having his baby.

But, feeling this way doesn't help the darkness stay away, and this is the only time I can let my emotions out. The tears come easily, hot streams down my face. I don't bother to wipe them away until I've had a good cry. This is a daily occurrence for me. I hate it, but I can't stop it. I don't know what I'm going to do when I move in with my parents and can't hide from them.

"Knock, knock."

"Just a sec." I scramble to wipe my face, knowing it'll be no use. I turn over, onto my back, surprised to see Ben standing in my doorway. "Ben! Hey, what're you doing here?"

"Well, I'm the lucky one who gets to deliver you some news." Ben chooses to sit on the edge of my bed as opposed to the chair. Not that I blame him. I've heard enough about that stupid hard plastic chair to last me a lifetime.

"What's that?"

"Tomorrow, you're out of here!" He throws his hands up in the air.

"No way... wait, why are you telling me?"

"Well, it seems your mom and sister are packing up your room, and your dad is making the necessary arrangements to fly us back to California."

"Well, this is great." I try to smile, but by the look on his face, I'm not fooling anyone.

"Wanna tell me what's wrong?"

"I'm in love with someone who doesn't or can't love me back," I blurt out, only to feel a bit of relief. Maybe talking about Noah is the right thing to do.

"Noah?"

I nod. "He told me he loves me but he's with Dessie and I don't understand, except I do because she's pregnant, but if you love someone..."

"You're supposed to set them free or whatever. I know how you feel, Peyton. Believe me, I really do."

"Because you love my sister?"

His eyes go wide, nodding slowly. It's not like any of us haven't figured it out, except for Elle. She seems to be blind or completely obtuse when it comes to Ben. It stinks because we love Ben, and we want them together.

I scoot over and invite Ben to sit next to me. He does, stretching his long legs out in front of him. Even sitting like this, I feel like a shrimp next to him. "Your sister is seeing someone. I don't know who because she won't tell me."

"How do you know?"

"When I'm here, waiting to visit you, she'll leave me for a bit, upwards to an hour or so. At first, I thought she was visiting you, but that wasn't the case. She's hiding her phone too, being secretive."

"Elle hasn't really visited much since I've been awake. Quinn says she's nervous around me, that the accident freaked her out."

"You guys have that weird twin thing going on, she probably felt some of your pain."

I hadn't thought about of it that way, but he's probably right, but it's not an excuse to avoid me. I'm her sister. I need her.

"So Noah, huh? For how long?"

I sigh and lean into my pillow. "For as long as I can remember. I don't know when it started or when the childhood crush turned into stupid adult feelings, but... always. I guess it doesn't matter anymore though because Dessie's pregnant and he went back to Portland with her."

"He may still come around." Ben's hopeful. It's a nice attribute.

"Not with a baby. Noah grew up not knowing his real father. He would never do that to his own child. I can't compete with a tiny human. I won't."

"Sounds like we're in the same boat, sharing the same paddle and going nowhere."

I rest my head on his shoulder and he places his hand in

mine. For as long as I've known Ben, I always thought he and my sister would end up together. At least for them, there's still hope.

NOAH

$\mathcal{I}$ stand in front of my living room window, watching as snowflakes fall from the sky. Down below, it doesn't look like anything is sticking, which means Dessie and I shouldn't have any problems flying.

My season is over and so is my career if I don't play my cards right. After I left Peyton in the hospital, breaking both our hearts, I continued to play like crap and was benched for the last game of the season. If that's not a slap in the face, I don't know what is.

Dessie comes into the room and turns on the Christmas tree. I study her profile through the reflection, looking hard to see if there's a baby bump yet. The one appointment she's had since she burst into Peyton's room and dropped the bomb, I was out of town for. Dessie gushed on how she was able to hear the heartbeat, but never thought to record the sound for me.

I avert my eyes so she doesn't see me looking and stare out into the city. At best, our relationship is strained. She tries. I avoid. And I'm the biggest ass for doing so. I should be happy she's carrying my child. Babies are miracles and I know there are millions out there who struggle to get pregnant. I just don't want her to be the one to have mine. Of course, I should have thought about that long before I ever slept with her.

"Do you think this snow is going to hamper our trip?"

I shake my head and take a sip of the whiskey I poured myself over an hour ago after I came back from meeting with my coach. He yelled. I listened. I came home and poured a drink, which is something I never do.

"I still don't understand why your father couldn't let us use the band's plane," Dessie says as she walks away. It's probably because I never asked him. When I told my mom I'd be home for Christmas, she didn't seem so thrilled to hear Dessie was coming with me. I have yet to tell my parents she's pregnant and I'm not sure if Peyton told anyone. If she did, my parents are doing a damn fine job of hiding it from me.

"My luggage is packed," she hollers from the room. I set my glass down on the table and head toward the bedroom. Since I returned from Chicago, I haven't slept in here, opting for the guest bedroom. I don't want Dessie to get the wrong idea. I may be here, but I don't have a clue about what I'm doing.

"The car will be here in an hour," I say, turning into my room. I stare into my closet. I used to look forward to going home, especially at Christmas. When I was ten, it became my favorite holiday, and now I have no desire to go at all.

"Do you want some help?" Dessie asks. She doesn't wait for me to answer before coming in. She starts pulling clothes out of my closet, setting them on my bed. "What do you think we'll do while we're there?"

"I'm not sure."

"Well, maybe it'd be a good time to get married since we'll be in your hometown."

I sit down on my bed and sigh. She's been pushing for marriage since we flew back to Portland, reminding me her friends often comment on how she's not engaged and now she's pregnant, this seems like the right time.

"I'm sure Beaumont is beautiful at Christmas time."

"It is. Listen, Dessie, I haven't told my parents yet about the baby."

"Why not?" she asks, sitting down next to me.

I rest my elbows on my knees and sigh. "I don't know," I tell her honestly. "Maybe because part of me wishes it weren't true, while the other part wishes our situations were different. It has nothing to do with you, and everything to do with me."

"Do you want me to leave?"

I glance at her from over my shoulder and shake my head. "No, I don't."

"Well, what can I do?"

"Nothing, Dessie. They're my demons I need to work through. I'll finish packing so we can go."

She stands and heads toward the door. "Everything will be okay, Noah."

I nod and feign a smile, waiting until she's gone before I pull out my phone and scroll through the calls I recently made. Each one is to Peyton. Each one unanswered. For all I know, she's changed her number. There isn't anyone I can ask though, except her. Everyone would question why, if she did, in fact, change her number, wasn't it given to me. I have a feeling she won't be in Beaumont for Christmas, which leaves me no choice but to dwell on the fact I screwed up big time and she's not willing to speak to me.

Pocketing my phone, I try to focus my attention on

packing. I throw a few dressy items in my bag, but most of what's going in there are jeans and sweats. I purposely leave my suit hanging in my closet. Maybe if I don't have it, she won't bring up marriage again.

By the door, her three pieces of luggage sit. I try not to think I'm under packing with my one bag, but clearly I am. Dessie comes out of the bedroom with another suitcase being towed behind her.

"Are you moving in with my parents or something?"

"These are presents."

Right, presents, for Christmas. I've been so caught up in my personal drama I completely forgot to buy presents.

"I picked up things for your parents, grandparents and your grandma, your sister, as well as Nick, Aubrey, Mack and Amelie."

"Wow. I think you thought of everyone." Except for Peyton, Elle and Quinn, but I can't imagine she wants to buy them anything. "I suppose we should go?"

"Or we wait another half hour until the car arrives," she suggests, laughing.

"I'll start taking these down."

I open the front door and use my foot to keep it open. Dessie helps pile luggage into my arms and follows me out to press the button for the elevator. "This is going to be a great trip, Noah," she says. I nod, thankful for the high-pitched ding that sounds when the doors are about to open.

When I arrive downstairs, I set our stuff down near the doorman. "Taking a trip, Mr. Westbury?"

"Heading home for the holidays now that the season is over."

"Ah, yes. Rough year, but the fans are confident."

I wish I were. "Thanks. I'll be back with the rest of our luggage. The car should be here in thirty minutes or so."

"Yes, sir, Mr. Westbury."

Instead of the elevator, I opt for the stairs. It seems to be the only way I can get my aggression out these days since I'm not actually allowed to go boxing or tackle anyone during practice. The thought of one-on-one with Trey Miller, my left tackle, is very appealing right about now. After my shitty performance to end the season, he'd probably take me up on the opportunity to kick my ass without repercussion.

I reach my floor with very little time to spare. Dessie is pacing the hallway with the rest of her luggage sitting outside our door. "I thought you forgot me," she says, rushing to give me a hug.

"Are you ready?" I know she is, but the alternate thought in my head would come off very snotty and the last thing I want to deal with is a pissed off Dessie. Since she broke the news of her pregnancy, she's done everything she can to appease me, while I've been a miserable jerk.

The ride to the airport is done in relative quietness. It's barely six and pitch black outside with the exception of the decorations. We'll arrive at my parents late, far too late for us to stay up and talk. I planned it this way. Tomorrow... well, it's another day and one I won't be able to dodge.

As soon as we get out of the car, someone screams out my name. I've been trained over the years to ignore the fans. I try with this one, but he's relentless.

"Hey, Noah, can I get a pic?" He puts his arm around me before I can even agree to the invasion. I smile and try to step away, but he pulls out a pen and scrambles in his pocket, searching for a piece of paper for me to write on.

"Here, babe," Dessie says, handing me a half sheet out of her oversized purse.

"Thanks," I say before turning to the guy. "What's your name?"

"Jeff, but can you make it to my little brother? He's in the hospital and you're his favorite player."

"What's his name?"

"Leo," he says, giving me pause.

"Leo, huh?" I can't say the name without smiling. I wish I had contact information for Leo back in Chicago. I could certainly use his advice right about now. "Can you Face-Time him?"

Jeff's eyes go wide. He starts to fumble with his phone. His face lights up when his brother comes on. "Leo, you're never going to guess who I ran into at the airport." He angles the phone so we're both in the screen.

"Holy shit," Leo says after he removes his oxygen mask. The way he looks reminds me of Peyton. "You're my fave."

"Thanks, Leo, for the support. I hope you get better, man."

"Yeah, me too. And I hope you kick ass next year."

"I'll do my best."

Jeff takes the phone and tells his brother he'll see him later. I don't know why I continue to watch their exchange but I do. When he hangs up, I hand him the sheet of paper I autographed and the card for my manager. "When you get a chance, call this number. It's my manager. Tell him we met and you're leaving word about your brother. I'd like to visit him when I get back in a week."

"Wow, really? Thank you."

"You're welcome. Merry Christmas, Jeff."

"Yes, you too. I can't thank you enough."

"It was my pleasure." I watch Jeff walk down toward the taxi line, waiting until he's out of sight before I turn my attention back to Dessie and all her luggage. "Sorry about that."

"It's fine. The porter took our stuff and security is ready to escort us to the first class lounge."

I nod and fall in line behind her. Now that we're inside the airport, both our names are called, but neither of us stops. For the past year and a half, we've been a high-profile couple, and the media is going to have a field day when they find out she's pregnant.

By the time we get through the TSA checkpoint, our flight is about to board. The security guard drops us off at our gate just as first class is being called. Dessie and I walk by, listening to the murmurs of people, wondering if it is in fact us.

"What you did back there for that kid, that was very nice of you," Dessie says once we're situated.

"It felt like the right thing to do. I'm going to go see him next week when we get back. Maybe round up a few of the guys if they're in town."

"You're going to make a great father, Noah." I turn away from her so she doesn't see the anger in my eyes. I want to be excited about this baby, I do, but I can't help to think we're doing the wrong thing by staying together for the sake of the baby. All I know is that when I get to Beaumont, my dad, Nick and I are having a long talk. I need their advice, their guidance and help. I don't want to make a mistake I'll regret later or make a rash decision that comes back to bite me in the ass. I have to remember, Dessie and I created this baby together, it's just shitty luck I don't want to be with his or her mom anymore.

23

PEYTON

I miss the snow. I miss the gloom of overcast days. The wind, rain and feel of Christmas that Chicago has. I never thought I would say those words, but it's true. I enjoy the beach, but being here in December seems all sorts of wrong. Watching my dad, brother and Ben surf, while carols play loudly from the surrounding houses, doesn't make sense.

In hindsight, I would've been home this week no matter what, but things would've been different. Normally, I'd be able to come and go as I please, but now I'm stuck, literally, in the sand, sitting in a wheelchair, without an escape.

After Christmas, I start physical therapy. Interesting considering I still have both casts on, but Xander says we need to strengthen my core and my left side. He's afraid the weakened state of my body will result in further injuries and he'd like to prevent those from happening. I agree. Being immobile and having to depend on others isn't my idea of a good time.

Ben comes out of the water and strips out of his wetsuit. The arms dangle at his sides, making him look like an odd octopus. He walks toward me, slamming his board into the sand, and sitting down next to me.

"I suppose your sister isn't home?"

"Nope, and you're here. Doesn't that make you feel sort of odd?"

"Quinn invited me." He nods toward the water where Quinn and my dad are riding a wave. "Not that I expect you to find out, but has Elle said anything about who she's dating?"

I shake my head slowly and glance down at Ben. Since our chat in the hospital, we've grown closer as friends. I can confide in him about my feelings for Noah, and he does the same when it comes to Elle. "Nothing. I even asked her one night and she became defensive."

"I don't know why she won't tell me. It's not like she hasn't dated before."

"Maybe it's someone you know or won't approve of."

Ben nods and lies back on the beach blanket. I feel bad for him. He's been in love with Elle for so long and the feeling isn't mutual. It sucks being in love with someone who doesn't love you back. It's worse when the other person loves you but chose someone else. I don't blame Noah, yet I do. I'm so mad at him for telling me how he feels, for kissing me, and then walking away without an explanation. But I know why he did it. I know how he struggled with Nick and Liam, both wanting to be his dad. He confided in me years ago about how class-mates used to tease him because Nick wasn't his real father. It's one of those things where everyone in town knew he was Liam Page's son, except for him, until my father died and Liam showed up. Everything changed then.

My mom comes out of the house and hollers to Dad and

Quinn, telling him lunch is ready. "Ben, are you joining us?"

"Yes, Mrs. KPJ."

I roll my eyes at the ridiculous nickname he's given her. Ben is polite and insists on calling my parents by their last names, but I'm sorry, Mr. and Mrs. Powell-James is a mouthful. He's been told numerous times to call them Katelyn and Harrison, but he refuses and instead started calling them by their initials. My parents don't seem to mind though because they really like Ben. I think they're waiting for Elle to open her eyes as well to see what's in front of her.

Quinn and my dad walk out of the water and drop their suits, much like Ben did. I giggle at my own inside joke, thinking we have a house full of squid.

"What's so funny?" Quinn asks as he rights his board.

"You look like an octopus," I tell him. He shakes his hair, letting the saltwater spray all over me. "A giant hairy one." I scream as he picks me up out of my wheelchair and starts running toward the water. "Quinn, Mom will kill you." I clutch onto his neck as hard as I can, but with one arm, it's about useless. If he wanted, he could drop me and there wouldn't be anything I could about it.

"I'm not going to drop you," he says as he wades out into the water. "I thought you'd like to come out and at least feel the breeze. You can tell me you don't miss this, but I know you do. You talk about missing Chicago, but it's peaceful here. No stress. No one's clamoring to take your photo when the band releases a new album. You can hear for miles with no traffic or noise."

"I can hide in Chicago."

"You can hide here, Peyton. He's not going to show up." As far as I know, Quinn has no knowledge of what went down between Noah and I, unless I talk in my sleep and he's been listening. I rest my head against his shoulder and close my eyes, getting lost in the ebb and flow of the waves. Quinn's grip on me is tight, never wavering.

We stay there until we hear our dad whistle. The spot where we were sitting is clean, my chair likely in our house. Inside, the smell of freshly baked bread and marinara sauce causes my stomach to growl loudly.

"Someone's hungry," Quinn says as he sets me down at the table.

"She needs her strength for when she starts PT." Dad places his hand on my head and smooths my hair down, careful not to touch the scar I now have. I've contemplated shaving my head, but the thought of being bald makes me cry. Still, I'm going to be forced to make a decision soon because it's going to take years for my hair to grow back to where the rest of it is now.

A mound of food is placed in front of me, and yet another gurgling sound emits from my stomach, causing everyone to laugh. If I never have to eat another meal at the hospital, it'll be too soon. Halfway through the meal, my cell vibrates. I look down at my lap and at the unfamiliar number, wondering if I should even read it. Very few people have my number and the one time I answered an unknown call, it was Dessie, telling me in some very unfavorable language to stay away from Noah. I didn't even know he was dating her at the time. It was shortly after prom... and I thought things were going to be different for us.

My cell vibrates again with another text. Everyone around the table is in full conversation so I open it up.

Hey, it's Kyle. My lawyer says we aren't

supposed to talk, but I have to know if you're okay.

I look around the table to make sure no one is watching me. My parents frown on us answering our phones at the table, but something tells me I should respond to Kyle.

I'm good. Sore. Can't walk. But I'm good.

No sooner do I send the message, does the conversation bubble pop up.

I'm unbelievably sorry, Peyton. If you'll let me, I'll make it up to you.

Do I want that? Do I want to see Kyle?

That'd be great.

I pocket my phone before anyone at the table gets suspicious. Everyone continues to talk, about Christmas, New Year's, whatever else is going on while I sit here in a daze, wondering what Kyle's doing and whether Noah went home for the holidays. What I really want to know is why Aunt Josie hasn't told my mom she's going to be a grandma.

Xander's gym is massive. I remember when I was younger and he started his own place in Beaumont, thinking it was huge. Elle and I used to go there and take dance classes with our aunt Yvie, but they soon moved to Los Angeles where Xander set his sights on becoming the premiere sports therapist. His client list is massive. Every professional athlete wants to work with him, and if they're not, they're using one of his employees.

The gym is private and mostly for the elite. Right now, it's bustling with celebrities. I'm in heaven, looking at all the football players I want to interview some day. A few come up to me, telling me they heard about the accident, saying things like how Kyle is a good guy and I should give him a chance. For the most part, I think nothing of it because I'm sure news has traveled. It's not like the players don't gossip. Most of them are worse than women.

Xander has me curling weight with my one good arm. Says I need upper arm strength first before I can start rehabbing my leg. He hasn't come out and said it, but I know I can't walk. I've tried when I'm in my room, to go from one side to the other by hopping. My left leg is weak. It wobbles under any amount of pressure, and if I set my bad foot on the ground, it does nothing. No amount of mind control can get it to move.

"Another set and we'll move on," Xander says. I pull the dumbbell toward my chest and release it slowly, feeling the ache in my arm. My forearm quivers as I grit my teeth, trying to keep it steady. "Good girl." He takes the weight from me and sets it back on the rack.

"I don't know, what do you think?" I flex and show off the fact I've gained zero muscle so far today.

"I think I need to know your secret?"

I turn at the voice behind me. Kyle is standing there, smiling. His foot is in a walking boot and I'm instantly jealous.

"My secret to what?" I ask, instead of saying hi.

He nods toward Xander, who doesn't look thrilled at the moment. "I tried to hire him, but was rejected."

I shrug. "Family obligation. Xander's my uncle. This is Kyle Zimmerman," I tell Xander.

"I know who he is. He should get back to training." Xander scoops me up and carries me to another machine. After he sets me down, he tells me we're going to work my right leg for a bit.

"You were rude to him."

"He almost killed you. I think I'm entitled. Now push."

I do as he says. "The truck almost killed me. Not Kyle. Did he really ask you to work with him?"

"Don't know. Everything goes through my assistant. I told her to clear time for you though." He stands next to the machine and adjusts my form with each push.

"Would you really have me with another trainer?" I ask, cocking my eyebrow at him.

"Never. You're too precious."

"You're mushy." I stop pushing so he'll look at me. "I love you. Thank you for fixing me."

Xander squats down. "I love you, P. Now push."

This is how the rest of my morning goes. Push, pull, sit-up, and repeat. By the end of my session, muscles I've never used before are screaming at me, telling me how much they hate me right now. What I hate is the embarrassment I feel sitting in my wheelchair while I wait for my driver to get here. Xander wouldn't let me sit outside, afraid I'd get kidnapped, my chair would get jacked or God forbid, someone snapped a picture of Harrison James' daughter panhandling on the street corner.

The only satisfying thing about being here right now is I get to watch others work. I've also noticed Kyle is moving closer and closer to where I'm waiting. A few of the other guys have stopped and talked to me, one of them being

Noah's friend, Julius. I was tempted to ask him about Noah, but I don't want to care. He clearly didn't care enough about me when he made his decision.

"Hey," Kyle says as he sets his towel on the machine near me. "How long are you in the chair for?"

"X-rays tomorrow. Maybe if I'm lucky I'll be in a boot like you." Even if I am, I doubt I'll be out of the chair.

Kyle looks down at his foot before back at me. "I'm really sorry, Peyton."

"I know."

He shakes his head and crouches down so we're eye level. "No, I don't think you do. I told my lawyer to pay for all your medical expenses. I don't care if doing so makes me look guilty. I feel responsible."

"You don't have to do that, Kyle. My dad—"

"Oh, I learned real quick who your dad is. When I asked you out, I didn't know you were Noah Westbury's girlfriend either."

My head snaps. "I'm sorry, what?"

"Westbury, he came to see me, told me to stay away."

I guffaw. "He's not my boyfriend. Never has been. I'm single and ready to mingle." My eyes go wide and I cover my mouth. "I didn't mean the last part."

Kyle smiles. "The part about being single?"

"No, I'm definitely single."

"Perfect." Kyle doesn't say anything else. He stands and turns toward his apparatus and starts his workout. I'm content to sit there and watch him, but as my luck would have it, my driver shows up.

"Oh hey, before I go. How'd you get my number?"

He pauses halfway through a pull-up. "Bob."

"The orderly?"

"Old friend of mine." He winks and continues to show

off his upper body strength.

"Bob, huh?" I say to myself.

"No, I'm Dale, your driver," the man standing next to me says.

"Right, well we can go now," I tell Dale, even though my eyes are set on Kyle.

24

NOAH

$\mathcal{J}$ can't remember the last time I drove my dad's truck to the water tower. Thinking back, it must've been at the end of my junior year or possibly homecoming my senior year. The carefree days of high school are long gone, replaced by the reality of being an adult and having to make decisions that affect everyone around you.

I finish my beer and let the bottle fall from my fingertips. The sound of shattering glass echoes over the empty field. Thankfully, I'm the only one here. I'm relieved I don't have to answer questions about my life and the NFL or be told how lucky I am to be dating Dessie. My life is a mess and I don't see it getting better anytime soon.

The moment Dessie and I walked into my parents' house, she spread her arms out wide and rushed to my mother, blurting out, "we're pregnant." The wide-eyed look my mother gave me spoke volumes. In fact, the screaming in her head was loud enough for my father and I to hear, and that's when I left. I hopped in his truck, stopped at the store for a case of beer and came to the only place where Dessie would never be able to find me.

Popping the top on another, I let the cold liquid pour down the back of my throat, swallowing as fast as I can. Beer escapes from the corner of my mouth and drips down my cheek and neck until my jacket catches it. I haven't been drunk in such a long time and I've forgotten what it feels like to start feeling numb. This kind of numbness is different from the way I felt when Peyton was lying there, helpless and dying. When I saw her, my world crashed. My heart stopped beating. It was like I was in a tunnel, chasing after her, but each mile I gained on her, she put two more between us.

Now, I'm just pissed. Pissed at myself for being incredibly stupid, for not listening to my heart years ago when I had Peyton. I could've told her how I felt, but let my brain convince me otherwise. If I did, things would be different. I know they would be. I have to believe we'd be together, celebrating Christmas with our families, watching the playoffs together and rooting against each other because honestly, what's the fun in cheering on the same team?

The roar of a motorcycle engine has me looking out into the field. There's a single headlight, followed by two more close behind it. I toss this bottle toward the truck, waiting to hear the satisfying crunch of glass breaking before I blindly reach for another.

Headlights are left on and one car door is slammed. The ladder groans under the weight of whoever has invited themselves to my pity party.

"Can't say I've been up here in a while," Nick says out into the darkness.

"That's because you aren't cool," my dad tells him.

My dads flank me, each coming at me from a different side of the tower. They both sit down and sigh. I don't know if it's because they're old or the fact that they're together.

Liam and Nick get along where I'm concerned, but I suspect each man still harbors some resentment toward the other.

I pull out my phone to check the time. It's well into the early hours of the morning and by all accounts, they should be home and fast asleep. Not climbing the water tower. "It's late. Shouldn't you guys be in bed?"

"We should, but we didn't want to miss the party," Nick says.

"How'd you find me?"

My dad sighs and Nick clears his throat. "Lucky guess," Dad says.

"Your dad called me, said you needed us."

I look from Nick to my dad, who shrugs. There have only been a handful of times where my dad has deferred family matters to Nick. The most important one was when my mom passed out during my little league baseball game while she was pregnant with my sister.

"Your dad thought you could use some company." Nick leans forward and lets his arms dangle over the railing. Someday this landing is going to give way and some unlucky bastard is going to crash to the ground. The city of Beaumont gave up on repairing this tower a long time ago, knowing full well what goes on here.

"Dessie's news is surprising," Dad says. "Your mom and I don't know what to think, especially considering what you told me in Chicago."

"I'm in love with Peyton," I say, looking at Nick, filling him in on my latest predicament. I sigh and rest my back against the tower. "I screwed up and now I'm—"

"Stuck," Nick states. "I'm saving you from saying you're screwed or whatever else you were going to use, because you're not. There are ways to make everyone happy."

Shaking my head, I reach for another bottle and pop the top. "Dessie wants to get married, like now, tomorrow, end of the week. Something about being embarrassed among her friends."

"And do you want to marry her?" Dad asks.

"Nope."

"Then why do it?"

I turn toward Nick and close my eyes. "She's pregnant." I shrug. "I don't want..." I let my words trail off. The last thing I want to do is insult either of the men sitting next to me, but the truth is, I don't want my child growing up without a father. Nick was always there, but everyone knew he wasn't my dad. I heard the whispers, saw the looks, and when Liam came to town, everything changed.

"The difference is, your dad didn't know about you, Noah."

"I would've never left had I known your mom was pregnant."

I've heard this before. From both my mom and dad. Doesn't make me feel any better, though. Why didn't she try harder to reach him? Why didn't she go to California and try to find him?

"I don't know if I can let another man raise my child." I avoid eye contact with my dad because I know he's going to take my comment personally.

"Fair enough," he says. "But tell me this. Would you rather your son or daughter grow up in a home where there isn't any love between the parents?"

"I... I love her."

"As much as you love Peyton?" Nick asks.

I shake my head. "It's different. I can't explain it, but when I look at her and think about my child growing inside, my stomach turns. I never thought of her being the mother of my children, and now that she is..."

"You know, I thought I was in love with your mom until I met Aubrey. One look at her and my whole world shifted. I no longer counted the days since I had seen you. Instead, I looked forward to bringing her back to Beaumont to meet you. Aubrey was who I was meant to be with and it took your dad coming back to get me to open my eyes. Can you imagine if I had never gone to Africa?"

"You wouldn't have Mack and Amelie."

"Well, I can do without Mack," my dad mutters but does so with a partial smile.

Nick glares at my dad and shakes his head. "Right, I'd be a shell of who I am now. Lost in a world of heartache and despair. I would've watched you grow up from the outside looking in and not been a part of your life. Aubrey... she encouraged me, guided me into looking deep within myself to find the man I was supposed to be.

"I know it wasn't easy for your dad to let me be a part of your life, but I'm beyond grateful he allowed it. Just because you're not with the mother of your child, doesn't make you any less of a father."

"As much as I hate saying this, Noah, Nick is right. Without him, where are you? Are you the standout baseball player in high school, the starting quarterback of a professional team? He started you on that path, not me. I jumped in and rode the coattails. Most of the time I hated it, but at least you had Nick, who I know loved you, who stepped up and raised a child that wasn't his own, only to lose him. Wouldn't you rather your child be loved by everyone?"

"Marriage shouldn't be out of obligation, Noah," Nick adds.

"And you shouldn't jump into anything until you're a hundred percent sure," Dad says.

"About what? Marriage? I'll never be sure, especially with her. I broke up with her before Peyton woke up, and days later she tells me she's pregnant."

"Are you sure she's pregnant?" Nick asks.

"I mean, she says she is."

My dad groans loudly. I know from his past experience, he's not always trusting of people and has good reasons not to be.

"You have every right to ask for proof, Noah," Nick suggests.

"She went to the doctor, but I had an away game." Even as I say the words out loud I'm starting to second-guess everything. Dessie wouldn't do this to me, would she? "She can't fake a pregnancy," I tell them. "We aren't sleeping together so it's not like she can suddenly get pregnant."

Neither of them say anything. They don't have to. There is already enough doubt in my mind. They don't need to add to it. Dessie told me she was months along, which should mean she should start showing soon. It also means there could be some damage to the baby because of her partying.

"Nick, is there a way to check and see if the baby is healthy?"

"Yeah, there is. Why, are you concerned?"

I nod. "Dessie parties, at least she had been up until she told me she was pregnant." I take a deep breath and let it out slowly. "What if there's something wrong with the baby?"

Nick places his hand on my back. "We can run a test to make sure. Dessie has to agree though."

"Right." I nod. I like to think she would, but I can't be sure.

"Noah, have you considered you might not be the father?"

I look at my dad and shake my head. "Why would you say that?"

He frowns and decides now is a good time for a beer. "I was in a similar situation. As soon as I was told there was a baby, I bailed. I thought there was no way in hell I was the father because we used protection. I refused to believe it."

"And where's the child now?" I ask, swallowing hard. I don't know how I'm going to feel if my dad tells me I have another sibling somewhere.

"There isn't one, or there wasn't. The woman… she caused a lot of problems for you, your mom, Harrison and me. I don't know if she ever was pregnant, but I knew I was going to wait until the baby arrived before I took responsibility."

"Because you didn't believe her?"

He nods. "I didn't. And I had good reason not to. She knew I would never be with her the way she wanted me to be, that I would never love her the way I loved your mother. I used her to cope, to numb my feelings, and when I came back here, she did everything she could to destroy what I was trying to build."

My father's words sink in. I don't want to believe Dessie would lie to me, but it seems convenient she just found out she's not only pregnant but also far enough along to miss a few cycles. I know she has a stressful job, but her body is her career, how would she not know she's months along?

"What am I going to do?" I ask both of them.

"Not make a decision at the water tower is my suggestion," Nick says.

"What do you say we head home? Your mom is probably pacing the floor and likely pulling her hair out. Don't be surprised if she wrings your neck and hugs you after the fact."

"Maybe I'll head to Nick's for the night," I say, laughing.

"You're more than welcome, Noah, but I think you should probably be wherever Dessie is, and at least talk to her about what you're feeling."

We climb down the ladder, leaving my beer behind with the intent to come back for it in the morning. I hug Nick and tell him I'll be by later to see everyone. Dad hands me a helmet and I slip it on before climbing on behind him. The roar of the engine reminds me of when I was a child and he'd take me out for rides. Oh, how I wish I could go back to being free again.

25

PEYTON

*M*y heart races as I wait for Kyle to show up. It wasn't easy to get here in the sense that my mother is watching me like a hawk. Seriously, she needs a hobby. I know she thinks I'm fragile, but I'm getting stronger every day and it's not because of the exercises Xander has me doing, it's because I know being with Noah is impossible. Deep down I've always known, but couldn't ever bring myself to separate my dreams from reality.

I watch Kyle as he walks by the window I'm sitting next to. Thankfully, they're tinted and he can't see me staring at his ass, let alone the other women who have happened to notice him. Suddenly I'm embarrassed and for the life of me I can't figure out why. Maybe it's the women at the other table, saying crude things about him or maybe it's that I'm embarrassed for Kyle because he has to put up with stuff like that.

The hostess escorts him to the table she sat me at earlier. She touches his arm and throws her head back in mock laughter, almost as if he's said something funny to her when he hasn't even taken his eyes off of me.

Being under his scrutiny is weird. Kyle's good-looking and a month or so ago, I would've jumped at the opportunity to be stared at by him or any other man for that matter, but knowing Noah's in love with me, leaves a gaping hole in my heart – the part where I would love another – and I'm not sure anyone is going to be able to fill it.

Kyle bypasses his chair and kisses me on my cheek. He lingers there for a moment, allowing me to breathe in his cologne. There's no denying my attraction for him, but right now it's not enough.

"Thank you for calling," he says as he sits down. Immediately, he puts his napkin on his lap and pushes his silverware aside so he can rest his elbows on the table.

"Technically, I texted," I point out as I try to mirror his posture, but I can't. Being in a wheelchair prevents me from sitting up higher. In fact, I feel short and awkward.

"Do you want to sit in the chair?" Kyle points to the vacant chair behind us, where the hostess moved it out of the way.

I nod eagerly and do my best to pull myself away from the table; all while the women not far from us watch our every move. Kyle picks me up effortlessly as if I weigh nothing and sets me down, maneuvering the chair until I'm pushed in and comfortable.

"Better?"

"Yes." How he knew I needed this, I'll never know because I don't plan on asking. It's better to leave the kind gesture alone instead of ruining it with an inquisition. "How do you ignore them?" I ask, motioning to the table behind him. The women have gone from a casual glance over their shoulder to full-on staring. Most likely trying to figure out where they know him.

"Same as you, probably."

"I'm not famous."

"Your father is though. You get hounded by the media too."

"How do you know? Did you Google me?"

Kyle smiles and ducks his head, almost as if he's been caught looking at something he shouldn't. "I was curious."

"Ah, I see. And what did you find?" I'm intrigued, yet I'm not. The one rule my dad imposed on us was that we never look him or our family members up online. He wants to protect us from seeing the negativity that comes with being a celebrity.

"Let's see, you have a twin sister and an older, but adopted brother? Your parents aren't married. You've been attending awards shows since you were little. You grew up in Beaumont, which is where Westbury grew up, but considering what you said the other day..."

He looks at me when he's done, but I can't tell if his last bit is a statement or a question. Does he want to know if Noah and I are friends? I'm not sure I can even answer him if that's the case. I suppose we'll always be something considering our families are close, but I don't know if I'll ever be able to think of him as extended family. I already told him Noah and I aren't dating, despite Kyle saying Noah told him to stay away from me.

"Let's see... My sister's name is Elle. My brother is Quinn. My dad adopted my sister and I, and my mom adopted Quinn. My biological father died in a car crash when I was five."

Kyle sits back in the chair and his body slumps. I don't think I need to divulge any more about my familial situation as telling him about my father is enough to shock anyone who knows what's going on with me. As for Noah, we grew up together, long before my parents got together.

He nods and reaches for my hand. I give it to him freely, expecting a spark or something when we touch, but there's nothing and that saddens me a little. "It took me a while to figure out why Liam Page was in the hospital. I kept hearing the nurses talk about him, but nothing online solved the mystery."

"He was there because of me. He's my uncle, more or less."

"And you said your real dad died in a car crash?"

I struggle to smile. Before the accident I never had any qualms speaking about my father, but since... since I saw him, my emotions are all over the place. It's like the wounds are fresh and even though I barely remembered him from before, I can now. "It's really not something I've ever talked about. For as long as I can remember, my dad Harrison, has been with us. But I know how he died. He was revered in the town we grew up in, and no one let us forget how much he meant to everyone."

"That had to be hard."

"It was." Before I can finish, the waitress stops at our table. Kyle hasn't had an opportunity to look at the menu but doesn't seem to be deterred. He opens the menu quickly and reels off what he wants.

"I'll have the ribeye, medium, potatoes, veggies and a side salad with Italian, and a Coke."

"And for you?"

Now I'm truly embarrassed. "I'll have the chicken strips and fries, please. And I'll have water."

The waitress glances at me as she writes it down, probably wondering why we're here if I'm ordering kiddie food. For good measure, I hold up my arm, as if I need the validation to eat finger foods. Once she leaves, Kyle goes back to holding my hand, and once again I feel nothing. "Being here is going against everything my lawyer says, but I don't care. I wanted to come see you in the hospital, but doing so was highly frowned upon. The police thought it was best if I kept my distance."

"So you followed me to California instead?" I jokingly ask.

"Pure luck. My trainer told me to head out here for rehab. He thought he could make a few calls, throw my name around and I'd get in with Knight, but—"

"But he's my uncle and doesn't have the time."

Kyle shakes his head. "You have no idea how lucky you are. He's like a God when it comes to rehabilitation. Every athlete wants to work with him. But I'm glad you have him."

The waitress returns with a basket of rolls and our drinks. Kyle takes one out and slathers it with butter, making my mouth water. I could do the same, but I have this phobia about my cast touching my food. As I start to reach for my own, Kyle extends his arm and in his hand is half the roll. "Thank you," I tell him before I bite into the warm bread. "Hmm, so good."

"It is. Here, I'll butter the rest. I know you said the other day, but when do you get that off? You said something about x-rays happening?"

"I thought the appointment was today, but it's next week. Fingers crossed. I'm ready to itch my arm and leg."

He gives me another half of the roll and sticks the other half in his mouth. We continue like this until the basket is empty, and I'm stuffed. "I used one of my dry cleaning coat hangers. You know they still use metal hangers?"

"I don't think I noticed, but I'll have to search my parents closet for one. The itching is out of control. I normally use a fork or spoon, but honestly, that grosses me out." Kyle laughs a little before continuing with the conversation.

"So tell me, Peyton. What do you like to do for fun? And don't say football!"

"No, why not?" I ask teasingly.

"Because it's my job and I'm off, and sometimes I want to talk about anything else other than work."

"Fair enough. I like to read, surf when I can, listen to music, go shopping. Watch sports."

"Oh yeah, which ones?"

"All of them, but mostly football. It's what I grew up with."

"Watching Westbury, right?"

I nod and lean forward. "I told you the other day, he's not my boyfriend. I don't know what he said to you, but maybe you took it out of context. But yes, I grew up with Noah. We used to throw the football around in his backyard and for awhile, our high school coach thought I was going to be his next quarterback, but I chose to join the school paper instead and became a sports reporter."

Kyle stares at me for a minute before reaching across the table. His fingers brush against my cheek until they slide behind my ear, securing a strand of hair. I've taken to wearing my hair on the opposite side to cover up the missing patch of hair and scar.

The waitress arrives, breaking the connection between us. Instantly, Kyle steals one of my fries, laughing as he does. "Do you want a bite?" he asks, holding a piece of meat on the end of his fork. I nod and lean forward.

"So good," I say, trying to keep my mouth covered. "I miss food."

"I'll make a deal with you. If your cast isn't off by the end of next week, I'll saw it off for you."

Shaking my head. "No, sorry. I'll tough it out. There's too much damage..."

As soon as the words are out of my mouth, I want to take them back. I see the look in his eyes and the pain he's dealing with. Now I'm the one reaching across the table to try and hold his hand. "I'm sorry, Kyle. I didn't mean to upset you."

"It's fine, Peyton. I've been meaning to ask about your injuries, but part of me doesn't want to know because I know I caused them."

"You didn't," I remind him. "The truck did."

He nods, but the damage is done. Halfway through our meal, my phone beeps. Normally I wouldn't check it, but being as I lied to my mom about where I was going, it's best that I do in case she's figured out I'm not at the library. Except it's not from my mom, it's from Noah.

You haven't answered my calls so you leave me with no choice. I'm coming to town after Xmas to see you.

"Everything okay?" Kyle asks.

I nod and smile before turning my attention back to the message.

I don't want you here.

I need to explain, Peyton.

There's nothing to explain. I write back. I slip it back into my bag. The last thing I want is for Noah to be here.

"So, where exactly do you live?" I ask Kyle.

"Ohio, but I'm staying here through rehab."

"What about your family? Christmas?"

"My parents are on a cruise, so it's just me. I think they were expecting I'd have practice or something." Kyle tries to play off his injury, but I know it has to be hard for him. Missing out on a season is something that can really mess with an athlete.

Another text comes in. I open my bag so that I can glance quickly at my screen and see that it's Dessie. Pulling my phone out I read her text quickly. **Noah and I thought you should know we're getting married after the New Year.** I read her message twice before I turn my phone off and try to keep the contents of my stomach where they belong. My immediate reaction is to cry, but I don't want Kyle to ask why. I really shouldn't shed any more tears over Noah Westbury. He's made his choice, and it wasn't me.

With a halfhearted smile, I say to Kyle, "You should spend Christmas with us. You can bunk with Quinn."

Kyle's eyes light up. "Seriously?"

I shrug. "As long as you like the beach, surfing, loud music and barbecues, why not? The more the merrier."

"I'd love to, Peyton."

I refuse to use Kyle to get over Noah, but that doesn't mean we can't hang out. I have to make things clear to him from the start though because neither of us can afford any more personal damage.

NOAH

*C*hristmas passed by in a blur. While everyone was celebrating, opening presents and gushing about the gifts they received, I sat by in a daze, wondering how my life changed on a dime. People tried to engage me in conversation, but their words fell on deaf ears. If they told me congratulations, I mumbled thanks and moved to the next room. If they asked me a question, I nodded and proceeded to stare at the floor, the tree or the muted television. If they told me my team sucked, I agreed and didn't bother to tell them how wrong they were.

I'm numb and it's because of Peyton and her text messages to me. I thought for sure I could talk to her, explain why I left her in her hospital room and ask her what I should do, but she doesn't want to see me. ***I don't want you here.*** Those words have stung hard; have hit me in my heart like no other. I know I deserve them and more, but seeing them typed out so I am forced to reread them over and over again, it does something else to me.

I'm numb because the woman at the end of the couch is writing down everything she can, with the help of my little sister as she leafs through a bridal magazine. I haven't found the courage to tell Dessie that the conversation she overheard, the one I was having with my grandma, was me telling her I have no plans to marry Dessie. She misconstrued every single word, screamed yes, kissed me and proceeded to tell everyone in my house we were getting married. Needless to say, you could hear a pin drop because of how quiet everyone was. You would think Dessie would catch on, but she didn't. She immediately started texting whoever she could, sharing the news.

The worst part is I can't seem to find the words to tell her it's not happening because each time I try, she brings up the baby, and the endless cycle of self-doubt starts all over again. I know she was expecting a ring to be under the tree or in her stocking, but there wasn't one. She hid her disappointment well though, more than I can say for myself.

I don't want to marry Dessie or even be the father of her baby, but I don't have a choice. The old adage is "stupidity doesn't get you far" but I can attest it does. Stupidity gets you so far up shit creek there's no amount of paddling to get you where you need to be.

The conversation I had with my dads has been nagging me for days. They've both tried to show me I could still be a part of the baby's life without being married to Dessie, but I don't see how. She lives in Portland because of me, choosing to travel back and forth for her shoots. She's better off in California or New York, which means she'd move and take the baby with her. Marriage keeps her in the same house, but I'm not sure how this would be fair to her. A loveless marriage isn't something either of us wants, and despite what she says, if she loved me, she'd see the turmoil I'm going through.

I look down at my phone, rereading the words I have

memorized over and over again. **I don't want you here. I don't want you here. I don't want you here.** Except that's exactly where I want to be. With Peyton, helping her recover. Not here, in my parents' home, hiding out because I'm too afraid of what might happen back in Portland. I'm using them as a buffer and they know it.

My dad walks into the family room and turns the television on. As luck would have it, there's a game and it seems like he's poised to watch it. I'm so pissed at myself for the way my season ended. Even if we didn't stand a chance at the wild card, getting benched for the last game of the season is a blow to my ego. It would be one thing if Coach was trying to save me for next year, but he wasn't. He was sending a message that he's done with my piss poor attitude. I half expect him to call me in after the first of the year and give me my walking papers.

"Daddy," Little B whines out his name. "We're trying to plan a wedding here."

I look away, not wanting to be a part of this conversation.

"Then go to the dining room or your bedroom."

"Daddy."

"Betty Paige, I want to watch the game. I'm sorry if it interrupts your play time, but you can go play make-believe somewhere else."

My dad's words are harsh, making me wish I could tell Dessie the same thing. By the time I glance over at her and Little B, they're gathering their books and leaving the room. Dessie stops in front of me. "Are you coming?"

I shake my head, which causes her to huff. The last thing I want to do is sit in a room and listen to them prattle on about wedding stuff. In fact, the more I think about it, the more I want to get on a plane and fly to California to see

Peyton, and maybe I should. She may be able to offer a little clarity and guidance on what I should do. If she agrees to see me, that is.

"Dessie, wait," I say as I get up. She's halfway up the stairs with Paige. "I have to head back for a meeting. Do you want to come or stay here?" The lie falls too easily.

She smiles widely. "I'll stay. I have a lot of preparations to do." Dessie gives me a little finger wave and continues on her way up the stairs. I wait until she's out of sight before I go to speak with my father. He's not exactly pleased because he's going to have to be the one to tell my mom I left Dessie here.

THE POWELL-JAMES CONDO looms in front of me. The wrought iron gate is locked and the code I used to use when we were all younger no longer works. I have no choice but to either access them from the beach or press the buzzer. The problem with walking along a private beach is someone is likely to see me and alert the authorities. Most of the neighbors around here know and look out for each other. The issue with being buzzed in though is the chance that Peyton is the one to answer the call and I have no doubt she'll tell me to go away.

In hindsight, I could've told my mother what I was doing so she could've called Katelyn and let her know I was coming, but I didn't want to have to explain to my mom what I was doing here, especially when I don't even know myself.

Somehow I think seeing Peyton will make everything better, that she'll tell me I'm making the right decision and she'll promise to always be there for me. As delusional as it all sounds, I need her to understand where I'm coming from. It's not like I could've accused Dessie of cheating on me without any proof or claim the baby she's carrying isn't mine. Leaving Peyton in the hospital that day was the hardest thing I've done to date, but I have a feeling facing her today is going to be even harder.

As luck would have it, a car pulls up along the sidewalk and Ben gets out. Surely, he'll have a code to get in.

"Noah, what're you doing here?"

I point toward the house. "I've come to visit the Powell-James family, with gifts," I say, holding up the bag of presents I swiped from behind our Christmas tree. I don't know how long it'll take before my mom realizes they're gone, but I'm hoping to be back in Beaumont before she does. I have no idea if she planned to fly out here herself or if Katelyn and Harrison are planning a trip to Beaumont. I needed a viable excuse and this was it.

"Anything in there for me?" Ben asks, pulling the edge of the bag a bit.

"Somehow I think they're for the twins and Quinn."

"Figures. Come on, they're expecting me and you'll be a nice surprise." Ben punches in a code and the door opens. I follow him through and into the house, which is empty, but as usual, the back wall of windows is wide open and the people I've known as my second family is outside. Their laughter is loud and inviting.

Ben steps out first and goes right to Peyton, while I watch from the entryway. He gives her a hug and she motions for someone to come over to them. I freeze at the sight of Kyle Zimmerman shaking hands with Ben, who happens to turn and look at me, followed by Peyton. She doesn't look happy to see me at all, which is going to make my plea even harder.

I slip my shoes off and step out onto the sand. It's a bit cold compared to what it usually is in the summer, but comfortable nonetheless. Elle comes over and gives me a hug, followed by Katelyn. "Quinn is out in the water," Katelyn says, pointing over her shoulder. I don't correct her. It's probably safer for her to assume I'm here to see Quinn and not her daughter.

Except, Peyton is exactly who I want to see. I hand Katelyn the bag and trudge my way over to Peyton. I lean down and kiss her on the cheek, letting my lips linger there for a minute. "Can we talk in private?"

She shakes her head and shies away from me. I stay there a beat longer, hiding my rejection. As soon as I right myself, Zimmerman sticks his hand toward me. "Westbury, it's good to see you again."

"You too. What brings you to California?"

He shows me his leg as if it's supposed to mean something to me. I shake my head, not understanding.

"He's doing PT at Xander's club," Peyton says.

"And what about you? Are you working with Xander?"

Peyton sticks her leg out, which is clearly in a cast, but her arm seems to be in a brace. "Does it look like I can do anything? Do you see me sitting in this chair?"

The hostility rolls off her in droves. I'm tempted to pick her up and carry her back into the house so we can have a conversation, but I have a feeling she'll kick me in the head with her leg if I even try to touch her.

Instead, I crouch down, so we're eye level. I look into

her baby blues, which she's trying desperately to hide from me. "Hey, I really want to talk to you, Peyton, without everyone lurking."

"Fine," she says. Peyton stretches her arms up, indicating I need to pick her up. I carry her into the house and down the hall to her bedroom where I set her down on her bed. As much as I want to sit next to her, I don't, but I do get on my knees and slide between her legs. She had unshed tears in her eyes, breaking my heart.

My hand rests on her waist, loving the way she feels. "Peyton, I'm so sorry about what I did in the hospital. Dessie's pregnant and I—"

"Chose her."

"I chose the baby."

"That might not even be yours," she says. I rock back and look at her. Peyton's face is cold and defiant.

"Why would you say that?"

"Because for as long as you've been with her, Noah, she's been doing everything she can to keep you away from me."

"How do you mean?"

"Why are you here?" she asks, evading the question.

"I don't know, honestly. I knew I had to come and see you. She's pressuring me to into getting married and I needed to talk to you."

"And you want me to what? Tell you not to marry her? Tell you to enjoy your life with her?" she sneers.

"I want my best friend back," I snap at her.

"I don't care what you want, Noah. You showed me exactly what you wanted when you left me right after professing your love for me. That's not love, Noah. I may not have ever been in love, outside of loving you that is, but I know you don't do something like that to people you claim to be in love with. You give them an opportunity to support you and be by your side. You don't leave."

"I'm sorry, Peyton."

"So am I, Noah. Now if you'd take me back outside, Kyle is waiting for me."

As much as it pains me, I do as she asks. Once she's settled in her chair, I quietly leave, not saying goodbye to anyone.

27

PEYTON

"Today's the day. Are you excited?" Dr. Colby asks as she comes into the room. I'm sitting on the exam room bed with the help of my dad, with my broken leg propped up on a pillow, waiting for the tech to come in with the handy dandy saw to remove the contraption from my leg. According to the doc, I'm ahead of schedule by weeks.

Excited would be the understatement. I'm nervous, anxious and afraid of how my body is going to respond later when I'm at PT. I want to walk. Crawl. Jump up and down. I want to feel human again. Showering by myself will be a blessing in disguise. I know not only for me but my mom as well. It's awkward as hell having to get undressed in front of her, to have her wash my body parts. I can't imagine how she feels, but she does it without question.

"You have no idea." Dad, Mom and the doc all laugh. If it weren't for my parents being diligent with my care, I'd probably still be in the hospital. Once I made it through the first night, my parents were shocked to find out I wasn't properly cared for. I get it to some extent. The surgeon probably thought having bulky casts in the way would prevent people from being able to touch me, but on the other hand, he had zero faith in me and he should've. He's the doctor. It's his job.

"How's therapy going?"

"It's good." I lift my arms and show her my tiny bit of muscle. Since I've started working out, I enjoy it. The draw to keep going is there, and I've asked Xander to find me a trainer in Chicago. Much to his and everyone else's dismay, I plan to return to school for summer classes. Missing a full semester, plus finals, is going to set me back a year, and I don't want that.

"Your uncle tells me you plan on trying to walk today?"

I nod happily. "I do. I'm tired of the chair. Being waited on is nice, but I'm an independent person and not having my freedom is really a blow to my ego."

"Okay," she says. "I've spoken to him about stabilization. You have a few options. We can transition from the chair to a cane until Xander clears you or we can go with the Rollator, which is the walker with the seat."

I blanch. My dad coughs. And I swear my mother snickers in the corner. I give them the side-eye, letting them know I'm not very happy with their non-verbal comments. "I think I'll stick with the chair until my uncle says I'm good." There is no way in hell will I be caught pushing a walker down the street. Imagine the looks I'd get. The tabloids would have a field day. They're already insisting Kyle and I are dating, even though we're clearly friend-zoning each other. And if it's not about Kyle and I, I'm either a druggie, a dropout or pregnant. Each time a new headline comes out, I cringe at what it might be. Let me say, it's been fun in my house lately.

I never bothered to tell my parents I invited Kyle over for Christmas so when he buzzed the gate, my dad was none too impressed to find it was the man who put me in the situation I'm in. They know he didn't cause the accident, but he was there, which in my parents' eyes means Kyle is guilty by association.

Christmas was awkward, at best. But as the day went, things got better. My mom was still hesitant around him, but I understood where she was coming from. Kyle and I both survived a very similar accident that took my father away from us – even for me, it's hard to grasp. However, Kyle has been over more frequently to visit and has even gone surfing with my dad.

And as uncomfortable as it was when Noah showed up, Kyle was a trooper. He hasn't fully come out to ask me about Noah. He's hinted with random statements, which I've ignored. I'm not in a place where I can fully say what Noah is or was to me because life is too short to play the what-if game. What if... Noah chose me over Dessie? What if... I was never in the accident?

What if... what if... what if...

The list can go on forever, and you'll never find the answer. I refuse to play the victim or be the one Noah seeks out because he's gotten himself into a situation. I *can't* be that person for him anymore, and I hate it. I hate that our friendship is over because of... well, everything. More so, I have so much animosity for his future wife, I refuse to go to their wedding. Of course, my entire family is making the trip, which means I will too, but I'm not leaving my house.

The tech comes in with his handy dandy saw, which I begged Kyle to find online so I could at least crack my cast open in order to scratch my leg. From our first luncheon, he told me he'd saw it off, but the jerk quickly changed his mind and gave me some spiel about healing and potential damage. I stuck my tongue out at him because being childish is the way to act when you don't get your way.

"I want to caution you, Peyton. This will be different from when we took the cast off your arm."

"I know. My leg is going to stink. There will be a lot of dead skin. And I have to be careful with how much itching I do."

Dr. Colby smiles. "The nurse will come in and give you a scrub down before you leave, which will help alleviate the issues."

"Perfect."

I wiggle my freshly painted toes, thanks to my sister, as the tech nears my leg. The saw switches on, and suddenly my mom is by my side. She grips my hand as the blade touches down on the cast. "I'm so proud of you," she whispers into my ear. I lean my head against her and watch with apt attention as the tech slowly cuts open my cast. I already know what my leg will look like. There's a nice scar running down the front of my shinbone, which matches the one on my chest and upper thigh. I joked, saying I was going to go as Frankenstein this year for Halloween, but the only one who found it funny was Quinn. He's really the only one not treating me with kid gloves but has been an overly amazing brother.

As soon as the cast is pulled open, I quickly pull my shirt over my nose. My eyes water and I'm tempted to tell the tech to put it back. "God, I stink."

"It's to be expected," Dr. Colby says.

My foot is lifted out and placed on the pillow. I stifle my laughter when a pool of sand falls out of the heel of my cast.

"Peyton, what is that?" Mom asks.

"Dunno." I shrug.

"Unbelievable. Who let you play in the sand?"

Let's see, Mom. Quinn. Dad. Kyle. "I think it's probably from the wind." There isn't any reason to tell her Kyle gave me piggyback rides while I tried to fly a kite. Or Quinn and I built a sand castle one day and I had to beg him to set me on the edge of the tub so I could remove all the sand from my shorts. And there's my dad who covered my arm and leg and took me out on his surfboard so I could feel human again.

"Definitely the wind. I mean we do live on the beach," I point out. She seems to agree. I chance a look at my dad who is in the corner. He winks; reminding me our secret is safe. Truthfully, my dad would never do anything to upset my mom. I can't recall a time when they've ever fought, and if they have it was never in front of us. But, that doesn't mean he won't do what we ask, even if it means upsetting her if she were to find out. Taking me out on the surfboard was one of those times.

It's five in the morning and I can't sleep. Elle and Quinn are back at school, leaving me to fend for myself which equates to having mom bug me every two minutes to see if I'm okay. I don't know if I ever will be, but I'm surviving. Behind me, the sliding door, or more fittingly named "the wall of windows," opens and my dad steps out. I can tell by his breathing and his cologne it's him.

"It's early, sweet pea."

"Couldn't sleep."

He pulls a patio chair close to me and sits down. Like me, he's staring out into the surf. Out there, it's where he loves to be. Every day, unless he's on tour, you'll find my dad in the water and normally my mom sitting in the sand watching him. I want a love like theirs. The all-consuming-never-wavering type of love.

"You okay, baby girl?"

I nod and lean toward him so I can rest my head on his shoulder. He's never been one to prod, always waiting for us to come to him with an issue or problem. It's like he stands back in the shadows, knowing eventually we'll confide in him. He knows mostly everything about me, except for when it comes to Noah. I don't think there will ever be a time when I can look my dad in the face and tell him I'm in love with Noah. Never mind the age difference, which isn't an issue the older I get, but it's the fact that it's Noah, his best friend's son.

"Want to go surfing?"

"I wish."

"I can make it happen." I look at my dad, who's smiling widely. "You know I would never do anything to jeopardize your recovery."

"I know," I tell him as my head starts to nod. "I never thought I'd miss it until I was told I couldn't."

My dad kisses me on the forehead and disappears to the side of our condo where the shed is. He comes back with his wetsuit on and sets his surfboard in the sand. "Be right back," he says as he goes into the house. My heart is beating rapidly with anticipation, wondering how this is going to work.

When he returns, he pulls off the blanket I was using to stay warm. As if he's in a hurry, he takes my leg and slips it into a heavy-duty trash bag and starts taping it up, like I'm about to take a shower. He turns and crouches down in front of me. "Get on." I climb onto his back and start laughing. "Ssh, your mother will kill me... but it'll be worth it to see you smile."

A lone tear escapes when he says that. I imagine the accident and subsequent recovery has been hard on everyone. When we get down to the surf, he slides me down to the sand.

"Okay. I'm going to set you on the board and we'll paddle out together. If you fall in, I'll save you."

I nod and reach my arms out to him. He cradles me for a minute before he sets me on the board. I expect him to get on behind me, but he doesn't. Instead, he pushes us out, treading water the deeper we get. The waves are minor but still exhilarating. Being out here and letting the sun hit my face as it wakes up, will be worth the wrath I receive from my mother.

By the time we're done, I'm soaked, and I love it. My clothes are waterlogged. My hair is drenched. But it was all worth it. When we get back to the house, thankfully Mom isn't awake yet. Dad does his best to get me fresh clothes and when Mom wakes up, he winks and presses his finger to his lips. Mom was none the wiser.

The nurse is gentle as she scrubs the dead skin off my leg. I'm smiling at the memory of my dad and I surfing, knowing that soon I'll be able to get back out there and ride next to him.

Even though my cast is off, I'm still in the chair. Everyone in the office claps for me as my dad pushes me out. Dr. Colby was hesitant to see if I could stand and wanted Xander to be the one to test out my leg, fearful it's too weak to withhold my weight. Bless her heart she never brought up the fact I may not be able to walk right away.

28

NOAH

I'm the definition of a chicken shit. For weeks I have avoided the inevitable. Dessie planned a wedding, invited people and somehow I haven't grown a set to tell her no or that we're making a mistake. Not only that, but she's delusional enough to think this is what I want. Maybe it is. Maybe I'm too blinded by my infatuation to see what's in front of me. Dessie is pregnant with my child, and at some point, I must've thought marriage was in the cards for us since I asked her to move in with me.

Needless to say, I have frozen feet solidly encased in cement being anchored to the ground. I don't know if I'm making the right decision or any decision at all for that matter.

Dessie's loving the attention she's getting from the local paper. Of course, it's big news when your former high school standout returns home to get married, which was never my intention, yet as my tuxedo pants are being yanked, pulled and I'm asked which side do I hang, I haven't found the words to tell her we can't do this.

"Everyone is so thrilled you chose Beaumont," Mrs.

Kline says. Her and her husband have owned the only wedding store in town for years. I was fitted here for each tuxedo I wore to prom. "Are you doing the flowers?" Mrs. Kline asks my mom, who is sitting in the corner, watching me as I get poked with needles.

"I'm not. I passed the job onto another florist in Allenville. I don't want to fret over the finer details while Noah is getting married."

My stomach rumbles just as Mr. Kline tells me I'm done. Ever so gingerly, I walk off the platform and into the dressing room where I carefully step out of my pants. I dress quickly and meet my mom by the door.

"Want to grab lunch?"

She smiles softly. "Sure, Noah."

After I open the car door for her, I run around to the other side. Beaumont is small. Everyone knows everyone. But they don't bother my dad or I for autographs, which is rather nice. However, small also means our options for lunch are limited. I decide to take her to Ralph's. Not the classiest place, but the lunch menu is decent and the place is big enough that we'll be able to talk.

My mom doesn't hide her emotions well. I know something is bothering her, and honestly, I've been avoiding her. In all the years I've been dating, I've never asked her if she's liked any of my girlfriends. Mostly, because I was afraid that whoever I was with at the time wouldn't live up to her standards. Not that she has crazy high expectations, but I'm her son, and I think it's hard for moms to let go.

A few years back, the owner of Ralph's died. The band did a huge tribute to him, mostly out of respect for my dad. It was here, when my dad played a song he had written for my mother, that everything changed for them.

We step into the pub that hasn't changed much over the

years. The lights are still fairly dim, the floor is some kind of tile, but no one knows what color it is. The stage is waiting for the next band to set-up. I wave at Ralph's son, who is now running the place. We call him Ralph, even though his name is Charlie, and he doesn't correct us, so I assume he doesn't mind.

"Hey Josie, Noah. What can I get you to drink?" Lonnie, the lone waitress asks.

Mom and I both order water.

"I haven't eaten here in years." I peruse the menu, trying to remember what's good. Honestly, most pub food is good as long as you don't try to get too fancy and order a steak or seafood.

"It's because you never come home." Mom sounds bitter, but I get it. "Paige loves the steak fries here."

I decide quickly on a burger, fries and a chocolate shake, and set my menu down so I can focus my attention on the woman across from me. For the longest time, she was my best friend and cheerleader, and while she's still my number one fan, something has shifted. Since Christmas, she's been unusually quiet and I have a feeling it's because of the situation I'm in.

As soon as she puts the menu down, I lean toward her. "Talk to me."

"I'm fine, Noah."

"Rule number one," I start to say, closing my mouth as the waitress arrives. We give her our orders and once she's out of sight, I look at my mom and smile. "As I was saying. Dad has always preached if a woman says fine, you know she's not. Don't make me use the word."

"You wouldn't."

"I would. I so would."

Mom squints her eyes as she looks at me, testing my

resolve. I cock my eyebrow at her and smirk. "Mommy, please tell me what's wrong." My lower lip juts out as her willpower crumbles. Only, she ends up covering her face. Her shoulder shakes and there's a soft whimper coming from behind her hands.

I'm up and out of my seat, sliding into her booth and wrapping her in my arms. "I'm sorry, Mom. Whatever it is. I'm so sorry."

She pulls her hands away and wipes away her tears. "I'm fine, Noah."

"Clearly, you're not."

"I don't want to hurt your feelings."

"Hurt them. I don't care." It's not like I'm feeling much these days anyway.

Mom takes a deep breath. She looks at me before she stares down at her napkin. "I don't like Dessie. I never have. I think she treats you poorly, is self-centered and I'm questioning if she's even pregnant."

My gaze lands on what was my seat until I moved to comfort my mom. The torn and worn out pleather shows its age. The inside lining of the booth is threadbare and it's only a matter of time until there's nothing left of the cushions. Her last statement replays through my mind. I can't make heads nor tails of it.

"Dessie told me you didn't like her, but I didn't believe it."

Mom shakes her head. "I've tried, Noah. I really have, but something about her rubs me the wrong way. She's superficial. I'm not the only one who sees it. Both your grandmothers feel the same way."

My jaw clenches. Wonderful. All the women in my life can't stand the soon to be mother of my... "Wait, why do you think she's not pregnant?"

"Because I've been there, Noah. Twice. There are signs and she doesn't show any of them."

"Everyone is different though, right?"

Mom nods but doesn't say anything else as our food is brought to the table. I excuse myself and slip back onto my side, picking at my fries. Mom takes a few bites of her cheesesteak and puts it down. "Noah, I love you more than life. I've been trying to tell myself I need to get over these feelings I have for Dessie, but I can't. Yes, everyone is different, but she shows very little signs of being pregnant. I've cooked garlic, onion, tomatoes – she's helped and eaten everything. When I was pregnant with you and Paige, garlic upset my stomach. I find it strange that she seems to be okay with everything, that nothing seems to make her feel queasy or she has no pregnancy-related sickness of any kind."

"Are you trying to make her sick?" I don't want to believe my mother would do something like that, but I'm starting to second-guess how well I know her, and I never thought I'd think that of my mother.

"I would never. But your girlfriend has been in the hot tub, and I'm sorry, but anyone who is pregnant knows you can't go in the hot tub."

"Maybe she forgot."

Mom nods and goes back to eating her food. The rest of lunch is done in silence, and so is the drive back to the house. She gets out of the car and instead of going to the front door, she runs down the back steps where my dad's studio is.

I contemplate going in and asking Dessie but have a feeling each answer will be opposite of my mom's and that'll force me to pick. Instead, I head back into town and stop at Nick's office. Inside, the receptionist he's had for years smiles.

"Hi, Noah. Your dad is with a patient. I'll let him know you're here."

"Actually, Jody. I'm here to see Aubrey."

Jody smiles and presses the buzzer for the door. "You know where to find her."

"Thank you." I walk down the hall where behind one closed door there's a baby crying. I can hear Nick and one of his nurses trying to soothe the child.

I find my stepmom at her desk, reading some manual. Knowing her, it's about some disease in Africa, and she's trying to find a way to help.

"Knock knock," I say as I lightly rap my knuckles on her door. Aubrey looks up in surprise and grins.

"Noah! What a pleasant surprise. What brings you by?"

"I need some advice."

She motions for me to sit down in the chair across from her desk, which is filled with pictures of all of us, including Betty Paige. A few years back, she and Nick had family photos taken and asked that Paige and I be included. I was an automatic yes and surprisingly my parents agreed to let Paige do it as well.

"So what's up?"

"As you know, Dessie's pregnant."

Aubrey nods.

"Would she be allowed to go into a hot tub?"

Her eyes widen. "Absolutely not. The temperature of the tub is more than the uterus can shield from the baby. In laymen's terms, the baby would essentially boil."

I rest my head in my hands. I'm sick to my stomach thinking Dessie would harm our child like this. "What about doctor's appointments? We've been here almost a month and she hasn't mentioned needing to go back to visit a doctor or anything."

Aubrey seems to think on this one a bit. "It really depends on when her last one was, but normal appointments are twenty-eight to thirty days apart so there's an accurate record of the baby's growth and how well nutritionally the other is doing. Why all the questions?"

I shrug. "My mom doesn't think Dessie is pregnant."

Aubrey sits back in her chair and sighs. "Women's intuition. We're not always right, but sometimes you can sense things. It's also a mother's sense. We suspect, always. It's why we're constantly asking you questions, it's because we have a suspicion something isn't right. And sometimes we're wrong."

"Dessie says she's heard the heartbeat—"

"When was this?"

"At her first appointment. I had a road game so I couldn't go."

Aubrey pulls some wheel type gizmo out and writes a few numbers down. "It's possible, but doctors normally don't check for a heartbeat at the first appointment unless the mother says she's farther along. Honestly, Dessie didn't share much when we saw her at Christmas, no due date or anything like that."

"Can't say I know either."

My stepmom leans forward with her hands clasped on her desk. "Are you having second thoughts?"

I nod. "About everything. I don't know what to do or who to believe. What questions to ask or what information to demand." I stand up and start pacing. "It's like my world is crashing all around me and I can't stop it. I'm in love with another woman and Dessie knows this, and now she's pregnant and I just..." My heart rate accelerates, causing my breathing to become sporadic. I bend at my waist, even though I know this isn't the answer. Aubrey is there to help me back to the chair.

"Noah, you're facing an uphill battle. Your feelings for Peyton are getting stronger, but your desire to do the right thing is also playing a heavy part in your decision-making. Have you spoken to Dessie about how you feel?"

"She knows I'm in love with Peyton."

"Is that when she told you she was pregnant?"

I nod. "We broke up. I told Peyton how I felt, and Dessie shows up in Chicago with the news."

"And just like that your happily ever after is swirling down the toilet."

I look at Aubrey, who is smiling. "Nice analogy."

She shrugs. "If I knew more about football, I'd use one of those, but this coach's wife is not well versed on the terminology. I only know that when Mack has the ball, he has to run fast."

Aubrey opens her arms and I fall into her embrace. "It'll all work out, Noah. I don't have the answers, but your dad and I have the resources. You could always bring her in to hear the heartbeat if you want."

Her suggestion gives me a lot to think about, but still, I don't know what to believe. Dessie has no reason to lie to me, but neither does my mom.

29

PEYTON

For the first time in my life, I hate Beaumont. It breaks my heart to even think this, but being in the same location as Noah and Dessie makes me long for the solitude of the condo or the active life of my sorority. The only positive is I can move about our former house with ease. Quinn thought it would be funny to, in fact, buy me the Rollator. It's hot pink with a bell. I hate it, and secretly love it because it gives me the ability to move from room to room without having my parents hovering, hoping I don't fall.

But being here makes it hard to escape. My mom has been going on and on about this wedding, mostly because my aunt Josie is stressed and my mom is trying to help her stay calm. With my mom constantly with Josie and my dad with Liam, I'm left to my own devices. I still can't drive and can barely walk on my own which makes me completely dependent upon others.

There used to be a time when I loved sitting out on our covered porch. Back when Noah was in high school, my parents had a massive sign in our yard letting everyone know we supported Beaumont High and Noah Westbury. I look around now and see the names of kids Elle and I used to babysit, being honored by their parents, reminding me of how simple life was when I was in high school. I didn't have to worry about anything and when I needed something, Noah was always there.

Quinn and Elle will arrive tomorrow. I don't know if either of them are a part of the ceremony, and honestly, I don't care. I'm not going. Even if I have to pretend I have the stomach flu or am in an incredible amount of make-believe pain – I'm not going. I refuse. Although, standing up when the minister asks if someone objects does sound like a fun way to ruin their wedding day. I'm not petty, even though I want to be. My parents would be shocked and I'm not sure I'm ready to explain myself to them where Noah is concerned.

Speaking of Noah, he's walking up my front steps. I knew sitting outside on the porch was a mistake, and as much as I'd love to run into the house, I'd never make it.

"Hey, Peyton," he says as he leans against the post with his hands pushed into the pockets of his track pants.

"Hey." I avoid eye contact as best I can. I don't want to look at his new haircut or wonder what it feels like to touch his five o'clock shadow.

"Your mom said you're doing really well in therapy." Noah sits down next to me but keeps a healthy space between us.

"I have a good therapist who doesn't care if he's killing me day after day."

"He loves you. Xander only wants to see you strong again."

How does he know what Xander wants? Who says I'm not strong now? I'm strong enough to stay away from him, to not bend and ask him to choose me over Dessie. If refraining from making a fool out of myself isn't some major strength, I don't know what is because saying those words, to beg him to give us a chance would be so easy.

"Look, Peyton. I know we're not on the same page right now and maybe we won't be for a long time, but I still value your opinion and I need your help."

I continue to stare at the road, the houses across from me, the tree branches swaying in the light breeze, anything but him.

Noah clears his throat. "I was benched for my last game. My performance... it took a hit after you were in the accident. I was afraid to lose you and even though I'm right here sitting next to you, I've lost you anyway. But that doesn't mean I don't need you. I do. For years, you've told me what's wrong with my game, and if I don't fix the issues this time, I'm likely going to be traded or regulated to being a backup. You and I both know I've worked too hard to let my career slip like this."

"Maybe you could try baseball. You wouldn't be the first player to do so. Bo Jackson had a pretty decent career in both sports."

"You're right, he did. I'm sure Nick would love it."

I'm sure all the women would love it, and you'd never be home with Dessie.

"I need your help, Peyton."

I look at him and scoff. "What? You want me to watch game film? Do you think I have time for that?" I do. I totally do because I have nothing else to do.

"Actually, I was thinking you could come with me. Nick gave me the keys to the storage shed and I thought I'd get the snap machine out, put the net up and even let you beat me with a bump stick."

"I do like the idea of beating you," I tell him. He smiles, but I don't because let's face it, I'm not joking. "However, I can't stand on my own for very long so I'd be useless."

He nods. "I asked your mom if it'd be okay, she said it was up to you. She thought you'd like to get out for a bit."

Of course she did because she wants to see me happy. She doesn't know Noah is the source of my pain and that my injuries pale in comparison to the heartache I feel. "I should tell you to figure it out yourself, and if you fail, it's on you."

"I know."

"But I won't, and you know this. You're playing on my weakness and I hate you right now."

"I know," he says softly with his eyes trained on me. I feel an onslaught of tears coming so I look away and nod.

"One condition."

"Anything."

"When I'm done, I'm done. You'll bring me home with no questions asked."

"Of course, Peyton." Noah smiles like he's been triumphant. He has, but I'll never tell him.

"I'm sorry, I have another condition."

"Let's hear it," he says, angling his body toward mine.

I look him square in the eyes, wishing I could get lost in his blue eyes. "No Dessie. If she's going to be there..." I don't know what I'll do considering I can't walk home. I could scoot home though, or at least far enough away from the school to wait for my parents.

Noah grabs for my hand, and I let him. "Just us, Peyton."

"Here's the deal. I can't do stairs so you have to carry

me. If you mock, tease or steal my walker, I'll maim you. Got it?"

Noah laughs. "I got it, captain."

Captain. He hasn't called me that in years. I haven't realized until this moment how much I've missed it. When he was named captain his sophomore year, he gave me the title, saying I earned it too, so we'd share it. Back then the five-year age difference was huge. My friends and I used to sit about and gush about how cute Noah was or they'd all want to come over when Quinn was having a birthday party so they could not only see my brother but his friend as well. Elle and I learned rather quickly that having an older brother was not beneficial in the friends department.

Noah takes my walker and sets it in the back of his truck. "Does this thing have brakes or something to keep it from rolling?"

"Yeah, on the wheels," I yell. I find myself laughing as I watch him fumble around.

"Got it." Noah shakes it back and forth for good measure, and then he goes to the door and opens it. Against my better judgment, my eyes are focused on him the entire time, at the way his shirt moves against his muscles and the long strides he takes to get up the stairs quickly. Everything about him is ingrained in my mind. "All right. Are you ready? Do you need anything?"

I shake my head and reach my arms out. I could walk a little with his assistance, but I don't want to pass up the opportunity to be held by him. It'll be my last time ever and as much as it'll torture me later, this is what I want.

Noah cradles me to his chest. I refuse to read anything into the gesture, and can't help but wonder if this is what it would be like to be carried to bed by him. If I'm going to survive today, I need to look at everything objectively and remind myself he's getting married this weekend. He chose someone else.

He sets me down in the truck and rushes around to the other side. "Do you remember the last time you were in here?" he asks as he pulls away from the curb.

Yes, I think but don't say it out loud.

Noah turns down the radio, so it's just us with our breathing, sighing, and the outside traffic to clog my brain with noise. He pulls up to the stoplight and someone yells his name. This is small town life at its best right here.

"My dad knows, Peyton."

"Knows what?"

"About us. Prom night."

I chose to stare out the window instead of him. I guess I didn't realize losing my virginity would be a hot topic for the Westbury men.

"When you were in the coma, I was talking to you. I was trying to bring up happy memories, at least those I consider happy, and prom night was one of them."

As he drives forward, I continue to stare out the window.

"My dad overheard me talking to you about it. He was pissed until I told him."

I don't want to know, but I ask anyway. "Told him what?"

"That I was in love with you and thought we'd be together after that night, but I screwed up by taking you to the cliffs. You see, I thought looking out over the ravine would be romantic, but then you started talking about college and how excited you were to finally be free. I started wondering how free you would be if we were together.

Would you feel comfortable going out? How would I feel? My mind went in a hundred different directions so I kept my mouth shut and my feelings to myself."

As much as I've tried to keep the tears away, I can't. Noah pulls into the parking lot by the football stadium and puts his truck into park. I know I should move, but I can't.

"Come to find out, taking a girl to the cliffs means different things for different people. Dad says you probably thought I was going to tell you that the night before shouldn't have happened, which is why you were going on about school and everything else."

I close my eyes as memories of prom, the night of and the day after flood my thoughts. I came onto him. I asked him to get us a room because I wanted him to be my first. I was finally eighteen and legal. No more silly thoughts or wasted hopes and dreams. Noah and I could be together. In my mind, it worked. He could live in Chicago until the season started, coming home on Sunday evenings and flying back for practice. But it wasn't meant to be.

Noah doesn't say anything as he gets out of the truck. He walks around the front and opens my door, resting his hand on my leg. "Peyton, that night meant everything to me."

"Me too." The words are out of my mouth and there's no taking them back.

He nods and steps away. I want him to come back and tell me how he feels, but I can't take much more heartbreak. Our moment, as brief as it was, has passed. I think about telling him about Dessie and the text message she sent me when they first started dating, but I bite my tongue. I'm not spiteful even though I want to be.

By the time he wakes up for his wedding, I'll be gone. I can't stay here and be a part of the ceremony of a man I love desperately, as he pledges his love to someone else. It'll kill me. Nursing my broken heart in the comfort of my own home is what's best for me. Telling my parents though, that'll be hard. They won't understand why I have the sudden urge to return to California.

30

NOAH

I never intended to stop by the Powell-James home until I heard Katelyn say Peyton was by herself. Driving over there was like second-nature. I knew each turn like the back of my hand, and each house I drove by, I could recall which teammate lived there along with his position.

Beaumont means something to me. It's home, and it's taken me days to figure this out. It's where I'm comfortable. Where I plan to retire or move to after I'm booted off the Pioneers for my lackluster performance on which I'm blaming Peyton in a roundabout way, even though it's not her fault.

She messes with my mind. Let's me dream about a time when we could've been together. Thinking about her and I together gives me a hope I'm not feeling right now. I'm getting married to a woman who's pregnant, or says she is, that I'm not in love with and I didn't even ask to marry me. If this isn't some jacked up version of life, I don't know what is. I can't even lie and say I never thought of Peyton and I together, walking down the aisle with our families looking on, because I have and more so recently. I know there's some saying about setting her free and she'll come back. I did that already, the morning after prom. She almost left me and just when I thought I could be free and be with her, someone showed me I'm not.

Peyton is sitting on her little cart thing at midfield. She's facing the broadcast booth, likely wondering if she'll ever call a game. It's her dream, and one I'd love to see fulfilled. Although there isn't a single doubt in my mind when she calls my game, she'll rip me apart. Thing is, I wouldn't expect anything less.

It takes me almost a half hour to get everything set up and the machine plugged in. Normally, I'd like to have a few of the high school players hanging out to shag balls, and Nick offered to make a few calls, but once I set my mind on seeing Peyton, I knew this had to be just the two of us.

I'm a glutton for punishment, spending time like this with her, telling her about prom night and my feelings. But I had to let her know our time together meant something to me, that I wasn't some cad who took advantage of her but truly cared about her. And care is probably the wrong word to use. I love her, but there isn't anything I can do about it right now.

"I don't remember Nick having this when I was in school?" Peyton says of the center machine.

"I bought it for him last year. Well, the Booster Club did after I made the donation. We use one in Portland and it's come in handy."

"How does it work?" She pulls herself over, using only her left leg.

"Aren't you supposed to use your right leg as well with that?" I ask, pointing to her scooter.

She shrugs and avoids my question. "So the machine."

"So your leg," I counter. "Tell you what, for every ball I get through the net, we walk ten yards together."

Peyton looks at me with dubious eyes. "My therapy is going fine."

"Prove it." I raise my eyebrows at her, sending her a challenge she'll never be able to back down from.

"Fine, and if I walk fifty yards, you run the snake."

I nod. "You're on." We shake on our newly minted deal. "Anyway. I place the ball on the tray, tap the pad and it releases."

"Sounds easy."

"Eh, the pad tends to resist so I have to really push on it, but the process is effective." As soon as I set the ball down, Peyton backs up. I look to see where she's at and maybe to see if she's staring at me, but her eyes are focused either on the machine or my feet. I take position behind the mechanical center and call out my cadence. Ahead of me is a net with multiple targets, each one representing a different route. I bump the pad and take my steps back, almost stumbling over my own feet.

"When did your footwork become sloppy?"

"When I left you in Chicago not knowing if I'd ever see you again." I'm blunt and to the point.

"Well I'm alive and well so it's time to come up with another excuse."

"Touché."

"Why don't you work on some footwork drills first?" Peyton suggests. She's right though. I hand her a whistle and get on the line, facing her. She blows into the whistle. I grapevine. She blows. I sprint. She blows. I shuffle. I use the hash marks for a makeshift ladder, twisting and turning my hips to make my feet move faster. For an hour we do this until I'm exhausted.

"Are you done blowing that whistle?" I ask, drinking down my bottle of water.

Peyton shrugs. "It was fun watching you sweat."

I nod and wink at her. "Right, back to the machine." This time my footwork is cleaner, but still not enough.

"You're overthinking. It's tap: one, two three. Look: four, five, six. Throw: seven, eight, nine."

I count off as she advised and find a decent rhythm. Balls are starting to hit their targets and my feet aren't crumbling beneath me. When the bucket is empty I tell her it's time to start walking.

Peyton sighs heavily, but stands, turns around and grips her handlebar almost effortlessly. I stay behind her in the event she starts to fall, but realize after ten yards she's doing really well.

"Has Xander said when you'll no longer need the walker?"

She shakes her head. "Nope. I can use a cane, sometimes. It's mostly when I'm walking from my room to the bathroom. Quinn bought me this because he thought he was being funny, but I actually like it because it affords me the ability to leave the house, although I'm not much for hanging out in public lately."

"Me neither."

"No? I thought for sure with the town getting ready for your wedding, you'd be loving every minute of it."

I step in front of her, halting her progression down the field. "What if I tell you I don't want to get married?"

"Then don't," she says as if calling off the wedding would be the easiest thing to do.

"Give me a reason, Peyton."

She shakes her head slowly. "I can't. I won't. She's pregnant. She wins."

"Was it a competition? Am I missing something?"

Peyton sighs and shifts so she can sit down. "It wasn't for me because I was waiting. I thought, someday you'll see me and realize... well, I don't know what because the morning after prom I was set to tell you how I felt, but yeah you took me to the cliffs and the last thing I wanted to hear was how you thought being with me was a mistake, so I went on about school even though I was so afraid to start and to be alone. I had this grand plan in my mind, which went swirling down the drain.

"Then you met Dessie. She wasn't your first girlfriend, but I had a feeling that anything I had hoped for was gone and I accepted it. I'm young, and you're playing professional football. The chips were stacked against us. But Dessie..."

I get down on my knees so we're eye level. "What is it, Peyton?"

She looks off into the distance and shakes her head. My fingers touch the softness of her face, pulling her chin toward me. "Tell me," I plead.

"She doesn't like me and never has, which wouldn't be a concern, but she gloats. She sends me messages. They're not kind. I should've blocked her number, but I never did."

"What kind of messages?"

"Trivial stuff, Noah. Pictures of you guys together, with you sleeping next to each other. Stupid comments about my age. How I'd never have you. After a tough game, she'd send me a picture of you and her together. I knew about your engagement because she told me. Like I said, I should've blocked her, but I didn't. The messages were sporadic, at best."

I stand up and step away from Peyton, running my

hand through my hair. I never gave Dessie Peyton's number, which means she went through my phone to get it.

"Peyton, I'm sorry. I had no idea."

She shrugs and offers me a thin-lipped smile. "I think I'm ready to go home."

I nod and head toward the fifty-yard line and start cleaning up. When I look down the field, Peyton is trying to pick up as many footballs as she can. I watch her as if she's some type of enigma. Everything within me is screaming to pick Peyton, but I can't leave my child. I can't stomach the idea of my son or daughter going from house to house on weekends and holidays, living off some schedule, instead of being a kid who gets to enjoy life. I know others do it and do so successfully, but I don't see Dessie and I being amicable.

What I do see is Peyton, the woman I'm in love with, stepping aside. What does that say about me? She's the one that'll make me happy and I'm letting her go – right into the hands of another man. I'm not stupid. Kyle Zimmerman is waiting in the wings for her. He'd be a fool not to.

After the equipment is all put away, I load Peyton back into the truck. The drive back to her house is done in silence. Anything I have to say is going to sound stupid. I screwed up. I should've been more selfish when she was eighteen, maybe then things would be different.

At her house, I make sure she's situated before leaving. With my hand on the doorknob, I turn and look at her. "Are you in love with me?" I ask her.

"I am, but it'll fade with time."

"Tell me not to marry her, Peyton."

She shakes her head. "I can't, Noah."

I nod and let myself out. The cab of my truck smells like her. I keep my windows rolled up so I can breathe her in and remember this one day because I have a feeling it'll be years until we have another one like it.

When I get back to my parents', I head into my bedroom and find Dessie's purse on the bed. I sit next to it, with my hand itching to go through her phone. I shouldn't, it's an invasion of privacy, but she must have done it to me, it's the only way she could get Peyton's number.

My hand reaches in and pulls it out. I type in the four-digit code used to get into my apartment building. When it doesn't work, I try another series of numbers finally figuring out she's used our upcoming wedding date as her passcode.

Her screen comes to life with folders of apps, and the background picture of her and I after one of my games. I press the text app and bring up the window. Searching for Peyton's name, I read the series of messages she's sent her. Peyton never responded. They seem harmless at first glance, but they're anything but.

A message comes in and against my better judgment, I open it. It's from her best friend, Isa. Immediately my throat tightens and my hand shakes so bad I have to squeeze the phone harder. I scroll up and start reading from the day I left to go to Chicago.

Noah left. The bitch was in a "car accident" of course he went running.

Isa: Maybe she'll die and you'll be free

I hope. Peyton this. Peyton that. I'm so over it.

Isa: She's always going to be a problem. He's got some perverse attachment to her.

The best friend line is overplayed. And dammit I want my ring

Isa: Has he mentioned it?

I'm tired of waiting. Seriously a year and a half. I don't know what else to do.

Isa: Trap him

How?

Isa: You said he has daddy issues. Get prego.

Ha. Sex is nonexistent. He's tired. Traveling. Sore. You name it. Excuses.

He broke up with me. Told me he's in love with Peyton. She's a vegetable. He left me.

Isa: I told you what to do.

He won't buy it.

Isa: Tell him you're "months" along. He'll rush into marriage to save his precious little image.

Isa: Did he buy it?

Hook. Line. Sinker.

Isa: When's the wedding? Invite? MoH?

In his hometown (gag) I have to be nice to his mother (shoot me) Bonus – dad's hot. Maybe I can do him, get knocked up and no one would know?

Isa: Dad *is* hot. I Googled. 3-some?

I get the seed!

As much as I want to stop reading, I can't. My stomach is in my throat. Tears of anger cloud my vision. She's destroying my life and for what? Because she doesn't like Peyton?

I'M PREGNANT

Isa: Noah? The DILF?

Nope. Doesn't matter. I'm pregnant. And he's none the wiser.

I swallow hard at the notion she's cheated on me. I chose her and the baby over my own happiness and she's been lying this entire time. She wasn't pregnant in Chicago.

Isa: What are you going to do when Noah finds out you're only eight weeks along and haven't slept together in months?

Idk. Haven't thought about it. Once we're married, half his money is mine. I'll deal with it later. Gotta go play nice with the mother-in-law from hell and his bratty sister. Peace.

"What are you doing?"

I look up to find Dessie standing in the doorway. Her face is stoic. No emotion. I clear my throat and half smile at her. "I was reading."

"On my phone?"

I nod and glance at the device in my hand. I don't know what to do with it, but somewhere deep in the recess of my brain, I'm being told to keep it. I stand and walk toward her, towering over her. "I'm going to keep this and uh... I really think you should go."

"We're getting married in two days."

Shaking my head, I bite the inside of my cheek. "No, I don't think we'll be doing that, Dessie. I really don't want to make a scene, especially in front of my 'bratty sister' so please get your things and leave. When I get back to Portland, you can get the rest of your stuff. By the time I get downstairs here and after you've packed, security will know not to let you in." I step out of my room and head toward the stairs.

"You left me no choice, Noah."

I pause and turn to look at her. "You lied to get me away from someone I'm in love with and because that wasn't enough, you cheated on me. I don't want to look at you right now. I don't want you in my house. I don't want you near my family, especially my father. I don't want you in my town, near my friends or the people I care about. My mom and Aubrey were right to suspect you, but I didn't want to believe them. I gave you the benefit of the doubt and you proved me wrong. Get out, Dessie."

I don't give her a chance to say anything else. Her sobs are enough to tell me how she's feeling. Thing is, I don't know if she's angry she got caught or truly heartbroken. I suppose there's a bit of both emotions mixed in there. I order her a car service and wait at the bottom of the stairs for her to leave. Once the front door slams, I lose it.

31

PEYTON

*T*elling my parents I needed to return to California immediately wasn't easy without causing an array of alarms to go off. After the few hours Noah and I had spent together, I had to get out of Beaumont. He was going to marry Dessie, and despite him begging me to tell him not to, I couldn't. There was no way I'd be able to live with the burden of him walking away from his child to be with me.

In hindsight, I should've told him. I should've yelled from the top of my lungs, but I didn't, and he's since called the wedding off. I thought my parents would tell me why, but I'm not sure they even know, and if they do, they're not saying anything. Not that I would expect them to. They probably figure Noah has told me himself since we're best friends and all.

But he hasn't, and I haven't heard from him and I've lost track of time. I stopped counting the hours, which turned into days. I had hoped he would've called, but if he's with Dessie, I'm going to be the furthest person from his mind. I imagine she's not very happy with him. As long as she doesn't blame me, I'm good.

Currently, I'm sitting on the couch while my mother runs around crazily packing. The band is going on a mini-tour. It's really not for them, but for an up and coming band called Little Queens who recently signed under the same label. The record company thought it would be nice if 4225 West accompanied them on tour. The funny thing is, they're opening for Little Queens. My dad, Liam and Jimmy were all eager to help out. Plus Dad says that being the headline act is too stressful and now they get to go out and just play for forty-five minutes.

Mom almost stayed home, but I told her to go, and she finally agreed to be away for a few weeks and then come home to check on me. While I'm not fully recovered, I have a driver to take me to therapy, an aunt and uncle who will come if I need them and a beach to stare at. Besides, I plan to call Quinn and ask him to come down to take me surfing. I figure he could do the same as our dad did, but this time I won't have to worry about getting wet. Even though I miss Chicago, I have to admit, being here during the winter has been very nice. I can't imagine trying to get around in the snow right now.

Honestly, I'm looking forward to the break from my parents. It'll give me time to relax, get my homework done and just be free without them hovering. Well, Mom hovers. Dad, he's just there, waiting in the wings for when I need him, and he always seems to know when that is.

My parents hug and kiss me goodbye, making me promise to call them if there's an emergency or if I need anything. I jokingly asked if pizza was included in the afore-mentioned category. Mom rolled her eyes and waved me off. Dad smiled and said to call him for anything. I'll likely take him up on that.

I wait for their car to pull away before yelling, "Freedom!" If I were crazy, I'd try some ridiculous stunt with my Rollator, but the idea of getting hurt doesn't sound too appealing. Calling my parents seconds after they left would defeat the purpose of having the house to myself.

Also defeating the purpose of is whoever is at my gate right now and pressing the button incessantly. "Hello, who's there?" I ask, even though I can see them on the video camera. It's Kyle and he's waving like crazy.

"I heard you were back in town."

I press the buzzer that unlocks our gate and open the door. He scoops me up into a hug and carries me into my living room while I desperately hold onto my cane. The hug is awkward and a bit over friendly. I thought I've been fairly clear about my feelings. Noah and I may not have ever been together, but for a brief glimmer, I thought we had a chance. And knowing Noah's in love with me, well, I don't know when I'll be ready to move past him.

"I missed you," he says as he reaches toward my face. I sidestep him as much as I can and hobble toward the kitchen.

"I wasn't gone very long. I actually came home a few days earlier."

"Oh yeah, why?" Kyle sits down on one of our bar stools. From where he is and the counter, there's more than enough space between us.

I shrug. "Not my scene. You know the 'whole go back to your hometown' thing. Besides, all my friends are away at school, and as much as I love my grandpa, hanging with him and his poker playing buddies isn't my idea of a good time."

"Can you play? I can teach you."

I shake my head. "Grandpa taught Elle and I, a long time ago. He says when we turn twenty-one he's taking us to Vegas so we can run the table. Something about twins at a table makes people nervous."

"I believe it."

"So what brings you by?"

Kyle runs his hand through his hair. "I mean, I guess I could say I was in the neighborhood, but you'd know it's a lie. It takes me an hour to get here from the gym and that's without traffic." He shrugs and stands up, making his way over to where I am and stopping in front of me. "Peyton, I was thinking we could go on a date, something real?"

I step, putting some space between us. "Kyle..."

"Is it Ben?" he asks as he steps further away. "I mean the guy is always whispering in your ear, but I thought he was a friend."

"Not Ben. Ben actually has turned out to be one of my best friends, surprisingly. He's in love with Elle."

"Really? But she's never around."

"I know. He comes over because our dad likes him, and he's been around for a long time."

"So if it's not Ben... It's Westbury isn't it?"

I honestly don't know how to answer his question. It is, and isn't. "I haven't been completely honest about Noah. I'm in love with him, but he's with Dessie and—"

"And you're not ready?"

I shake my head and expect him to leave, but he steps forward and pulls me into his arms. "Friend-zoned. I can dig it."

"The only other better place is the end zone."

"Watch out people, Peyton's on fire."

I hug him back, thankful he's understanding, at least he's acting that way. With my direction and guidance, Kyle loads his arms up with junk food and sets it out on the table. I challenge him to a game of Madden, which he happily accepts.

"I hope you're ready to lose," I tell him as I get situated. I have residual pain in my right side and my reflexes are a bit slow, but I can still video game with the best of them.

"I've never lost to a chick before and I'm not about to today."

"We'll see about that."

"Remind me, how is it you're so well versed in football? I've met your dad and brother, they don't seem like the type."

I turn slightly to face him. "Remember when I told you my dad died when I was five?"

He nods.

"Big time football guy. Football gave me a way to stay connected to him. My uncle Liam filled the gap left behind and I went to all of Noah's practices and games."

"Do you ever get star struck when it comes to your family?"

I start laughing. "No, why? Because my dad and uncles have a band?"

"Well, yeah! And your brother is a pretty good musician. You're... whatever with Westbury. It's like Beaumont-bred stardom."

I roll my eyes at him and turn my attention toward the television. It's time to pick teams. Kyle picks the Bears, earning an odd look from me. I pick the Patriots, because why not. Brady is the best.

"My dad and Quinn are from here."

"Which makes the majority of you from Beaumont."

I've never thought of it that way before. To me, everyone is family. It doesn't matter what we do for a living or who we're surrounded by. Kyle is famous in his own right as well.

Within seconds of the game starting, I'm up by two touchdowns. Normally, I'd get up and do a little dance, but it'd take me too long and I'm rather comfortable. I easily win the first and second games, but now Kyle has switched his team to Denver and is giving me a run for my money.

"You can try to beat her, but it'll never happen."

I hit pause on the game and look toward the sliding glass door. Noah is standing there, staring at the television. "How'd you get in?"

"Ben gave me his code." My eyebrows shoot up and Noah shrugs.

"Is he supposed to be here?" Kyle asks.

"More than you are, I'm sure. Harrison and Katelyn won't care I'm here." Noah pushes off the doorframe and saunters into the living room. He stares at the TV for a minute before turning his attention to me. "I need to speak with you, Peyton. In private."

"I have company," I state the obvious.

Noah pushes his hands into his pockets and nods. "It's urgent. Maybe we can go outside and talk? Or to your room?"

Definitely not my room.

"Do you want to talk to him, babe?" I look at Kyle oddly. Why would he call me babe? He leans forward and kisses me. It's chaste, but still, it's a kiss. "I'll call you after my appointment. Maybe stop by later?" He speaks low, but I know Noah can hear him.

Kyle gets up from the couch, leaving me stunned. Once the door slams, I slowly turn my attention to Noah, who is still standing in the same spot.

"Are you dating him?"

"What would it matter?"

"It'd make all the difference in the world. If you tell me you're with Zimmerman, I'll walk out the door right now."

"And if I tell you I'm not?"

Noah steps closer. "Then I'm going to drop down on my knees and beg you to give me a chance to prove I'm worthy of your love."

"I think you're forgetting about your girlfriend, Noah. I told you before, I won't be a side chick." I manage to get up on my first try and maneuver my way outside. It's been so hot the past few days and there are people milling around everywhere.

Noah stands next to me, close enough I can feel him, but far enough way we're not touching. "The day you and I spent together at the field, you told me something about text messages. When I got back to my house, I did the unthinkable and went through her phone. I saw what she was sending to you, but I saw and read some other messages... Dessie and I aren't together anymore."

"But she's pregnant."

He nods. "She is, but it's not mine. She cheated on me sometime after telling me she was pregnant and before we left for Beaumont."

"Noah, I'm so sorry." I fight the urge to pull Noah into my arms.

His head drops, but he turns it slightly to look at me. "Better now, right? I mean, Nick raised a kid that wasn't his, but he knew it. I don't know how I would've coped down the road." He clears his throat and straightens up. "However, I've taken some time to clear my head."

"Was it foggy?" It's a stupid joke, but humor is always needed.

Noah laughs. "I miss you, Peyton. I miss everything we

had and believe it or not I miss what we could've had because I think about it all the time. I had an opportunity with you and I screwed it up, but it'll never happen again. You see, I've been in love with you for as long as I can remember. I'm not willing to state an age because let's face it, five years was a big gap when we were growing up. Now, it's nothing.

"So here's the deal. I'm going to chase you, woo you, romance you, and beat your ass at Madden because you know I can. And when I'm done, I want you to look me in the eyes and tell me you don't feel the same way. I'm *in love* with you, Peyton. It's crazy, ridiculous and unconventional, and it may have taken an accident for me to see the light, but I'm not fighting it."

Noah stands before me looking sexy and kissable. It'd be so easy to jump into his arms and ask him to take me to bed. But I don't. I shrug and say, "Okay." Much to his dismay.

NOAH

$\mathcal{J}$ can feel my eyes bug out of my head at her nonchalant response. Is she for real? I just poured my heart and soul out to her and all she can say is "okay." I must be living in some twisted version of the Twilight Zone because the last I knew, this woman was in love with me. And color me stupid, but I thought when two people were in love, despite one of them being an idiot, they usually fall into each other's arms after they've declared their feelings for each other and start to live happily ever after.

Granted, I did tell her I was going to woo her, and maybe she needs some romance in her life. For all I know, the guys she's dated before were dweebs who think being romantic is pizza and a lava lamp for ambiance. The only reason I know this is an option is because of my college teammates. They would share their big plans with us about their date nights. That's not me, it never was and it never will be. If I learned anything from my dad, it's how to show the woman you're in love with the fact that you are completely head over heels in love with them. I'm going to pull out all the stops and show Peyton I mean what I say.

My dad told me earlier that Katelyn had decided to go on tour with the band, otherwise I probably wouldn't be here. I needed her to be alone when I told her my plan, and having her parents lurking by wasn't going to do. My dad thinks I'm crazy, and I probably am, but I'm going to spend as long as it takes in order to win her heart. If she makes me wait until after she graduates, so be it. I'll be the one in the crowd holding a sign proclaiming my love for her. Either way, I'm here until she tells me I don't stand a chance.

"Bet I can beat you," I say, motioning toward the house where her Madden game is still paused. "I'll even take his sorry ass team."

"You're on."

Peyton steps forward and I use this opportunity to scoop her up into my arms. Her cane falls to the ground, clanking against the patio a few times before coming to a rest. "I can walk," she says with a bit of bite to her words.

"I'm fully aware of your abilities, but this gives me a chance to feel you next to me, even if it's only for a few seconds." No sooner are the words out of my mouth, am I setting her down on the couch. "Do you want anything? Water, juice, a kiss?" I throw the kiss out there, thinking maybe she'd like a little make-out session. I know I would, but I have a feeling it's still too early for her.

Peyton laughs and cracks a smile. "Kissing is off limits, but water is good."

"For how long?"

"Water is always good. It's a necessary staple for survival. I can't imagine we'll live to see when water is bad for you."

"Smart ass," I mutter as I start looking through the

cupboards to see what's there. "Are you hungry? Do you want something to eat?" Despite nothing jumping out at me, the shelves are fully stocked.

"Are you going to make something?" she asks.

I smile and tilt my head to the side so I can see her better. "I will if you want me to."

"Don't."

"Don't what?" I ask.

"Don't be like that," she says. "I don't want you to cater to me because you think it'll make me happy. Are you hungry, Noah? Do you want to make something to eat or get take-out?" Peyton looks fierce as she gives me the riot act. It's duly noted she doesn't want to be waited on. I'm not sure I'll be able to stop though because I feel like I need to do this for her.

"Take-out it is." The first thing I do when I pull my phone out is send her a text message. After the fiasco with Dessie, I changed my number. Her nonstop calling grew tiresome, as did her excuses. Telling me she only cheated so I would be happy because she thought she *was* pregnant when she blurted it out in Peyton's hospital room. Too bad the messages on her phone told me the truth. She was trapping me into marriage. My dad and Nick say I dodged a bullet. I say I dodged a lot more than that.

I'm in love with you. Someday, you'll be ready to tell me the same.

I stay back in the kitchen, watching as Peyton opens her phone. From where I'm standing it looks like she's concentrating, possibly trying to figure out who sent her the message.

Peyton: Stop skulking in the kitchen

"Skulking? What kind of word is that? I'm not skulking."

"It's a perfectly fine word for what you're doing and it's creepy. Why'd you get a new number?"

Returning to the couch, I set her water down on the table. "Too many unwanted phone calls and text messages. I moved on."

"Has she?"

Peyton's question gives me pause, but she's right to ask it. I can't expect her to become involved with me when Dessie could be an issue for her. "Has she texted you?"

She shakes her head. "No. In fact, I thought you were still with her."

I sigh. "Things got ugly. The stuff that she said to her friend... I couldn't even look at her after I read what I did. I took her phone as evidence in the event she gives birth and tries to pin it on me."

"Do you think she will?"

"I'm an optimist. Everything will work out in our favor." I look at her and wink. She holds my gaze for a few seconds, maybe even a minute or so before turning away with blushed cheeks. "I'm thinking Chinese for dinner."

"Sounds good."

I place the order quickly and reach for the controller. "You're the Patriots?"

"Of course," she says as she scrolls through the many options for her offense.

"Why not the Pioneers?"

Peyton shrugs. "I heard their quarterback has sloppy footwork."

I try not to laugh, but there's no use. "Touché."

It's been days since I made my intentions known to Peyton, and she's still keeping me at an arm's length. I'm fine with it because it means I have to work harder and I'm not afraid to put in the effort. She's worth it. *We're worth it.* However, something has been weighing heavily on my mind, and while her parents know we've been spending time together, they're under the impression I've been checking on her, making sure she's eating, getting to her therapy appointments, all the stuff Katelyn's worried about.

Not the case. I haven't left. When Peyton goes to bed, I sleep on the couch. It wasn't a decision I consciously made, but that first day, which turned into night, we fell asleep watching a movie. I wish I could say a few of my dreams about her turned into reality, but the truth is, we both stayed on our own sides of the sectional. I'm not even upset about it. As much as I'd love to hold her at night, knowing she's safe and not alone is far more important.

I hate leaving her and she knows it. In fact, she's called me out on what she says is obsessive hovering. My girl is fiercely independent and doesn't understand that I *need* to be near her. It's not because she's recovering, but because she makes me feel like I have a place in this world, that I'm not Liam Page's son or the starting quarterback (at least last season) of the Portland Pioneers. To Peyton, I'm Noah. The guy she's known her entire life and once called her best friend. To me, she's everything.

And that's why I've left her in the hands of Quinn. It wasn't easy trying to find out when he'd be home without giving much away, but I couldn't very well leave her all alone for a few days. I've told Peyton my last lie. At best, it could be considered a fib. I told her I had to fly home to take care of business. I didn't specify said business had to do with her.

If she were any other woman, talking to her parents about pursuing a relationship with her would never cross my mind, but as luck would have it, her father and mine are best friends. Her mother is my aunt purely in the sense our mothers are also best friends. I owe it to Harrison and Katelyn to seek their permission.

I haven't thought about what I'll do if they say no. I suppose I'm counting on them saying yes and wishing me luck because they probably know I'll need it. If they're not happy... well, I'll cross the proverbial bridge when I come to it.

The lady at the ticket booth smiles as she hands me my pass. My dad was excited to hear I wanted to attend their concert. When I told him why, he grew silent on the phone, but told me my credentials would be waiting for me.

By the time I make it to backstage, my dad and the band are well into their set. My mom, Katelyn and Jenna give me hugs. I look around and find Eden and Betty Paige sitting in the corner, focusing on their iPads, most likely doing homework. Honestly, I'm surprised to see the girls. I would think school is more important than traveling with the band while they help out an up and coming act.

I tap Paige on the shoulder and motion for her to move over so I can sit between them. Eden smiles and sets the device in my lap and both girls lean into me. Looking at us from the outside shows how tight-knit of a family we are, and some may balk at Peyton and I dating, but to me, it's the only thing that makes sense. For years, she followed me around and I never discouraged her. I loved having her by my side, on the sidelines for football and in the dugout when I was playing baseball. We were meant to be.

Once the show's over, we all head to the dressing room. I'm nervous. My palms are sweating. My heart's racing. And the words I had planned to say to Harrison no longer exist. Inside, champagne is poured and another successful show is celebrated, all while I stand in the corner contemplating what my life would be like without Peyton.

I can't even begin to imagine.

I didn't while she was lying in the hospital bed and I won't now.

"Excuse me, Harrison. Do you think I could speak to you in the other room?"

He looks at me oddly, as he should.

"What's going on, Noah? Is Peyton okay?" Katelyn asks, her face full of worry.

"Peyton's great. In fact, Quinn should be with her. Don't worry, she's in good hands." I immediately regret those words even though I've yet to touch her.

"Maybe we could go to the hall?" I motion toward the door as I try to avoid eye contact with my mother, whose beaming smile is distracting me. One look at my dad tells me he knows what I'm about to do and for the life of me, I can't decipher if he's okay with it or not.

Harrison follows me out into the hall where two security guards block access to the dressing room. I clear my throat, square my shoulders and look into his eyes, while my stomach twists, turns and threatens to expel its contents all over his Doc Martens.

"So you're probably wondering why I needed to speak with you."

"I am. Are you in some sort of trouble?"

"No, sir." I clear my throat again. "I'd like your permission to date Peyton." The words seem to come out in a rush.

"Say again?" he asks, cocking his eyebrow. "I'm not sure I heard you correctly."

Taking a deep breath, I make eye contact with him again. "Sir, I'm seeking your permission to pursue Peyton in a romantic relationship. I'm not even going to beat around the bush..." *Bad choice of words, Noah!* "I'm in love with her and I have been for a long time. I understand your hesitation in giving me an answer because of the situation I was in over the holidays, but I assure you, Peyton is my only priority and nothing will keep me from her... unless of course you tell me no."

Harrison crosses his arms and glares at me. We're about the same height, but right now I feel like I'm two feet shorter. "And if I say no?"

"Um... If you say no, I will do whatever I have to in order to prove to you that Peyton is the love of my life. I love her, Harrison. I mean, sir."

He stands there staring at me. I don't know for how long, but it's enough for my stomach to heave and my bladder to beg for relief.

"Are you sleeping with my daughter, Noah?"

Kill. Me. Now.

"No, sir."

"Waiting for marriage?"

Please don't tell me to wait.

"If you tell me so, yes we will."

He nods and runs his hand over his face and adjusts his beanie. "Honestly, Noah, you're not who I pictured as

257

someone my daughter would be interested in, but I know for a fact she loves you, and I'm not really one to stand in the way of love, so you have my blessing. But, if you hurt her—"

"I won't."

Harrison steps closer. "Remember, I know where you live," he says as he pulls me into his arms. "Let me just say, it's about damn time."

I don't know if I should rejoice or be relieved. I do know Harrison can hug and is squeezing the life out of me right now. "Can't breathe," I eek out. He finally lets go and starts laughing.

"That was your one and only warning. Don't mess this up."

He puts his arm around me and takes me back into the dressing room. Everyone is looking at us with expectant eyes, but he goes right to Katelyn and pulls her into his arms and whispers into her ear. She looks over and smiles, before rushing over to give me a hug.

"I've known it all along," she whispers in my ear. "Hold onto her, Noah."

"I plan to," I say back to her.

33

PEYTON

The humidity is stifling and the usual breeze that makes Chicago windy is nowhere to be felt. When Professor Fowler asked if I could come see him, I jumped at the opportunity. Not only to get away from California but to also give Noah and I a weekend alone.

Our relationship is progressing...slowly. I don't know if he's scared to touch me, thinking I might fall apart or if he's afraid of my parents. The latter is a bit far-fetched because I know he went and asked my dad for permission to date me. It may have been a bit old-fashioned, but to me it was perfect.

It also made sense for Noah to come with me. His season will be starting soon, and we'll see less and less of each other, although he's promised to move to Chicago. I don't want to burden him, but on the other hand, I want him near me as much as possible.

As our driver takes us toward my campus, I point out landmarks to Noah, along with my favorite coffee shop and where I watch the games on the weekends. He seems interested in every spot, even if he's only doing so to placate me.

It's times like this where I question the age difference and wonder if Noah will stick around. I know I shouldn't second-guess what he tells me, but I do, and it's for obvious reasons. I mean, look at the man! He's gorgeous, sexy, and unbelievably sweet. He cares for me, showers me with love, but so reserved when it comes to affection.

Maybe he's waiting for a sign, for the sky to open and start raining Peytons. Or footballs would be a better fit for us. Short of throwing myself at him, I don't know what else to do.

Elle thinks he's scared because of the Dessie mess. I get that, I do. But I'm not Dessie. I have no desire to trap Noah, and honestly, I feel like I don't have to. He's in love with me and while he knows I love him, I haven't told him yet. Maybe that's what he's waiting for.

Noah opens his door as soon as the car comes to a stop. He reaches in and seeks my hand in order to help me out. Aside from the humidity, I love being back in Chicago. I turn my face toward the mid-day sun and close my eyes. Not only am I back on campus, but Noah's here and that means everything to me.

With our hands joined, I direct him toward the journalism building. When Fowler called, I thought he was going to tell me I'd been kicked out of the program. It would make sense considering the amount of work I missed, despite trying to keep up online. My grades weren't on par with what they had been before my accident and I petitioned the school to make them void in exchange for going for another year. This should've been the decision I made from the start, but I was stubborn and thought I was mentally strong enough to not only recover from my life-threatening injuries but also carry a full workload. I was so wrong.

"Sometimes I miss college, even high school," Noah says as he holds the door open for me.

"Me too. When I first started here, no one knew who I was. The band goes on tour, pictures are posted and bam, everyone wants to be my friend. In Beaumont, people were my friend because of you and Quinn. This one time I made a mistake and told someone we went to prom together. Of course, any such evidence is somewhere in my room in the condo, so I could never prove it."

"You could've asked me to send you a picture."

I shake my head and grip his hand a bit tighter. "You were with Dessie. At best, we spoke maybe once a month with a quick 'how are you' text and nothing more."

Thankfully, Dessie hasn't tried to contact Noah. Even though he changed his number, we both expected her to somehow get her hands on it and contact him. Through the tabloids, we learned she's gotten married to the father of her baby, who happened to be Noah's neighbor.

He nods and continues to walk alongside me. "Well, I guess everyone has no choice but to believe you now."

Noah takes my hand and swings it out in front of him, as if he's spinning me around a dance floor, only now I'm in his arms and cradled to his chest. Our eyes are locked on each other as the back of his fingers brush along my cheek. My body temperature begins to rise in anticipation of what could come next.

Only I don't wait. I rise up on my tippy toes and press my lips to his. His hand moves to my hair, soft and gentle, as he opens his mouth to deepen the kiss. We haven't kissed like this since the hospital and while that kiss was amazing, this one's eager.

"Now that I've kissed you, I won't be able to stop," he says, pressing his lips to my cheeks and finally my forehead. His arms wrap around me tightly, holding me to his chest.

"I don't want you to stop, Noah. Not now. Not ever."

He pulls back and tips my chin up with his index finger and runs his thumb along my bottom lip. "Are you sure? I don't want to hurt you."

"Is that what you've been waiting for? To know whether I'm healed or not?"

He nods and seeks my eyes for the truth.

"I'm healed, but—"

"You're beautiful," he says, moving a strand of hair away from my eye. He's careful not to touch the side of my head where it was shaved. It's tender and while my hair is growing back, it's doing so rather slowly. "I'm so in love with you, Peyton. I know you're cautious about the scars. I can tell you over and over to not pay attention to them, but I know you see them when you look in the mirror."

"They're ugly."

Noah smiles. "It's impossible for anything to be ugly when it comes to you. We move at your pace, Peyton. I'm not in a rush."

I nod but frown instantly. He must've missed my confusion because he's walking us down the hall again. I'm done waiting. I want to make-out with him. Score a touchdown. Kick a field goal. He just needs to touch me. I want to feel human again, desirable. Doesn't he get it?

There isn't time to ask because we're at Professor Fowler's door. I don't know what to expect, but I square my shoulders anyway and knock.

"Come in," he hollers from inside the room.

Slowly, I turn the doorknob and step in. I look back at Noah who is standing on the other side and beckon him forward. It may be unprofessional for him to come in, but I'll need him with me if the news is bad.

"Good afternoon Professor Fowler."

He looks at us from over the top of his glasses. "Do I know you from somewhere?" he directs his question toward Noah who looks down at me. I nod, giving him the go ahead.

"Noah Westbury," he says, extending his hand to shake my professor's.

"Quarterback from the Pioneers?"

"Yes, sir."

"Huh, I heard rumblings that Miss Powell-James knew you, but—"

"But no one believed her," Noah says. "It's been hard for me to get to campus to see her, but I've recently relocated to Chicago and will be living not far from here so I imagine you'll be seeing me a lot more, especially once the season ends."

My mouth drops open as I look at Noah. He's talked about moving, but I hadn't heard any definitive plans, and he definitely didn't tell me about renting a place.

"Well, I'm sure Peyton will enjoy having her friend around."

Friend with benefits, I hope.

"I was very sorry to hear about the accident, but am very pleased you'll be rejoining us in the fall. Your last assignment was to write a recap of the game and while it took you a few months to turn it in, I was very impressed with not only your knowledge of the players but your understanding of the game."

"She gets that from me," Noah interjects. I poke him in the side, causing him to flinch. "What?" he asks innocently.

"What Noah is trying to say is I come from a long line

of football fanatics and while I may be female, the men in my life taught me everything they know." I glance from my professor to Noah, giving him a silent thank you.

"It's paid off. At the start of the semester, you will continue to represent your class on the sideline of the Bears."

"Seriously?" Noah pulls me into his arms as I try to process what this means.

"You also came highly recommended by Kyle Zimmerman. He wrote a letter to the department on your behalf. We weren't sure why until we found out he was the driver of the car you were in. He made a sizable donation that will be used as scholarships for any female who applies and is accepted into the sports journalism program."

Noah groans, but stops after I tap his stomach. The night after Kyle kissed me, which he says he did only to make Noah jealous, we had a long talk and both agreed we were better off as friends. He told me he was trying to come onto me, hoping to ignite a spark, but felt nothing and I was right to turn him down. This was easily the best rejection ever and instead, I've found a friend for life.

"Do you want this assignment?"

"Yeah, she does," Noah answers for me. He pulls me into his arms again, clearly happy for me. We stay and talk to Professor Fowler for a bit longer until Noah tells me he has a surprise for me.

"You mean other than telling me you're moving here?"

He puts his arm on my shoulders and pulls me close. Looking around, we're walking like any other couple, and I like it. We take the path to the edge of campus and cross the street, entering into a non-descript building. Inside, there's a security guard behind a white marble desk.

Noah comes to a screeching halt as soon as he enters. "Leo?"

"Westbury?"

Noah leaves me standing there as he rushes to the security guard. They hug as if they're long lost friends. "What are you doing here?" Noah asks him.

"This past winter some nice man was having a real hard time and bought me a cup a coffee. Coffee was nasty, but he also gave me the money in his wallet. Now he probably thought I was going to buy some drugs, but I found me a place to live with some running water and found a job sweeping floors. Just got promoted yesterday to man the front desk."

Noah shakes his head. "Must've been some coffee."

"Must've been some man to help a stranger out like that."

I stand there watching the both of them and have a sense of déjà vu wash over me. I've seen Noah and Leo together before, but can't place where. Noah turns to me and holds out his hand. "Leo, allow me to introduce you to Peyton Powell-James. Peyton, this is my friend Leo."

"Well, I know all about you, Ms. Peyton. I'm happy to say it's nice to meet you." Leo holds onto my hand as if it's his lifeline. Strangely enough, I don't want him to let go.

"I'm sorry, but I'm at a loss. I'll have to make Noah spill about you so we can be friends."

Noah places his arm around me again and pulls me to his side. "We're the new tenants in 5A, so you'll be seeing a lot more of her."

"Is that so? Well, my day is made."

"Mine too, Leo. Mine too." Noah hugs Leo again before directing me toward the elevator. This building isn't super fancy, and while both of us can afford to live in penthouses and high-rises, we weren't raised that way.

"How do you know Leo?"

"I met him at the hospital while you were in a coma." Noah's statement gives me pause. Since I've woken, I've remembered random moments that don't have an explanation. The only person I can talk to them about is my dad. My mom refuses to believe me, but Dad is more open about what happened. Somehow, Leo fits in, but I don't know how.

Noah opens the door to the apartment and scoops me into his arms to carry me over the threshold. "I don't think I'll ever get tired of carrying you," he says, as he kisses my cheek. He carries me through the hallway and into the living room where two large picture windows overlook the city.

"Wow."

"Yeah, I thought you'd like this. As soon as I saw it online, I saw you curled up on the couch with the fire lit, doing your homework."

"You see me living here?"

"With me," he says looking into my eyes.

"As roommates?"

Noah starts walking toward another hall and steps into a bedroom. It's tastefully decorated in various shades of purple, but it's the view that has me falling in love. He sets me on the bed and stands in front of me.

"I'd like you to live here as my girlfriend, as my lover."

"Noah..."

"For months I've been trying to get you alone, but someone is always around. I take you on a date, Quinn shows up. We're alone at the condo and Elle comes home. I take you to my hotel, your mom calls. Ever since I asked your dad for permission to date you, something has been preventing me from... well, from being with you."

"You've never told me what my dad said?"

Noah sits down next to me. "I think that's between your dad and I, and while I still think that, I have a feeling he's been plotting against us."

I start laughing, but Noah frowns. "I thought you weren't attracted to me."

His eyes go wide. "Are you serious?" Noah shakes his head. "I've been walking around with a raging hard-on for months. I mean, at first I was waiting because I wanted to make sure you wanted to be with me, and sometimes I still question—"

I don't let Noah finish his statement before attacking him with as much vigor as I can muster. For two people who are in love, we're horrible about reading each other's cues, but not anymore. Noah deftly moves us up the bed without breaking our kiss. I'm tugging and pulling at his clothes, trying to get his shirt off and his jeans unbuttoned.

"Eager?" he asks. I nod and shimmy out of my shorts. "What about this?" he pulls at the hem of my shirt, but I shake my head. I'm not comfortable taking my top off, and he knows that. Noah nods and pulls his shirt off slowly, revealing his washboard abs. I've seen him bare-chested many times, but everything seems different now.

He slides his jeans down his legs, pausing only to remove a condom from his pocket. I take it from him and examine the packaging.

"It's valid, don't worry."

"I'm not worried because I know you would never do anything to hurt me."

Noah cups my face and brings his lips to mine. "I love

you, so much it hurts sometimes when I think about heading back to work and leaving you."

"I love you, Noah. I love you so much." Our lips and tongue meet again, but now he's exploring. His hand moves up my shirt and grazes over my scar. My body tenses until his fingers slide under my bra. His large hand easily covers my breast while his other moves to my center. My legs spread, welcoming him. The first brush of his thumb over my sensitive bud sends a quake of shivers over my body.

Noah is everywhere. And so am I. His mouth is on my neck. My hands are roaming his body, pulling at him to get closer to me. His hands push and grab in all the right places and his fingers... I cry out when they enter me. My hand finds his erection, tugging gently at his smooth-skinned shaft. And when he groans in my ear, I smile.

He searches for the condom, ripping the package open and sliding the rubber over his hard-on. "This will be fast, Captain. I've been waiting for this to happen again since your prom."

"Really?"

Noah answers by pushing himself into my sex and pausing. "You have no idea. I've waited for a long time for you, Peyton."

Not as long as I have, Noah.

"I'm yours now," I tell him as I cup his face. He tilts his head and kisses my palm as he slides into me. My eyes close from the sensation.

"Open your eyes. I want to see you," he tells me as he moves languidly. Every thrust, his eyes are on me, and when they're not, he's kissing me deeply. I've never been made love to before, and I'm thankful I waited for this moment because being with Noah is like no other feeling in the world.

Our first time, we don't climax together because let's get real, we haven't been together in years. But every time after that, through every room in our new apartment, he plays my body like it's the two-minute warning and scores each and every time.

Sometime during the night, he whispers, "I love you. I'm going to love you forever."

"Same," I reply.

34

NOAH

*E*ven though I rented a place for Peyton and I in Chicago, I had to convince her to move to Portland with me for a little bit while I prepared for the season. When I wasn't working my ass off with the team, we would find a deserted field and work on my passing and footwork. Let me tell you something, there's nothing like watching your girl run after a ball, knowing that months prior she couldn't even stand on her own.

My girl's a superhero.

My girl's also back at school and I'm missing her terribly. I bow down to Steve Jobs and the Apple crew for creating FaceTime because without it I'd be going stir crazy. I never thought I was an obsessive sort of guy until Peyton and I finally figured it out. Now it's like I can't get enough of her, and the days I am home in Chicago are spent being domesticated. We created a rule in our home when it comes to football. I love that she's walking the sidelines for the Bears, but hate it as well. Selfishly, I want her in Portland, but know it's not possible and likely never will be. If she were there, I'd be distracted and worried about whether she's out of harm's way all the time. When we're together for the few short days each week – it's no football – just us. We cook together, take walks through the city, watch movies with the fire roaring in the background, and I help her study. I didn't want our relationship to be based off the sport we love. It had to be based on everything else that makes us who we are.

Today is our season opener. The weather is utter crap. It's cold and overcast. Everyone is here though, making the trek for the first game. The last time we were all together was when news of Peyton's accident brought us all to Chicago. So much has changed since the moment my dad told me Peyton wasn't going to make it. Spiritually, I battled for her and begged her to stay, but at that time I had nothing to offer her. Emotionally, I was a wreck. I couldn't fathom not having Peyton in my life and hated that our friendship had dwindled because of the relationship I was in. After seeing Peyton lying there, dying, I realized life was too short to wait idly for something to happen and despite the turmoil I was caught up in, my thoughts never strayed away from the life I wanted with her.

And now I have it.

The Pioneers take the field under the loud thunderous applause of the Portland faithful. I love this city, but my heart is in Chicago. Peyton and I haven't talked about what will happen when she graduates, but I'm expecting my girl to have a plethora of jobs to choose from. I'm confident in her ability to call a game. Unless it's mine in which case I'll stay on the bench.

I look out over the stands at the sea of people dressed in our colors of green, blue and yellow. Bringing football to Oregon was the best decision the state made. Of course, drafting me is also on the top of my list.

Today, I'm the starting quarterback. For a while, I thought my career was hanging by a thread, but I worked my butt off to prove to the organization that their investment in me would be worth it. We have a few new faces with our new draft picks and a couple of off-season trades, all of which excite me. Rookie running back, Brandon Garrison, is supposed to be legit. I watched him a little in college and liked what I saw. Happy to say I'll have no problems giving him the ball.

As I warm up, the normal game day activities are going on around me. The media is clamoring for early interviews, fans are filling the seats and the smell of popcorn is making my stomach growl. I look over and see my family, taking them all in. Nick and Aubrey are here with the kids, and sure enough, Mack is sitting next to Betty Paige. My mom thinks it's cute that they have a little crush on each other. My dad, on the other hand, is onto the "game" Mack is playing. As the big brother, who loves them both, I want Mack far, far away from Little B.

Right smack in the middle, next to my mom is Peyton. She gives me a small wave, likely thinking she's being shy. I'm tempted to go to her and pull her over the railing to kiss her senseless, but I refrain. I'm beyond in love with my girl and can't wait for this game to be over so I can show her.

Our warm-up clock winds down and the nerves start to set in. There's some ceremonial stuff happening on the field. Someone's getting a key to the city, another won season tickets, and there's a speech about how the city of Portland is the best place to play football.

Before the coin toss, my name is called and I'm asked to come out to the center of the field. Coach hands me the microphone and pats me on the back.

"Is this thing on?" I ask, earning a raucous roar from the

crowd. One quick glance up and I see my mug all over the JumboTron. I wave and the fans go wild. "Last year I let you down as your starting quarterback. My life was thrown into a tailspin when my best friend was in an accident that almost claimed her life. I couldn't think, sleep, eat or even focus on football, all because she was lying in a bed with machines fighting to keep her alive while I was here, trying to play a game that she and I share an immense love for."

Once again, I look up at the big screen and catch Peyton wiping her tears. "There she is. That's my girl."

The crowd, who was already loud, raises the decibel of noise up a notch.

"Peyton's accident opened my eyes. Not only to what I was missing out on but to what I was doing wrong. I was here, surviving. Taking each day as it came and never planning for the next step. Because of her, I am no longer that person. Because of Peyton and her will to live and learn to walk again, I'm stronger, braver and have better footwork, all thanks to her."

The crowd erupts.

"I'd like to invite Peyton down to join me out here."

The fans start chanting her name as security helps her navigate her way through the mess of wires, cameras, media and players on the field. "As she's making her way onto the field, I want to thank our families, who are with us today, for being the best parents, aunts, uncles, cousins and siblings that either of us could ask for."

When Peyton steps into our logo, I smile brightly and drop to one knee. In my hand is a black velvet box with her engagement ring, if she'll marry me. "Captain, you have been my best friend since forever. We may have been brought together by our mothers and forced to hang out, but secretly I have loved every single minute of it. It never bothered me that you were younger; it only bothered me when you weren't around. You've shown me what determination looks like, how to persevere through whatever life throws at you, and how true love feels. Without you, I'm a shell of the man I need to be. With you though, I'm confident, self-assured and the man I *want* to be. With that, I want to tell you that I love you and I'm going to hold onto you forever."

Peyton's hand covers her mouth and she starts nodding. "Yes, Noah."

"Yes, what?" I ask as her eyes go wide.

"Oh my God." She looks around and covers her face.

"Hey, Peyton?"

She looks at me through her fingers. "Will you marry me? Maybe add Westbury to your already long last name?"

This time she tackles me to the ground and peppers me with kisses. Thankfully, I dropped the microphone or everyone would've heard it when she called me an ass. When I'm finally able to slip the ring on her finger, I keep her with me for the coin toss before I help her back to the stands, where our families congratulate us.

Before heading back to the field she calls my name.

"Yeah, Captain?"

"Did you ask my dad?"

I nod. "Both of them," I say, winking and pointing my finger up to the sky. After I asked Harrison for his permission to marry Peyton, I took a trip to Beaumont and had an in-depth conversation with Mason.

"I love her." It's difficult to talk to someone who isn't here. I did this with Peyton when she was lying in her bed, wondering if she could hear me. Over the past few months, I've dropped hints about things I told her, hoping she'd remember or feel like I've said these things to her before, but she hasn't said anything.

I read a book on dying and the afterlife, wondering what Peyton might be experiencing, and also curious if she saw anyone. Where was she? And is there a bright light waiting for us? I don't want to ask her though because I feel like it's her personal journey, something only she can relate to. It's not like taking a trip to the zoo and sharing it with your friend who has also been there.

But this journey I had to take alone. I can't recall the last time I visited Mason's grave. Probably with Peyton on his birthday before I left for college. Even with Katelyn living in California, Mason's marker and plot are taken care of. Mr. Powell is too old to do it, but I know Katelyn pays for someone to make sure it's pristine.

I lay next to him with my ankles crossed, telling him about Peyton, and how amazing she is. I want to believe he knows this, and that maybe he was there with her in the hospital. Would he have told her to stay? Or encourage her to come with him? The latter I can't even think about because not having her in my life would kill me.

"She's beautiful and smart. You'd be so proud of her," I tell him. "I'm sure you never thought I would be here to ask this, but I'm seeking your permission to marry Peyton. Now you're probably thinking I'm nuts because I'm older and we grew up together, but I've been in love with her for as long as I can remember. I want her to be my wife, have my children, be my voice of reason and call me out on my shit when I need it. You know, she's really good at that, by the way. My girl doesn't have an ounce of fear in her body."

The cemetery is peaceful. There are a few people milling around, but no one bothers you here. The trees sway in the wind and off into the distance car doors slam, music plays softly and voices carry over the acres of land. I don't expect an answer or a sign, but knowing I've been here and have asked the question; it gives me a peace of mind. I imagine I'll have to tell Peyton about coming here, and have a feeling this is where we'll get married... Beaumont, not the cemetery, so she has both her dads with her on her big day. Honestly, I wouldn't want it any other way.

She covers her face once more, hiding the tears I know she's shedding. But it's in that moment where I'm watching her and she's watching me, that the sky opens up and the sun starts to shine, and everyone in my family turns their faces toward the warmth, welcoming Mason to the game.

The End.

ACKNOWLEDGMENTS

When I first wrote FOREVER MY GIRL (The Beaumont Series), I never thought about expanding it until I wrote the scene where Harrison saw Katelyn for the first time. But also developing within the pages was a story between Noah and Peyton. Deep down I always knew they would end up together, even though a few people begged me not to do it.

I've been asked a few times over the past few years what their story would be. I had a rough idea, but it never felt right. This storyline didn't come about until earlier this year when I was driving down the road. I had to pull over and type some notes out so I wouldn't forget, and when I arrived home, I started plotting.

I knew there would be tears. I cried as well. Writing anything with Mason is hard, and just think Elle will have a book so there will be more!

As with every acknowledgment I write, I have to thank my best friend, Yvette. We live thousands of miles away from each other and don't get to see one another as often as we want. Our relationship is mostly texts and emails. We talk about everything from work, to stories and characters as if they were real. To us, they are. She's been with me from day one.

Many thanks to those who helped with this story: Amy & Amber thank you for pre-reading and providing feedback. Thank you, Sarah, for another amazing cover. And Ellie: thank you for dropping everything to editing. It's only fitting you were the one since you've been there from the beginning. End & Amanda, thank you! I really appreciate all your help.

To all the bloggers who have been with the Beaumont crew for what seems like *forever*... thank you!

With the mention of the band touring with 4225 West – Little Queens – I hope you check out the sneak peek of Royal Protection by Amy Briggs! Liam, Harrison, and JD would appreciate it if you do!

Beaumont Babes – Enjoy Beautober!

If you want to be included on all Beaumont news, join my Beaumont only newsletter.

ABOUT HEIDI MCLAUGHLIN

Heidi McLaughlin is a New York Times, Wall Street Journal, and USA Today Bestselling author of The Beaumont Series, The Boys of Summer, and The Archers.

Originally, from the Pacific Northwest, she now lives in picturesque Vermont, with her husband, two daughters, and their three dogs.

In 2012, Heidi turned her passion for reading into a full-fledged literary career, writing over twenty novels, including the acclaimed Forever My Girl.

When writing isn't occupying her time, you can find her sitting courtside at either of her daughters' basketball games.

Heidi's first novel, Forever My Girl, has been adapted into a motion picture with LD Entertainment and Roadside Attractions, starring Alex Roe and Jessica Rothe, and opened in theaters on January 19, 2018.

Don't miss more books by Heidi McLaughlin! Sign up for her newsletter, or join the fun in her fan group!

Connect with Heidi!
www.heidimclaughlin.com

ALSO BY HEIDI MCLAUGHLIN

THE BEAUMONT SERIES

Forever My Girl – Beaumont Series #1

My Everything – Beaumont Series #1.5

My Unexpected Forever – Beaumont Series #2

Finding My Forever – Beaumont Series #3

Finding My Way – Beaumont Series #4

12 Days of Forever – Beaumont Series #4.5

My Kind of Forever – Beaumont Series #5

Forever Our Boys - Beaumont Series #5.5

The Beaumont Boxed Set - #1

THE BEAUMONT SERIES: NEXT GENERATION

Holding Onto Forever

My Unexpected Love

THE ARCHER BROTHERS

Here with Me

Choose Me

Save Me

LOST IN YOU SERIES

Lost in You

Lost in Us

THE BOYS OF SUMMER

Third Base

Home Run

Grand Slam

THE REALITY DUET

Blind Reality

Twisted Reality

SOCIETY X

Dark Room

Viewing Room

Play Room

THE CLUTCH SERIES

Roman

STANDALONE NOVELS

Stripped Bare

Blow

Sexcation

Santa's Secret

SNEAK PEEK OF ROYAL PROTECTION

BY: AMY BRIGGS

Ryan

I stared at Mr. Royal with a raised eyebrow, both shocked and amused at his request. Not only was it unorthodox, and as much as I wanted the money that came with a gig like that, deception wasn't something I was entirely comfortable with. Lying to get your job done made doing your job more difficult. His gray hair only highlighted his bright blue eyes, and as I glanced around his office, checking out all the awards and records on the wall, he continued to justify his request.

"I can see your apprehension, son," he interrupted my thoughts. "What you need to understand is that I'd do absolutely anything to protect my daughters, but they are stubborn. I'm far less concerned with Carmen, to be honest; she is a bit of a scrapper and doesn't trust anyone, but Miranda..." He sighed before continuing, "Miranda isn't taking these threats seriously, and I've tried doing this the right way." The concern on his face was apparent, but I was still on the fence and had questions.

"So, they've blatantly refused to have a security detail on this tour? And Miranda is receiving specific threats from a stalker or fan? You've already been down this road?" My trepidation was centered around being undercover on a cross-country music tour with these chicks. Unless I had full access, it would be almost impossible to protect either of them.

Rolling his eyes, and stifling a chuckle, he replied, "Oh, yes. Yes, I have. When you meet them, you'll see."

"And you believe this is the only way?" I questioned.

"I do," .He paused and leaned forward over his desk. "Look, I realize that being undercover security and on tour at the same time is an unusual request, and it's probably not the easiest gig, but I'm willing to compensate you generously. You come highly recommended from other people in the industry. It has to be just you. If I try to set up some kind of detail, they'll be onto us; as it stands, Carmen will probably doubt you, right out of the gate. Discretion is critical, and obviously, the girls cannot find out about this or they'll kill us both," .He let out a half-hearted chuckle, causing me to grin. "Her mother and I have tried everything from begging to demanding, and at the end of the day, I'm still their manager and have the ability to make some of these decisions in their best interest. And I'll be paying you from my own personal funds so that you work for me, not them." That seemed to be important to him, from the stern and stoic expression on his face.

"Okay, so let's say I'm in - which I'm not saying yet. What's the cover you had in mind, and what's the expectation here?" I didn't have any reason not to go. My private security firm was doing extremely well since I'd been in the business, and my team was one hundred percent trustworthy. With a high profile set of clients like we had with in the Little Queens, I understood why their dad wanted me, but before I agreed to anything, I wanted him to lay out his plan for how this would work, and decide whether or not it was legit.

"I want you to pose as a journalist," he stated, causing me to laugh out loud.

"A journalist?" He had to be crazy.

"Yes, a journalist," he replied.

"How do you propose that work?" Mr. Royal certainly had me entertained.

"You're going to go on tour with them, as if you were chronicling the tour for a magazine. You'll stick with Miranda, but you'll also spend some time with Carmen, obviously. So, you'll ask a lot of questions, get to know them all, and you'll find yourself part of the crew essentially. I'll instruct the girls that it's my decision as their manager to have a journalist out on tour with them, because it's fantastic PR for them."

"So, you think they'll buy it?" I was intrigued by this whole proposition.

"I do. Miranda is a smart businesswoman, and she'll agree with me on this. Carmen... well, she is probably going to give you a hard time. That's just her way. She's my little girl, but she'll likely put you through the ringer at some point," he explained.

"Okay, but Miranda is the one you want me to watch. She's the one with a stalker of some kind?" I asked.

"Yes. Miranda has been receiving threatening letters, and they've gotten worse. I'm concerned for her safety, and that's why I'm willing to deceive them to do it. Mr. King --" I interrupted him.

"You can call me Ryan."

"Ryan," he paused, "If you ever have the opportunity to have children, you'll understand what it's like to be a parent. I would do anything to protect them." He let out a sigh. "Anyway, are you in? What do you think?"

I contemplated the pros and cons of taking on the job, and even though I somehow knew it would be trouble, I heard myself say, "Sir, I'm in."

CPSIA information can be obtained
at www.ICGtesting.com
Printed in the USA
LVHW021442121218
600214LV00001B/30/P